THE
REINCARNATION
LIBRARY

MOON
OF
ISRAEL

A TALE OF THE EXODUS

H. RIDER HAGGARD

Æ

AEON PUBLISHING COMPANY
Mamaroneck · New York

First Published November 1918

This edition has been designed and typeset
exclusively for The Reincarnation Library.
Book cover artwork and title page artwork
©, Aeon Publishing Company, LLC 2001.
All rights reserved.

ISBN: 1-893766-20-9
Library of Congress Control Number: 00-134143

PRINTED AND BOUND IN
THE UNITED STATES
OF AMERICA

AUTHOR'S NOTE

This book suggests that the real Pharaoh of the Exodus was not Meneptah, or Merenptah, son of Rameses the Great, but the mysterious usurper, Amenmeses, who for a year or two occupied the throne between the death of Meneptah and the accession of his son the heir-apparent, the gentle-natured Seti II.

Of the fate of Amenmeses history says nothing; he may well have perished in the Red Sea or rather the Sea of Reeds, for, unlike those of Meneptah and the second Seti, his body has not been found.

Students of Egyptology will be familiar with the writings of the scribe and novelist Anana, or Ana as he is here called.

It was the Author's hope to dedicate this story to Sir Gaston Maspero, K.C.M.G., Director of the Cairo Museum, with whom on several occasions he discussed its plot some years ago. Unhappily, however, weighed down by one of the bereavements of the war, this great Egyptologist died in the interval between its writing and its publication. Still, since Lady Maspero informs him that such is the wish of his family, he adds the Dedication which he had proposed to offer to that eminent writer and student of the past.

Dear Sir Gaston Maspero,

When you assured me as to a romance of mine concerning ancient Egypt, that it was so full of the "inner spirit of the old Egyptians" that, after kindred efforts of your own and a lifetime of study, you could not conceive how it had been possible for it to spring from the brain of a modern man, I thought your verdict, coming from such a judge, one of the greatest compliments that ever I received. It is this opinion of yours indeed which induces me to offer you another tale of a like complexion. Especially am I encouraged thereto by a certain conversation between us in Cairo, while we gazed at the majestic countenance of Pharaoh Meneptah, for then it was, as you may recall, that you said you thought the plan of this book probable and that it commended itself to your knowledge of those dim days.

With gratitude for your help and kindness and the sincerest homage to your accumulated lore concerning the most mysterious of all the perished peoples of the earth,

Believe me to remain

Your true admirer,

H. RIDER HAGGARD

CONTENTS

MOON OF ISRAEL

1

SCRIBE ANA COMES TO TANIS

This is the story of me, Ana the scribe, son of Meri, and of certain of the days that I have spent upon the earth. These things I have written down now that I am very old in the reign of Rameses, the third of that name, when Egypt is once more strong and as she was in the ancient time. I have written them before death takes me, that they may be buried with me in death, for as my spirit shall arise in the hour of resurrection, so also these my words may arise in their hour and tell to those who shall come after me upon the earth of what I knew upon the earth. Let it be as Those in heaven shall decree. At least I write and what I write is true.

I tell of his divine Majesty whom I loved and love as my own soul, Seti Meneptah the second, whose day of birth was my day of birth, the Hawk who has flown to heaven before me; of Userti the Proud, his queen, she who afterwards married his divine Majesty, Saptah, whom I saw laid in her tomb at Thebes. I tell of Merapi, who was named

Moon of Israel, and of her people, the Hebrews, who dwelt for long in Egypt and departed thence, having paid us back in loss and shame for all the good and ill we gave them. I tell of the war between the gods of Egypt and the god of Israel, and of much that befell therein.

Also I, the King's Companion, the great scribe, the beloved of the Pharaohs who have lived beneath the sun with me, tell of other men and matters. Behold! is it not written in this roll? Read, ye who shall find in the days unborn, if your gods have given you skill. Read, O children of the future, and learn the secrets of that past which to you is so far away and yet in truth so near.

As it chanced, although the Prince Seti and I were born upon the same day and therefore, like the other mothers of gentle rank whose children saw the light upon that day, my mother received Pharaoh's gift and I received the title of Royal Twin in Ra, never did I set eyes upon the divine Prince Seti until the thirtieth birthday of both of us. All of which happened thus.

In those days the great Pharaoh, Rameses the second, and after him his son Meneptah who succeeded when he was already old, since the mighty Rameses was taken to Osiris after he had counted one hundred risings of the Nile, dwelt for the most part at the city of Tanis in the desert, whereas I dwelt with my parents at the ancient, white-walled city of Memphis on the Nile. At times Meneptah and his court visited Memphis, as also they visited Thebes, where this king lies in his royal tomb to-day. But save on one occasion, the young Prince Seti, the heir-apparent, the Hope of Egypt, came not with them, because his mother, Asnefert, did not favour Memphis, where some trouble had befallen her in youth—they say it was a love matter that cost the lover his life and her a sore heart—and Seti stayed with his mother who would not suffer him out of sight of her eyes.

Once he came indeed when he was fifteen years of age, to be proclaimed to the people as son of his father, as Son of the Sun, as the future wearer of the Double Crown, and then we, his twins in Ra—there were nineteen of us who were gently born—were called by name to meet him and to kiss his royal feet. I made ready to go in a fine new robe embroidered in purple with the name of Seti and my own. But on that very morning by the gift of some evil god I was smitten with spots all over my face and body, a common sickness that affects the young. So it happened that I did not see the Prince, for before I was well again he had left Memphis.

Now my father Meri was a scribe of the great temple of Ptah, and I was brought up to his trade in the school of the temple, where I copied many rolls and also wrote out Books of the Dead which I adorned with paintings. Indeed, in this business I became so clever that, after my father went blind some years before his death, I earned enough to keep him, and my sisters also until they married. Mother I had none, for she was gathered to Osiris while I was still very little. So life went on from year to year, but in my heart I hated my lot. While I was still a boy there rose up in me a desire—not to copy what others had written, but to write what others should copy. I became a dreamer of dreams. Walking at night beneath the palm-trees upon the banks of Nile I watched the moon shining upon the waters, and in its rays I seemed to see many beautiful things. Pictures appeared there which were different from any that I saw in the world of men, although in them were men and women and even gods.

Of these pictures I made stories in my heart and at last, although that was not for some years, I began to write these stories down in my spare hours. My sisters found me doing so and told my father, who scolded me for such foolishness which he said would never furnish me with bread and beer. But still I wrote on in secret by the light of the lamp in my chamber at night. Then my sisters married, and one day my father died suddenly while he was reciting prayers in the temple. I caused him to be embalmed in the best fashion and buried with honour in the tomb he had made ready for himself, although to pay the costs I was obliged to copy Books of the Dead for nearly two years, working so hard that I found no time for the writing of stories.

When at length I was free from debt I met a maiden from Thebes with a beautiful face that always seemed to smile, and she took my heart from my breast into her own. In the end, after I returned from fighting in the war against the Ninebow Barbarians, to which I was summoned like other young men, I married her. As for her name, let it be, I will not think of it even to myself. We had one child, a little girl which died within two years of her birth, and then I learned what sorrow can mean to man. At first my wife was sad, but her grief departed with time and she smiled again as she used to do. Only she said that she would bear no more children for the gods to take. Having little to do she began to go about the city and make friends whom I did not know, for of these, being a beautiful woman, she found many. The end of it was that she departed back to Thebes with a soldier whom I had never even seen, for I was always working at home thinking of the babe who was dead and how happiness is a bird that no man can snare, though sometimes, of its own will, it flies in at his window-place.

It was after this that my hair went white before I had counted thirty years.

Now, as I had none to work for and my wants were few and simple, I found more time for the writing of stories which, for the most part, were somewhat sad. One of these stories a fellow scribe borrowed from me and read aloud to a company, whom it pleased so much that there were many who asked leave to copy it and publish it abroad. So by degrees I became known as a teller of tales, which tales I caused to be copied and sold, though out of them I made but little. Still my fame grew till on a day I received a message from the Prince Seti, my twin in Ra, saying that he had read certain of my writings which pleased him much and that it was his wish to look upon my face. I thanked him humbly by the messenger and answered that I would travel to Tanis and wait upon his Highness. First, however, I finished the longest story which I had yet written. It was called the Tale of Two Brothers, and told how the faithless wife of one of them brought trouble on the other, so that he was killed. Of how, also, the just gods brought him to life again, and many other matters. This story I dedicated to his Highness, the Prince Seti, and with it in the bosom of my robe I travelled to Tanis, having hidden about me a sum of gold that I had saved.

So I came to Tanis at the beginning of winter and, walking to the palace of the Prince, boldly demanded an audience. But now my troubles began, for the guards and watchmen thrust me from the doors. In the end I bribed them and was admitted to the antechambers, where were merchants, jugglers, dancing-women, officers, and many others, all of them, it seemed, waiting to see the Prince; folk who, having nothing to do, pleased themselves by making mock of me, a stranger. When I had mixed with them for several days, I gained their friendship by telling to them one of my stories, after which I was always welcome among them. Still I could come no nearer to the Prince, and as my store of money was beginning to run low, I bethought me that I would return to Memphis.

One day, however, a long-bearded old man, with a gold-tipped wand of office, who had a bull's head embroidered on his robe, stopped in front of me and, calling me a white-headed crow, asked me what I was doing hopping day by day about the chambers of the palace. I told him my name and business and he told me his, which it seemed was Pambasa, one of the Prince's chamberlains. When I asked him to take me to the Prince, he laughed in my face and said darkly that the road to his Highness's presence was paved with gold. I understood what he meant and gave him a gift which he took as readily as a cock picks corn, saying that he would speak of me to his master and that I must come back again.

I came thrice and each time that old cock picked more

corn. At last I grew enraged and, forgetting where I was, began to shout at him and call him a thief, so that folks gathered round to listen. This seemed to frighten him. At first he looked towards the door as though to summon the guard to thrust me out; then changed his mind, and in a grumbling voice bade me follow him. We went down long passages, past soldiers who stood at watch in them still as mummies in their coffins, till at length we came to some broidered curtains. Here Pambasa whispered to me to wait, and passed through the curtains which he left not quite closed, so that I could see the room beyond and hear all that took place there.

It was a small room like to that of any scribe, for on the tables were palettes, pens of reed, ink in alabaster vases, and sheets of papyrus pinned upon boards. The walls were painted, not as I was wont to paint the Books of the Dead, but after the fashion of an earlier time, such as I have seen in certain ancient tombs, with pictures of wild fowl rising from the swamps and of trees and plants as they grow. Against the walls hung racks in which were papyrus rolls, and on the hearth burned a fire of cedar-wood.

By this fire stood the Prince, whom I knew from his statues. His years appeared fewer than mine although we were born upon the same day, and he was tall and thin, very fair also for one of our people, perhaps because of the Syrian blood that ran in his veins. His hair was straight and brown like to that of northern folk who come to trade in the markets of Egypt, and his eyes were grey rather than black, set beneath somewhat prominent brows such as those of his father, Meneptah. His face was sweet as a woman's, but made curious by certain wrinkles which ran from the corners of the eyes towards the ears. I think that these came from the bending of the brow in thought, but others say that they were inherited from an ancestress on the female side. Bakenkhonsu my friend, the old prophet who served under the first Seti and died but the other day, having lived a hundred and twenty years, told me that he knew her before she was married, and that she and her descendant, Seti, might have been twins.

In his hand the Prince held an open roll, a very ancient writing as I, who am skilled in such matters that have to do with my trade, knew from its appearance. Lifting his eyes suddenly from the study of this roll, he saw the chamberlain standing before him.

'You come at a good time, Pambasa,' he said in a voice that was very soft and pleasant, and yet most manlike. 'You are old and doubtless wise. Say, are you wise, Pambasa?'

'Yes, your Highness. I am wise like your Highness's uncle, Khaemuas the mighty magician, whose sandals I used to clean when I was young.'

'Is it so? Then why are you so careful to hide your wisdom which should be open like a flower for us poor bees to suck at? Well, I am glad to learn that you are wise, for in this book of magic that I have been reading I find problems worthy of Khaemuas the departed, whom I only remember as a brooding, black-browed man much like my cousin, Amenmeses his son—save that no one can call Amenmeses wise.'

'Why is your Highness glad?'

'Because you, being by your own account his equal, can

now interpret the matter as Khaemuas would have done. You know, Pambasa, that had he lived he would have been Pharaoh in place of my father. He died too soon, however, which proves to me that there was something in this tale of his wisdom, since no really wise man would ever wish to be Pharaoh of Egypt.'

Pambasa stared with his mouth open.

'Not wish to be Pharaoh!' he began—

'Now, Pambasa the Wise,' went on the Prince as though he had not heard him. 'Listen. This old book gives a charm "to empty the heart of its weariness," that it says is the oldest and most common sickness in the world from which only kittens, some children, and mad people are free. It appears that the cure for this sickness, so says the book, is to stand on the top of the pyramid of Khufu at midnight at that moment when the moon is largest in the whole year, and drink from the cup of dreams, reciting meanwhile a spell written here at length in language which I cannot read.'

'There is no virtue in spells, Prince, if anyone can read them.'

'And no use, it would seem, if they can be read by none.'

'Moreover, how can any one climb the pyramid of Khufu, which is covered with polished marble, even in the day let alone at midnight, your Highness, and there drink of the cup of dreams?'

'I do not know, Pambasa. All I know is that I weary of this foolishness, and of the world. Tell me of something that will lighten my heart, for it is heavy.'

'There are jugglers without, Prince, one of whom says

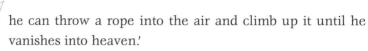

he can throw a rope into the air and climb up it until he vanishes into heaven.'

'When he has done it in your sight, Pambasa, bring him to me, but not before. Death is the only rope by which we can climb to heaven—or be lowered into hell. For remember there is a god called Set, after whom, like my great-grandfather, I am named by the way—the priests alone know why—as well as one called Osiris.'

'Then there are the dancers, Prince, and among them some very finely made girls, for I saw them bathing in the palace lake, such as would have delighted the heart of your grandfather, the great Rameses.'

'They do not delight my heart who want no naked women prancing here. Try again, Pambasa.'

'I can think of nothing else, Prince. Yet, stay. There is a scribe without named Ana, a thin, sharp-nosed man who says he is your Highness's twin in Ra.'

'Ana!' said the Prince. 'He of Memphis who writes stories? Why did you not say so before, you old fool? Let him enter at once, at once.'

Now hearing this I, Ana, walked through the curtains and prostrated myself, saying,

'I am that scribe, O Royal Son of the Sun.'

'How dare you enter the Prince's presence without being bidden——' began Pambasa, but Seti broke in with a stern voice, saying,

'And how dare you, Pambasa, keep this learned man waiting at my door like a dog? Rise, Ana, and cease from giving me titles, for we are not at Court. Tell me, how long have you been in Tanis?'

'Many days, O Prince,' I answered, 'seeking your presence and in vain.'

'And how did you win it at last?'

'By payment, O Prince,' I answered innocently, 'as it seems is usual. The doorkeepers——'

'I understand,' said Seti, 'the doorkeepers! Pambasa, you will ascertain what amount this learned scribe has disbursed to "the doorkeepers" and refund him double. Begone now and see to the matter.'

So Pambasa went, casting a piteous look at me out of the corner of his eye.

'Tell me,' said Seti when he was gone, 'you who must be wise in your fashion, why does a Court always breed thieves?'

'I suppose for the same reason, O Prince, that a dog's back breeds fleas. Fleas must live, and there is the dog.'

'True,' he answered, 'and these palace fleas are not paid enough. If ever I have power I will see to it. They shall be fewer but better fed. Now, Ana, be seated. I know you though you do not know me, and already I have learned to love you through your writings. Tell me of yourself.'

So I told him all my simple tale, to which he listened without a word, and then asked me why I had come to see him. I replied that it was because he had sent for me, which he had forgotten; also because I brought him a story that I had dared to dedicate to him. Then I laid the roll before him on the table.

'I am honoured,' he said in a pleased voice, 'I am greatly honoured. If I like it well, your story shall go to the tomb with me for my Ka to read and re-read until the day of res-

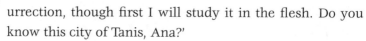

urrection, though first I will study it in the flesh. Do you know this city of Tanis, Ana?'

I answered that I knew little of it, who had spent my time here haunting the doors of his Highness.

'Then with your leave I will be your guide through it this night, and afterwards we will sup and talk.'

I bowed and he clapped his hands, whereon a servant appeared, not Pambasa, but another.

'Bring two cloaks,' said the Prince, 'I go abroad with the scribe, Ana. Let a guard of four Nubians, no more, follow us, but at a distance and disguised. Let them wait at the private entrance.'

The man bowed and departed swiftly.

Almost immediately a black slave appeared with two long hooded cloaks, such as camel-drivers wear, which he helped us to put on. Then, taking a lamp, he led us from the room through a doorway opposite to that by which I had entered, down passages and a narrow stair that ended in a courtyard. Crossing this we came to a wall, great and thick, in which were double doors sheathed with copper that opened mysteriously at our approach. Outside of these doors stood four tall men, also wrapped in cloaks, who seemed to take no note of us. Still, looking back when we had gone a little way, I observed that they were following us, as though by chance.

How fine a thing, thought I to myself, it is to be a Prince who by lifting a finger can thus command service at any moment of the day or night.

Just at that moment Seti said to me,

'See, Ana, how sad a thing it is to be a Prince, who cannot even stir abroad without notice to his household and commanding the service of a secret guard to spy upon his every action, and doubtless to make report thereof to the police of Pharaoh.'

There are two faces to everything, thought I to myself again.

2

THE
BREAKING
OF THE CUP

We walked down a broad street bordered by trees, beyond which were lime-washed, flat-roofed houses built of sun-dried brick, standing, each of them, in its own garden, till at length we came to the great market-place just as the full moon rose above the palm-trees, making the world almost as light as day. Tanis, or Rameses as it is also called, was a very fine city then, if only half the size of Memphis, though now that the Court has left it I hear it is much deserted. About this market-place stood great temples of the gods, with pylons and avenues of sphinxes, also that wonder of the world, the colossal statue of the second Rameses, while to the north upon a mound was the glorious palace of Pharaoh. Other palaces there were also, inhabited by the nobles and officers of the Court, and between them ran long streets where dwelt the citizens, ending, some of them, on that branch of the Nile by which the ancient city stood.

Seti halted to gaze at these wondrous buildings.

'They are very old,' he said, 'but most of them, like the walls and those temples of Amon and of Ptah, have been rebuilt in the time of my grandfather or since his day by the labour of Israelitish slaves who dwell yonder in the rich land of Goshen.'

'They must have cost much gold,' I answered.

'The Kings of Egypt do not pay their slaves,' replied the Prince shortly.

Then we went on and mingled with the thousands of the people who were wandering to and fro seeking rest after the business of the day. Here on the frontier of Egypt were gathered folk of every race; Bedouins from the desert, Syrians from beyond the Red Sea, merchants from the rich Isle of Chittim, travellers from the coast, and traders from the land of Punt and from the unknown countries of the north. All were talking, laughing and making merry, save some who gathered in circles to listen to a teller of tales or wandering musicians, or to watch women who danced half naked for gifts.

Now and again the crowd would part to let pass the chariot of some noble or lady before which went running footmen who shouted, 'Make way, Make way!' and laid about them with their long wands. Then came a procession of the white-robed priests of Isis travelling by moonlight as was fitting for the servants of the Lady of the Moon, and bearing aloft the holy image of the goddess before which all men bowed and for a little while were silent. After this followed the corpse of some great one newly dead, preceded by a troop of hired mourners who rent the air with their lamentations as they conducted it to the quarter of the embalmers. Lastly, from out of one of the side streets emerged a gang of several hundred hook-nosed and bearded men, among whom were a few women, loosely roped together and escorted by a company of armed guards.

'Who are these?' I asked, for I had never seen their like.

'Slaves of the people of Israel who return from their labour at the digging of the new canal which is to run to the Red Sea,' answered the Prince.

We stood still to watch them go by, and I noted how proudly their eyes flashed and how fierce was their bearing although they were but men in bonds, very weary too and stained by toil in mud and water. Presently this happened. A white-bearded man lagged behind, dragging on the line and checking the march. Thereupon an overseer ran up and flogged him with a cruel whip cut from the hide of the sea-horse. The man turned and, lifting a wooden spade which he carried, struck the overseer such a blow that he cracked his skull so that he fell down dead. Other overseers rushed at the Hebrew, as these Israelites were called, and beat him till he also fell. Then a soldier appeared and, seeing what had happened, drew his bronze sword. From among the throng sprang out a girl, young and very lovely although she was but roughly clad.

Since then I have seen Merapi, Moon of Israel, as she was called, clad in the proud raiment of a queen, and once even of a goddess, but never, I think, did she look more beauteous than in this hour of her slavery. Her large eyes, neither blue nor black, caught the light of the moon and were aswim with tears. Her plenteous bronze-hued hair flowed in great curls over the snow-white bosom that her

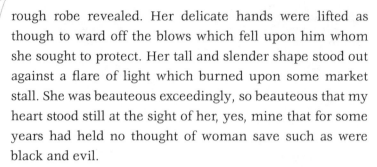

rough robe revealed. Her delicate hands were lifted as though to ward off the blows which fell upon him whom she sought to protect. Her tall and slender shape stood out against a flare of light which burned upon some market stall. She was beauteous exceedingly, so beauteous that my heart stood still at the sight of her, yes, mine that for some years had held no thought of woman save such as were black and evil.

She cried aloud. Standing over the fallen man she appealed to the soldier for mercy. Then, seeing that there was none to hope for from him, she cast her great eyes around until they fell upon the Prince Seti.

'Oh! Sir,' she wailed, 'you have a noble air. Will you stand by and see my father murdered for no fault?'

'Drag her off, or I smite through her,' shouted the captain, for now she had thrown herself down upon the fallen Israelite. The overseers obeyed, tearing her away.

'Hold, butcher!' cried the Prince.

'Who are you, dog, that dare to teach Pharaoh's officer his duty?' answered the captain, smiting the Prince in the face with his left hand.

Then swiftly he struck downwards and I saw the bronze sword pass through the body of the Israelite who quivered and lay still. It was all done in an instant, and on the silence that followed rang out the sound of a woman's wail. For a moment Seti choked—with rage, I think. Then he spoke a single word—'Guards!'

The four Nubians, who, as ordered, had kept at a distance, burst through the gathered throng. Ere they reached us I, who till now had stood amazed, sprang at the captain and gripped him by the throat. He struck at me with his bloody sword, but the blow, falling on my long cloak, only bruised me on the left thigh. Then I, who was strong in those days, grappled with him and we rolled together on the ground.

After this there was great tumult. The Hebrew slaves burst their rope and flung themselves upon the soldiers like dogs upon a jackal, battering them with their bare fists. The soldiers defended themselves with swords; the overseers plied their hide whips; women screamed, men shouted. The captain whom I had seized began to get the better of me; at least I saw his sword flash above me and thought that all was over. Doubtless it would have been, had not Seti himself dragged the man backwards and thus given the four Nubian guards time to seize him. Next I heard the Prince cry out in a ringing voice,

'Hold! It is Seti, the son of Pharaoh, the Governor of Tanis, with whom you have to do. See,' and he threw back the hood of his cloak so that the moon shone upon his face.

Instantly there was a great quiet. Now, first one and then another as the truth sank into them, men began to fall upon their knees, and I heard one say in an awed voice,

'The royal Son, the Prince of Egypt struck in the face by a soldier! Blood must pay for it.'

'How is that officer named?' asked Seti, pointing to the man who had killed the Israelite and well-nigh killed me.

Someone answered that he was named Khuaka.

'Bring him to the steps of the temple of Amon,' said Seti to the Nubians who held him fast. 'Follow me, friend Ana, if you have the strength. Nay, lean upon my shoulder.'

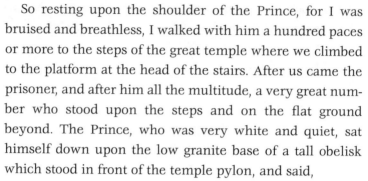

So resting upon the shoulder of the Prince, for I was bruised and breathless, I walked with him a hundred paces or more to the steps of the great temple where we climbed to the platform at the head of the stairs. After us came the prisoner, and after him all the multitude, a very great number who stood upon the steps and on the flat ground beyond. The Prince, who was very white and quiet, sat himself down upon the low granite base of a tall obelisk which stood in front of the temple pylon, and said,

'As Governor of Tanis, the City of Rameses, with power of life and death at all hours and in all places, I declare my Court open.'

'The Royal Court is open!' cried the multitude in the accustomed form.

'This is the case,' said the Prince. 'Yonder man who is named Khuaka, by his dress a captain of Pharaoh's army, is charged with the murder of a certain Hebrew, and with the attempted murder of Ana the scribe. Let witnesses be called. Bring the body of the dead man and lay it here before me. Bring the woman who strove to protect him, that she may speak.'

The body was brought and laid upon the platform, its wide eyes staring up at the moon. Then soldiers who had gathered thrust forward the weeping girl.

'Cease from tears,' said Seti, 'and swear by Kephera the creator, and by Maat the goddess of truth and law, to speak nothing but the truth.'

The girl looked up and said in a rich low voice that in some way reminded me of honey being poured from a jar, perhaps because it was thick with strangled sobs,

'O Royal Son of Egypt, I cannot swear by those gods who am a daughter of Israel.'

The Prince looked at her attentively and asked,

'By what god then can you swear, O Daughter of Israel?'

'By Jahveh, O Prince, whom we hold to be the one and only God, the Maker of the world and all that is therein.'

'Then perhaps his other name is Kephera,' said the Prince with a little smile. 'But have it as you will. Swear, then, by your god Jahveh.'

Then she lifted both her hands above her head and said,

'I, Merapi, daughter of Nathan of the tribe of Levi of the people of Israel, swear that I will speak the truth and all the truth in the name of Jahveh, the God of Israel.'

'Tell us what you know of the matter of the death of this man, O Merapi.'

'Nothing that you do not know yourself, O Prince. He who lies there,' and she swept her hand towards the corpse, turning her eyes away, 'was my father, an elder of Israel. The captain Khuaka came when the corn was young to the Land of Goshen to choose those who should work for Pharaoh. He wished to take me into his house. My father refused because from my childhood I had been affianced to a man of Israel; also because it is not lawful under our law for our people to intermarry with your people. Then the captain Khuaka seized my father, although he was of high rank and beyond the age to work for Pharaoh, and he was taken away, as I think, because he would not suffer me to wed Khuaka. A while later I dreamed that my father was sick. Thrice I dreamed it and ran away to Tanis to visit him. But this morning I found him and, O Prince, you know the rest.'

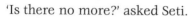

'Is there no more?' asked Seti.

The girl hesitated, then answered,

'Only this, O Prince. This man saw me with my father giving him food, for he was weak and overcome with the toil of digging the mud in the heat of the sun, he who being a noble of our people knew nothing of such labour from his youth. In my presence Khuaka asked my father if now he would give me to him. My father answered that sooner would he see me kissed by snakes and devoured by crocodiles. "I hear you," answered Khuaka. "Learn, now, slave Nathan, before to-morrow's sun arises, you shall be kissed by swords and devoured by crocodiles or jackals." "So be it," said my father, "but learn, O Khuaka, that if so, it is revealed to me who am a priest and a prophet of Jahveh, that before to-morrow's sun you also shall be kissed by swords and of the rest we will talk at the foot of Jahveh's throne."

'Afterwards, as you know, Prince, the overseer flogged my father as I heard Khuaka order him to do if he lagged through weariness, and then Khuaka killed him because my father in his madness struck the overseer with a mattock. I have no more to say, save that I pray that I may be sent back to my own people there to mourn my father according to our custom.'

'To whom would you be sent? Your mother?'

'Nay, O Prince, my mother, a lady of Syria, is dead. I will go to my uncle, Jabez the Levite.'

'Stand aside,' said Seti. 'The matter shall be seen to later. Appear, O Ana the Scribe. Swear the oath and tell us what you have seen of this man's death, since two witnesses are needful.'

So I swore and repeated all this story that I have written down.

'Now, Khuaka,' said the Prince when I had finished, 'have you aught to say?'

'Only this, O Royal One,' answered the captain throwing himself upon his knees, 'that I struck you by accident, not knowing that the person of your Highness was hidden in that long cloak. For this deed it is true I am worthy of death, but I pray you to pardon me because I knew not what I did. The rest is nothing, since I only slew a mutinous slave of the Israelites, as such are slain every day.'

'Tell me, O Khuaka, who are being tried for this man's death and not for the striking of one of royal blood by chance, under which law it is lawful for you to kill an Israelite without trial before the appointed officers of Pharaoh.'

'I am not learned. I do not know the law, O Prince. All that this woman said is false.'

'At least it is not false that yonder man lies dead and that you slew him, as you yourself admit. Learn now, and let all Egypt learn, that even an Israelite may not be murdered for no offence save that of weariness and of paying back unearned blow with blow. Your blood shall answer for his blood. Soldiers! Strike off his head.'

The Nubians leapt upon him, and when I looked again Khuaka's headless corpse lay by the corpse of the Hebrew Nathan and their blood was mingled upon the steps of the temple.

'The business of the Court is finished,' said the Prince. 'Officers, see that this woman is escorted to her own peo-

ple, and with her the body of her father for burial. See, too, upon your lives that no insult or harm is done to her. Scribe Ana, accompany me hence to my house where I would speak with you. Let guards precede and follow me.'

He rose and all the people bowed. As he turned to go the lady Merapi stepped forward, and falling upon her knees, said,

'O most just Prince, now and ever I am your servant.'

Then we set out, and as we left the market-place on our way to the palace of the Prince, I heard a tumult of voices rise behind us, some in praise and some in blame of what had been done. We walked on in silence broken only by the measured tramp of the guards. Presently the moon passed behind a cloud and the world was dark. Then from the edge of the cloud sprang out a ray of light that lay straight and narrow above us on the heavens. Seti studied it a while and said,

'Tell me, O Ana, of what does that moonbeam put you in mind?'

'Of a sword, O Prince,' I answered, 'stretched out over Egypt and held in the black hand of some mighty god or spirit. See, there is the blade from which fall little clouds like drops of blood, there the hilt of gold, and look! there beneath is the face of the god. Fire streams from his eye-holes and his brow is black and awful. I am afraid, though what I fear I know not.'

'You have a poet's mind, Ana. Still, what you see I see and of this I am sure, that some sword of vengeance is indeed stretched out over Egypt because of its evil doings, whereof this light may be the symbol. Behold! it seems to fall upon the temples of the gods and the palace of

Pharaoh, and to cleave them. Now it is gone and the night is as nights were from the beginning of the world. Come to my chamber and let us eat. I am weary, I need food and wine, as you must after struggling with that lustful murderer whom I have sent to his own place.'

The guards saluted and were dismissed. We mounted to the Prince's private chambers, in one of which his servants clad me in fine linen robes after a skilled physician of the household had doctored the bruises upon my thigh over which he tied a bandage spread with balm. Then I was led to a small dining-hall, where I found the Prince waiting for me as though I were some honoured guest and not a poor scribe who had wandered hence from Memphis with my wares. He caused me to sit down at his right hand and even drew up the chair for me himself, whereat I felt abashed. To this day I remember that leather-seated chair. The arms of it ended in ivory sphinxes and on its back of black wood in an oval was inlaid the name of the great Rameses, to whom indeed it had once belonged. Dishes were handed to us—only two of them and those quite simple, for Seti was no great eater—by a young Nubian slave of a very merry face, and with them wine more delicious than any I had ever tasted.

We ate and drank and the Prince talked to me of my business as a scribe and of the making of tales, which seemed to interest him very much. Indeed one might have thought that he was a pupil in the schools and I the teacher, so humbly and with such care did he weigh everything that I said about my art. Of matters of state or of the dreadful scene of blood through which we had just passed he spoke no word. At the end, however, after a little pause

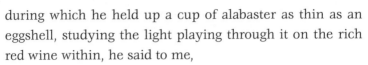

during which he held up a cup of alabaster as thin as an eggshell, studying the light playing through it on the rich red wine within, he said to me,

'Friend Ana, we have passed a stirring hour together, the first perhaps of many, or mayhap the last. Also we were born upon the same day and therefore, unless the astrologers lie, as do other men—and women—beneath the same star. Lastly, if I may say it, I like you well, though I know not how you like me, and when you are in the room with me I feel at ease, which is strange, for I know of no other with whom it is so.

'Now by a chance only this morning I found in some old records which I was studying, that the heir to the throne of Egypt a thousand years ago, had, and therefore, as nothing ever changes in Egypt, still has, a right to a private librari-an for which the State, that is, the toilers of the land, must pay as in the end they pay for all. Some dynasties have gone by, it seems, since there was such a librarian, I think because most of the heirs to the throne could not, or did not, read. Also by chance I mentioned the matter to the Vizier Nehesi who grudges me every ounce of gold I spend, as though it were one taken out of his own pouch, which perhaps it is. He answered with that crooked smile of his,

' "Since I know well, Prince, that there is no scribe in Egypt whom you would suffer about you for a single month, I will set the cost of a librarian at the figure at which it stood in the Eleventh Dynasty upon the roll of your Highness's household and defray it from the Royal Treasury until he is discharged."

'Therefore, Scribe Ana, I offer you this post for one

month; that is all for which I can promise you will be paid whatever it may be, for I forget the sum.'

'I thank you, O Prince,' I exclaimed.

'Do not thank me. Indeed if you are wise you will refuse. You have met Pambasa. Well, Nehesi is Pambasa multiplied by ten, a rogue, a thief, a bully, and one who has Pharaoh's ear. He will make your life a torment to you and clip every ring of gold that at length you wring out of his grip. Moreover the place is wearisome, and I am fanciful and often ill-humoured. Do not thank me, I say. Refuse; return to Memphis and write stories. Shun courts and their plottings. Pharaoh himself is but a face and a puppet through which other voices talk and other eyes shine, and the sceptre which he wields is pulled by strings. And if this is so with Pharaoh, what is the case with his son? Then there are the women, Ana. They will make love to you, Ana, they even do so to me, and I think you told me that you know something of women. Do not accept, go back to Memphis. I will send you some old manuscripts to copy and pay you whatever it is Nehesi allows for the librarian.'

'Yet I accept, O Prince. As for Nehesi I fear him not at all, since at the worst I can write a story about him at which the world would laugh, and rather than that he will pay me my salary.'

'You have more wisdom than I thought, Ana. It never came into my mind to put Nehesi in a story, though it is true I tell tales about him which is much the same thing.'

He bent forward, leaning his head upon his hand, and

ceasing from his bantering tone, looked me in the eyes and asked,

'Why do you accept? Let me think now. It is not because you care for wealth if that is to be won here; nor for the pomp and show of courts; nor for the company of the great who really are so small. For all these things you, Ana, have no craving if I read your heart aright, you who are an artist, nothing less and nothing more. Tell me, then, why will you, a free man who can earn your living, linger round a throne and set your neck beneath the heel of princes to be crushed into the common mould of servitors and King's Companions and Bearers of the Footstool?'

'I will tell you, Prince. First, because thrones make history, as history makes thrones, and I think that great events are on foot in Egypt in which I would have my share. Secondly, because the gods bring gifts to men only once or twice in their lives and to refuse them is to offend the gods who gave them those lives to use to ends of which we know nothing. And thirdly'—here I hesitated.

'And thirdly—out with the thirdly for, doubtless, it is the real reason.'

'And thirdly, O Prince—well, the word sounds strangely upon a man's lips—but thirdly because I love you. From the moment that my eyes fell upon your face I loved you as I never loved any other man—not even my father. I know not why. Certainly it is not because you are a prince.'

When he heard these words Seti sat brooding and so silent that, fearing lest I, a humble scribe, had been too bold, I added hastily,

'Let your Highness pardon his servant for his presumptuous words. It was his servant's heart that spoke and not his lips.'

He lifted his hand and I stopped.

'Ana, my twin in Ra,' he said, 'do you know that I never had a friend?'

'A prince who has no friend!'

'Never, none. Now I begin to think that I have found one. The thought is strange and warms me. Do you know also that when my eyes fell upon your face I loved you also, the gods know why. It was as though I had found one who was dear to me thousands of years ago but whom I had lost and forgotten. Perhaps this is but foolishness, or perhaps here we have the shadow of something great and beautiful which dwells elsewhere, in the place we call the Kingdom of Osiris, beyond the grave, Ana.'

'Such thoughts have come to me at times, Prince. I mean that all we see is shadow; that we ourselves are shadows and that the realities who cast them live in a different home which is lit by some spirit sun that never sets.'

The Prince nodded his head and again was silent for a while. Then he took his beautiful alabaster cup, and pouring wine into it, he drank a little and passed the cup to me.

'Drink also, Ana,' he said, 'and pledge me as I pledge you, in token that by decree of the Creator who made the hearts of men, henceforward our two hearts are as the same heart through good and ill, through triumph and defeat, till death takes one of us. Henceforward, Ana, unless you show yourself unworthy, I hide no thought from you.'

Flushing with joy I took the cup, saying,

'I add to your words, O Prince. We are one, not for this life alone but for all the lives to be. Death, O Prince, is, I think, but a single step in the pylon stair which leads at last to that dizzy height whence we see the face of God and hear his voice tell us what and why we are.'

Then I pledged him, and drank, bowing, and he bowed back to me.

'What shall we do with the cup, Ana, the sacred cup that has held this rich heart-wine? Shall I keep it? No, it no longer belongs to me. Shall I give it to you? No, it can never be yours alone. See, we will break the priceless thing.'

Seizing it by its stem with all his strength he struck the cup upon the table. Then what seemed to me to be a marvel happened, for instead of shattering as I thought it surely would, it split in two from rim to foot. Whether this was by chance, or whether the artist who fashioned it in some bygone generation had worked the two halves separately and cunningly cemented them together, to this hour I do not know. At least so it befell.

'This is fortunate, Ana,' said the Prince, laughing a little in his light way. 'Now take you the half that lies nearest to you and I will take mine. If you die first I will lay my half upon your breast, and if I die first you shall do the same by me, or if the priests forbid it because I am royal and may not be profaned, cast the thing into my tomb. What should we have done had the alabaster shattered into fragments, Ana, and what omen should we have read in them?'

'Why ask, O Prince, seeing that it has befallen otherwise?'

Then I took my half, laid it against my forehead and hid it in the bosom of my robe, and as I did, so did Seti.

So in this strange fashion the royal Seti and I sealed the holy compact of our brotherhood, as I think not for the first time or the last.

3

USERTI

S eti rose, stretching out his arms.

'That is finished,' he said, 'as everything finishes, and for once I am sorry. Now what next? Sleep, I suppose, in which all ends, or perhaps you would say, all begins.'

As he spoke the curtains at the end of the room were drawn and between them appeared the chamberlain, Pambasa, holding his gold-tipped wand ceremoniously before him.

'What is it now, man?' asked Seti. 'Can I not even sup in peace? Stay, before you answer tell me, do things end or begin in sleep? The learned Ana and I differ on the matter and would hear your wisdom. Bear in mind, Pambasa, that before we are born we must have slept, since of that time we remember nothing, and after we are dead we certainly seem to sleep, as any who have looked on mummies know. Now answer.'

The chamberlain stared at the wine flask on the table as

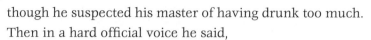

though he suspected his master of having drunk too much. Then in a hard official voice he said,

'She comes! She comes! She comes, offering greetings and adoration to the Royal Son of Ra.'

'Does she indeed?' asked Seti. 'If so, why say it three times? And who comes?'

'The high Princess, the heiress of Egypt, the daughter of Pharaoh, your Highness's royal half-sister, the great lady Userti.'

'Let her enter then. Ana, stand you behind me. If you grow weary and I give leave you can depart; the slaves will show you your sleeping-place.'

Pambasa went, and presently through the curtain appeared a royal-looking lady splendidly apparelled. She was accompanied by four waiting women who fell back on the threshold and were no more seen. The Prince stepped forward, took both her hands in his and kissed her on the brow, then drew back again, after which they stood a moment looking at each other. While they remained thus I studied her who was known throughout the land as the 'Beautiful Royal Daughter,' but whom till now I had never seen. In truth I did not think her beautiful, although even had she been clad in a peasant's robe I should have been sure that she was royal. Her face was too hard for beauty and her black eyes, with a tinge of grey in them, were too small. Also her nose was too sharp and her lips were too thin. Indeed, had it not been for the delicately and finely-shaped woman's form beneath, I might have thought that a prince and not a princess stood before me. For the rest in most ways she resembled her half-brother Seti, though her countenance lacked the kindliness of his; or rather both of them resembled their father, Meneptah.

'Greeting, Sister,' he said, eyeing her with a smile in which I caught a gleam of mockery. 'Purple-bordered robes, emerald necklace and enamelled crown of gold, rings and pectoral, everything except a sceptre—why are you so royally arrayed to visit one so humble as your loving brother? You come like sunlight into the darkness of a hermit's cell and dazzle the poor hermit, or rather hermits,' and he pointed to me.

'Cease your jests, Seti,' she replied in a full, strong voice. 'I wear these ornaments because they please me. Also I have supped with our father, and those who sit at Pharaoh's table must be suitably arrayed, though I have noted that sometimes you think otherwise.'

'Indeed. I trust that the good god, our divine parent, is well to-night as you leave him so early.'

'I leave him because he sent me with a message to you.' She paused, looking at me sharply, then asked, 'Who is that man? I do not know him.'

'It is your misfortune, Userti, but one which can be mended. He is named Ana the Scribe, who writes strange stories of great interest which you would do well to read who dwell too much upon the outside of life. He is from Memphis and his father's name was—I forget what. Ana, what was your father's name?'

'One too humble for royal ears, Prince,' I answered, 'but my grandfather was Pentaur the poet who wrote of the deeds of the mighty Rameses.'

'Is it so? Why did you not tell me that before? The

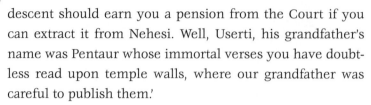

descent should earn you a pension from the Court if you can extract it from Nehesi. Well, Userti, his grandfather's name was Pentaur whose immortal verses you have doubtless read upon temple walls, where our grandfather was careful to publish them.'

'I have—to my sorrow—and thought them poor, boastful stuff,' she answered coldly.

'To be honest, if Ana will forgive me, so do I. I can assure you that his stories are a great improvement on them. Friend Ana, this is my sister, Userti, my father's daughter though our mothers were not the same.'

'I pray you, Seti, to be so good as to give me my rightful titles in speaking of me to scribes and other of your servants.'

'Your pardon, Userti. This, Ana, is the first Lady of Egypt, the Royal Heiress, the Princess of the Two Lands, the High-priestess of Amon, the Cherished of the Gods, the half-sister of the Heir-apparent, the Daughter of Hathor, the Lotus Bloom of Love, the Queen to be of—Userti, whose queen will you be? Have you made up your mind? For myself I know no one worthy of so much beauty, excellence, learning and—what shall I add—sweetness, yes, sweetness.'

'Seti,' she said stamping her foot, 'if it pleases you to make a mock of me before a stranger, I suppose that I must submit. Send him away, I would speak with you.'

'Make a mock of you! Oh! mine is a hard fate. When truth gushes from the well of my heart, I am told I mock, and when I mock, all say—he speaks truth. Be seated, Sister, and talk on freely. This Ana is my sworn friend who saved my life but now, for which deed perhaps he should be my enemy. His memory is excellent also and he will remember what you say and write it down afterwards, whereas I might forget. Therefore, with your leave, I will ask him to stay here.'

'My Prince,' I broke in, 'I pray you suffer me to go.'

'My Secretary,' he answered with a note of command in his voice, 'I pray you to remain where you are.'

So I sat myself on the ground after the fashion of a scribe, having no choice, and the Princess sat herself on a couch at the end of the table, but Seti remained standing. Then the Princess said,

'Since it is your will, Brother, that I should talk secrets into other ears than yours, I obey you. Still'—here she looked at me wrathfully—'let the tongue be careful that it does not repeat what the ears have heard, lest there should be neither ears nor tongue. My Brother, it has been reported to Pharaoh, while we ate together, that there is tumult in this town. It has been reported to him that because of a trouble about some base Israelite you caused one of his officers to be beheaded, after which there came a riot which still rages.'

'Strange that truth should have come to the ears of Pharaoh so quickly. Now, my Sister, if he had heard it three moons hence I could have believed you—almost.'

'Then you did behead the officer?'

'Yes, I beheaded him about two hours ago.'

'Pharaoh will demand an account of the matter.'

'Pharaoh,' answered Seti lifting his eyes, 'has no power to question the justice of the Governor of Tanis in the north.'

'You are in error, Seti. Pharaoh has all power.'

'Nay, Sister, Pharaoh is but one man among millions of other men, and though he speaks it is their spirit which

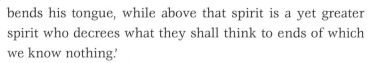

bends his tongue, while above that spirit is a yet greater spirit who decrees what they shall think to ends of which we know nothing.'

'I do not understand, Seti.'

'I never thought you would, Userti, but when you have leisure, ask Ana here to explain the matter to you. I am sure that *he* understands.'

'Oh! I have borne enough,' exclaimed Userti rising. 'Hearken to the command of Pharaoh, Prince Seti. It is that you wait upon him to-morrow in full council, at an hour before noon, there to talk with him of this question of the Israelitish slaves and the officer whom it has pleased you to kill. I came to speak other words to you also, but as they were for your private ear, these can bide a more fitting opportunity. Farewell, my Brother.'

'What, are you going so soon, Sister? I wished to to tell you the story about those Israelites, and especially of the maid whose name is—what was her name, Ana?'

'Merapi, Moon of Israel, Prince,' I answered with a groan.

'About the maid called Merapi, Moon of Israel, I think the sweetest that ever I have looked upon, whose father the dead captain murdered in my sight.'

'So there is a woman in the business? Well, I guessed it.'

'In what business is there not a woman, Userti, even in that of a message from Pharaoh. Pambasa, Pambasa, escort the Princess and summon her servants, women everyone of them, unless my senses mock me. Good-night to you, O Sister and Lady of the Two Lands, and forgive me—that coronet of yours is somewhat awry.'

At last she was gone and I rose, wiping my brow with a

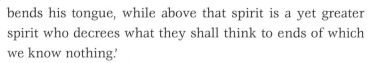

corner of my robe, and looked at the Prince who stood before the fire laughing softly.

'Make a note of all this talk, Ana,' he said; 'there is more in it than meets the ear.'

'I need no note, Prince,' I answered; 'every word is burnt upon my mind as a hot iron burns a tablet of wood. With reason too, since now her Highness will hate me for all her life.'

'Much better so, Ana, than that she should pretend to love you, which she never would have done while you are my friend. Women ofttimes respect those whom they hate and even will advance them because of policy, but let those whom they pretend to love beware. The time may come when you will yet be Userti's most trusted councillor.'

Now here, I, Ana the Scribe, will state that in after days, when this same queen was the wife of Pharaoh Siptah, I did, as it chanced, become her most trusted councillor. Moreover, in those times, yes, and even in the hour of her death, she swore that from the moment her eyes first fell on me she had known me to be true-hearted and held me in esteem as no self-seeker. More, I think she believed what she said, having forgotten that once she looked upon me as her enemy. This indeed I never was, who always held her in regard and honour as a great lady who loved her country, though one who sometimes was not wise. But as I could not foresee these things on that night of long ago, I only stared at the Prince and said,

'Oh! why did you not allow me to depart as your Highness said I might at the beginning? Soon or late my head will pay the price of this night's work.'

'Then she must take mine with it. Listen, Ana. I kept

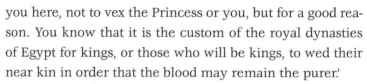

you here, not to vex the Princess or you, but for a good reason. You know that it is the custom of the royal dynasties of Egypt for kings, or those who will be kings, to wed their near kin in order that the blood may remain the purer.'

'Yes, Prince, and not only among those who are royal. Still, I think it an evil custom.'

'As I do, since the race wherein it is practised grows ever weaker in body and in mind; which is why, perhaps, my father is not what his father was and I am not what my father is.'

'Also, Prince, it is hard to mingle the love of the sister and of the wife.'

'Very hard, Ana; so hard that when it is attempted both are apt to vanish. Well, our mothers having been true royal wives, though hers died before mine was wedded by my father, Pharaoh desires that I should marry my half-sister, Userti, and what is worse, she desires it also. Moreover, the people, who fear trouble ahead in Egypt if we, who alone are left of the true royal race born of queens, remain apart and she takes another lord, or I take another wife, demand that it should be brought about, since they believe that whoever calls Userti the Strong his spouse will one day rule the land.'

'Why does the Princess wish it—that she may be a queen?'

'Yes, Ana, though were she to wed my cousin, Amenmeses, the son of Pharaoh's elder brother Khaemuas, she might still be a queen, if I chose to stand aside as I should not be loth to do.'

'Would Egypt suffer this, Prince?'

'I do not know, nor does it matter since she hates Amenmeses, who is strong-willed and ambitious, and will have none of him. Also he is already married.'

'Is there no other royal one whom she might take, Prince?'

'None. Moreover she wishes me alone.'

'Why, Prince?'

'Because of ancient custom which she worships. Also because she knows me well and in her fashion is fond of me, whom she believes to be a gentle-minded dreamer that she can rule. Lastly, because I am the lawful heir to the Crown and without me to share it, she thinks that she would never be safe upon the Throne, especially if I should marry some other woman, of whom she would be jealous. It is the Throne she desires and would wed, not the Prince Seti, her half-brother, whom she takes with it to be in name her husband, as Pharaoh commands that she should do. Love plays no part in Userti's breast, Ana, which makes her the more dangerous, since what she seeks with a cold heart of policy, that she will surely find.'

'Then it would seem, Prince, that the cage is built about you. After all it is a very splendid cage and made of gold.'

'Yes, Ana, yet not one in which I would live. Still, except by death how can I escape from the threefold chain of the will of Pharaoh, of Egypt, and of Userti? Oh!' he went on in a new voice, one that had in it both sorrow and passion, 'this is a matter in which I would have chosen for myself who in all others must be a servant. And I may not choose!'

'Is there perchance some other lady, Prince?'

'None! By Hathor, none—at least I think not. Yet I would have been free to search for such a one and take her when I found her, if she were but a fishergirl.'

'The Kings of Egypt can have large households, Prince.'

'I know it. Are there not still scores whom I should call aunt and uncle? I think that my grandsire, Rameses, blessed Egypt with quite three hundred children, and in so doing in a way was wise, since thus he might be sure that, while the world endures, in it will flow some of the blood that once was his.'

'Yet in life or death how will that help him, Prince? Some must beget the multitudes of the earth, what does it matter who these may have been?'

'Nothing at all, Ana, since by good or evil fortune they are born. Therefore, why talk of large households? Though, like any man who can pay for it, Pharaoh may have a large household, I seek a queen who shall reign in my heart as well as on my throne, not a "large household," Ana. Oh! I am weary. Pambasa, come hither and conduct my secretary, Ana, to the empty room that is next my own, the painted chamber which looks toward the north, and bid my slaves attend to all his wants as they would to mine.'

'Why did you tell me you were a scribe, my lord Ana?' asked Pambasa, as he led me to my beautiful sleeping-place.

'Because that is my trade, Chamberlain.'

He looked at me, shaking his great head till the long white beard waved across his breast like a temple banner in the faint evening breeze, and answered,

'You are no scribe, you are a magician who can win the love and favour of his Highness in an hour which others cannot do between two risings of the Nile. Had you said so at once, you would have been differently treated yonder in the hall of waiting. Forgive me therefore what I did in ignorance, and, my lord, I pray it may please you not to melt away in the night, lest my feet should answer for it beneath the sticks.'

It was the fourth hour from sunrise of the following day that, for the first time in my life I found myself in the Court of Pharaoh standing with other members of his household in the train of his Highness, the Prince Seti. It was a very great place, for Pharaoh sat in the judgment hall, whereof the roof is upheld by round and sculptured columns, between which were set statues of Pharaohs who had been. Save at the throne end of the hall, where the light flowed down through clerestories, the vast chamber was dim almost to darkness; at least so it seemed to me entering there out of the brilliant sunshine. Through this gloom many folk moved like shadows; captains, nobles, and state officers who had been summoned to the Court, and among them white-robed and shaven priests. Also there were others of whom I took no count, such as Arab headmen from the desert, traders with jewels and other wares to sell, farmers and even peasants with petitions to present, lawyers and their clients, and I know not who besides, though of all these none were suffered to advance beyond a certain mark where the light began to fall. Speaking in whispers all of these folk flitted to and fro like bats in a tomb.

We waited between two Hathor-headed pillars in one of the vestibules of the hall, the Prince Seti, who was clad in purple-bordered garments and wore upon his brow a fillet

of gold from which rose the uræus or hooded snake, also of
gold, that royal ones alone might wear, leaning against the
base of a statue, while the rest of us stood silent behind
him. For a time he was silent also, as a man might be
whose thoughts were otherwhere. At length he turned and
said to me,

'This is weary work. Would I had asked you to bring that
new tale of yours, Scribe Ana, that we might have read it
together.'

'Shall I tell you the plot of it, Prince?'

'Yes. I mean, not now, lest I should forget my manners
listening to you. Look,' and he pointed to a dark-browed,
fierce-eyed man of middle age who passed up the hall as
though he did not see us, 'there goes my cousin, Amenmeses. You know him, do you not?'

I shook my head.

'Then tell me what you think of him, at once before the
first judgment fades.'

'I think he is a royal-looking lord, obstinate in mind and
strong in body, handsome too in his way.'

'All can see that, Ana. What else?'

'I think,' I said in a low voice so that none might over-
hear, 'that his heart is as black as his brow; that he has
grown wicked with jealousy and hate and will do you
evil.'

'Can a man grow wicked, Ana? Is he not as he was born
till the end? I do not know, nor do you. Still you are right,
he is jealous and will do me evil if it brings him good. But
tell me, which of us will triumph at the last?'

While I hesitated what to answer I became aware that

someone had joined us. Looking round I perceived a very ancient man clad in a white robe. He was broad-faced and bald-headed, and his eyes burned beneath his shaggy eyebrows like two coals in ashes. He supported himself on a staff of cedar-wood, gripping it with both hands that for thinness were like to those of a mummy. For a while he considered us both as though he were reading our souls, then said in a full and jovial voice,

'Greeting, Prince.'

Seti turned, looked at him, and answered,

'Greeting, Bakenkhonsu. How comes it that you are still alive? When we parted at Thebes I made sure——'

'That on your return you would find me in my tomb. Not so, Prince, it is I who shall live to look upon you in your tomb, yes, and on others who are yet to sit in the seat of Pharaoh. Why not? Ho! ho! Why not, seeing that I am but a hundred and seven, I who remember the first Rameses and have played with his grandson, your grandsire, as a boy? Why should I not live, Prince, to nurse your grandson—if the gods should grant you one who as yet have neither wife nor child?'

'Because you will get tired of life, Bakenkhonsu, as I am already, and the gods will not be able to spare you much longer.'

'The gods can endure yet a while without me, Prince, when so many are flocking to their table. Indeed it is their desire that one good priest should be left in Egypt. Ki the Magician told me so only this morning. He had it straight from Heaven in a dream last night.'

'Why have you been to visit Ki?' asked Seti, looking at

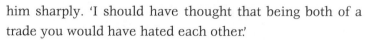

him sharply. 'I should have thought that being both of a trade you would have hated each other.'

'Not so, Prince. On the contrary we add up each other's account; I mean, check and interpret each other's visions, with which we are both of us much troubled just now. Is that young man a scribe from Memphis?'

'Yes, and my friend. His grandsire was Pentaur the poet.'

'Indeed. I knew Pentaur well. Often has he read me to sleep with his long poems, rank stuff that grew like coarse grass upon a deep but half-drained soil. Are you sure, young man, that Pentaur was your grandfather? You are not like him. Quite a different kind of herbage, and you know that is a matter upon which we must take a woman's word.'

Seti burst out laughing and I looked at the old priest angrily, though now that I came to think of it my father always said that his mother was one of the biggest liars in Egypt.

'Well, let it be,' went on Bakenkhonsu, 'till we find out the truth before Thoth. Ki was speaking of you, young man. I did not pay much attention to him, but it was something about a sudden vow of friendship between you and the Prince here. There was a cup in the story too, an alabaster cup that seemed familiar to me. Ki said it was broken.'

Seti started and I began angrily,

'What do you know of that cup? Where were you hid, O Priest?'

'Oh, in your souls, I suppose,' he answered dreamily, 'or rather Ki was. But I know nothing and am not curious. If you had broken the cup with a woman now, it would have been more interesting, even to an old man. Be so good as to answer the Prince's question as to whether he or his cousin Amenmeses will triumph at the last, for on that matter both Ki and I are curious.'

'Am I a seer,' I began again still more angrily, 'that I should read the future?'

'I think so, a little, but that is what I want to find out.'

He hobbled towards me, laid one of his claw-like hands upon my arm, and said in a new voice of command,

'Look now upon that throne and tell me what you see there.'

I obeyed him because I must, staring up the hall at the empty throne. At first I saw nothing. Then figures seemed to flit around it. From among these figures emerged the shape of the Count Amenmeses. He sat upon the throne, looking about him proudly, and I noted that he was no longer clad as a prince but as Pharaoh himself. Presently hook-nosed men appeared who dragged him from his seat. He fell, as I thought, into water, for it seemed to splash up about him. Next Seti the Prince appeared to mount the throne, led thither by a woman, of whom I could only see the back. I saw him distinctly wearing the double crown and holding a sceptre in his hand. He also melted away and others came whom I did not know, though I thought that one of them was like to the Princess Userti.

Now all were gone and I was telling Bakenkhonsu everything I had witnessed like a man who speaks in his sleep, not by his own will. Suddenly I woke up and laughed at my own foolishness. But the other two did not laugh; they regarded me very gravely.

'I thought that you were something of a seer,' said the old

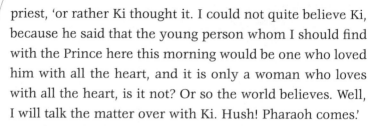

priest, 'or rather Ki thought it. I could not quite believe Ki, because he said that the young person whom I should find with the Prince here this morning would be one who loved him with all the heart, and it is only a woman who loves with all the heart, is it not? Or so the world believes. Well, I will talk the matter over with Ki. Hush! Pharaoh comes.'

As he spoke from far away rose a cry of—

'Life! Blood! Strength! Pharaoh! Pharaoh! Pharaoh!'

4

THE
COURT OF
BETROTHAL

'Life! Blood! Strength!' echoed everyone in the great hall, falling to their knees and bending their foreheads to the ground. Even the Prince and the aged Bakenkhonsu prostrated themselves thus as though before the presence of a god. And, indeed, Pharaoh Meneptah, passing through the patch of sunlight at the head of the hall, wearing the double crown upon his head and arrayed in royal robes and ornaments, looked like a god, no less, as the multitude of the people of Egypt held him to be. He was an old man with the face of one worn by years and care, but from his person majesty seemed to flow.

With him, walking a step or two behind, went Nehesi his Vizier, a shrivelled, parchment-faced officer whose cunning eyes rolled about the place, and Roy the High-priest, and Hora the Chamberlain of the Table, and Meranu the Washer of the King's Hands, and Yuy the private scribe, and many others whom Bakenkhonsu named to me as

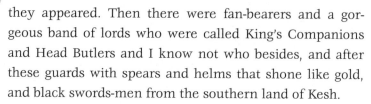

they appeared. Then there were fan-bearers and a gor-
geous band of lords who were called King's Companions
and Head Butlers and I know not who besides, and after
these guards with spears and helms that shone like gold,
and black swords-men from the southern land of Kesh.

But one woman accompanied his Majesty, walking
alone immediately behind him in front of the Vizier and
the High-priest. She was the Royal Daughter, the Princess
Userti, who looked, I thought, prouder and more splendid
than any there, though somewhat pale and anxious.

Pharaoh came to the steps of the throne. The Vizier and
the High-priest advanced to help him up the steps, for he
was feeble with age. He waved them aside, and beckoning
to his daughter, rested his hand upon her shoulder and by
her aid mounted the throne. I thought that there was
meaning in this; it was as though he would show to all the
assembly that this princess was the prop of Egypt.

For a little while he stood still and Userti sat herself
down on the topmost step, resting her chin upon her jewelled hand. There he stood searching the place with his
eyes. He lifted his sceptre and all rose, hundreds and hundreds of them throughout the hall, their garments rustling
as they rose like leaves in a sudden wind. He seated himself and once more from every throat went up the regal
salutation that was the king's alone, of—

'Life! Blood! Strength! Pharaoh! Pharaoh! Pharaoh!'

In the silence that followed I heard him say, to the
Princess, I think,

'Amenmeses I see, and others of our kin, but where is
my son Seti, the Prince of Egypt?'

'Watching us no doubt from some vestibule. My brother loves not ceremonials,' answered Userti.

Then, with a little sigh, Seti stepped forward, followed by Bakenkhonsu and myself, and at a distance by other members of his household. As he marched up the long hall all drew to this side or that, saluting him with low bows. Arriving in front of the throne he bent till his knee touched the ground, saying,

'I give greeting, O King and Father.'

'I give greeting, O Prince and Son. Be seated,' answered Meneptah.

Seti seated himself in a chair that had been made ready for him at the foot of the throne, and on its right, and in another chair to the left, but set farther from the steps, Amenmeses seated himself also. At a motion from the Prince I took my stand behind his chair.

The formal business of the Court began. At the beckoning of an usher people of all sorts appeared singly and handed in petitions written on rolled-up papyri, which the Vizier Nehesi took and threw into a leathern sack that was held open by a black slave. In some cases an answer to his petition, whereof this was only the formal delivery, was handed back to the suppliant, who touched his brow with the roll that perhaps meant everything to him, and bowed himself away to learn his fate. Then appeared sheiks of the desert tribes, and captains from fortresses in Syria, and traders who had been harmed by enemies, and even peasants who had suffered violence from officers, each to make his prayer. Of all of these supplications the scribes took notes, while to some the Vizier and councillors made

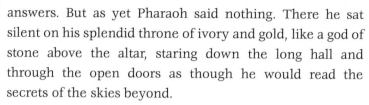

answers. But as yet Pharaoh said nothing. There he sat silent on his splendid throne of ivory and gold, like a god of stone above the altar, staring down the long hall and through the open doors as though he would read the secrets of the skies beyond.

'I told you that courts were wearisome, friend Ana,' whispered the Prince to me without turning his head. 'Do you not already begin to wish that you were back writing tales at Memphis?'

Before I could answer some movement in the throng at the end of the hall drew the eyes of the Prince and of all of us. I looked, and saw advancing towards the throne a tall, bearded man already old, although his black hair was but grizzled with grey. He was arrayed in a white linen robe, over which hung a woollen cloak such as shepherds wear, and he carried in his hand a long thornwood staff. His face was splendid and very handsome, and his black eyes flashed like fire. He walked forward slowly, looking neither to the left nor the right, and the throng made way for him as though he were a prince. Indeed, I thought that they showed more fear of him than of any prince, since they shrank from him as he came. Nor was he alone, for after him walked another man who was very like to him, but as I judged, still older, for his beard, which hung down to his middle, was snow-white as was the hair of his head. He also was dressed in a sheepskin cloak and carried a staff in his hand. Now a whisper rose among the people and the whisper said,

'The prophets of the men of Israel! The prophets of the men of Israel!'

The two stood before the throne and looked at Pharaoh, making no obeisance. Pharaoh looked at them and was silent. For a long space they stood thus in the midst of a great quiet but Pharaoh would not speak, and none of his officers seemed to dare to open their mouths. At length the first of the prophets spoke in a clear, cold voice as some conqueror might do.

'You know me, Pharaoh, and my errand.'

'I know you,' answered Pharaoh slowly, 'as well I may, seeing that we played together when we were little. You are that Hebrew whom my sister, she who sleeps in Osiris, took to be as a son to her, giving to you a name that means "drawn forth" because she drew you forth as an infant from among the reeds of Nile. Aye, I know you and your brother also, but your errand I know not.'

'This is my errand, Pharaoh, or rather the errand of Jahveh, God of Israel, for whom I speak. Have you not heard it before? It is that you should let his people go to do sacrifice to him in the wilderness.'

'Who is Jahveh? I know not Jahveh who serves Amon and the gods of Egypt, and why should I let your people go?'

'Jahveh is the God of Israel, the great God of all gods whose power you shall learn if you will not hearken, Pharaoh. As for why you should let the people go, ask it of the Prince your son who sits yonder. Ask him of what he saw in the streets of this city but last night, and of a certain judgment that he passed upon one of the officers of Pharaoh. Or if he will not tell you, learn it from the lips of the maiden who is named Merapi, Moon of Israel, the daughter of Nathan the Levite. Stand forward, Merapi, daughter of Nathan.'

Then from the throng at the back of the hall came forward Merapi, clad in a white robe and with a black veil thrown about her head in token of mourning, but not so as to hide her face. Up the hall she glided and made obeisance to Pharaoh, as she did so, casting one swift look at Seti where he sat. Then she stood still, looking, as I thought, wonderfully beautiful in that simple robe of white and the veil of black.

'Speak, woman,' said Pharaoh.

She obeyed, telling all the tale in her low and honeyed voice, nor did any seem to think it long or wearisome. At length she ended, and Pharaoh said,

'Say, Seti my son, is this truth?'

'It is truth, O my Father. By virtue of my powers as Governor of this city I caused the captain Khuaka to be put to death for the crime of murder done by him before my eyes in the streets of the city.'

'Perchance you did right and perchance you did wrong, Son Seti. At least you are the best judge, and because he struck your royal person, this Khuaka deserved to die.'

Again he was silent for a while staring through the open doors at the sky beyond. Then he said,

'What would ye more, Prophets of Jahveh? Justice has been done upon my officer who slew the man of your people. A life has been taken for a life according to the strict letter of the law. The matter is finished. Unless you have aught to say, get you gone.'

'By the command of the Lord our God,' answered the prophet, 'we have this to say to you, O Pharaoh. Lift the heavy yoke from off the neck of the people of Israel. Bid that they cease from the labour of the making of bricks to build your walls and cities.'

'And if I refuse, what then?'

'Then the curse of Jahveh shall be on you, Pharaoh, and with plague upon plague shall he smite this land of Egypt.'

Now a sudden rage seized Meneptah.

'What!' he cried. 'Do you dare to threaten me in my own palace, and would ye cause all the multitude of the people of Israel who have grown fat in the land to cease from their labours? Hearken, my servants, and, scribes, write down my decree. Go ye to the country of Goshen and say to the Israelites that the bricks they made they shall make us aforetime and more work shall they do than aforetime in the days of my father, Rameses. Only no more straw shall be given to them for the making of the bricks. Because they are idle, let them go forth and gather the straw for themselves; let them gather it from the face of the fields.'

There was silence for a while. Then with one voice both the prophets spoke, pointing with their wands to Pharaoh,

'In the Name of the Lord God we curse you, Pharaoh, who soon shall die and make answer for this sin. The people of Egypt we curse also. Ruin shall be their portion; death shall be their bread and blood shall they drink in a great darkness. Moreover, at the last Pharaoh shall let the people go.'

Then, waiting no answer, they turned and strode away side by side, nor did any man hinder them in their goings. Again there was silence in the hall, the silence of fear, for these were awful words that the prophets had spoken. Pharaoh knew it, for his chin sank upon his breast and his

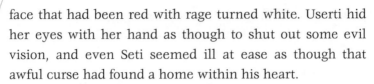

face that had been red with rage turned white. Userti hid her eyes with her hand as though to shut out some evil vision, and even Seti seemed ill at ease as though that awful curse had found a home within his heart.

At a motion of Pharaoh's hand the Vizier Nehesi struck the ground thrice with his wand of office and pointed to the door, thus giving the accustomed sign that the Court was finished, whereon all the people turned and went away with bent heads speaking no words one to another. Presently the great hall was emptied save for the officers and guards and those who attended upon Pharaoh. When everyone had gone Seti the Prince rose and bowed before the throne.

'O Pharaoh,' he said, 'be pleased to hearken. We have heard very evil words spoken by these Hebrew men, words that threaten your divine life, O Pharaoh, and call down a curse upon the Upper and the Lower Land. Pharaoh, these people of Israel hold that they suffer wrong and are oppressed. Now give me, your son, a writing under your hand and seal, by virtue of which I shall have power to go down to the Land of Goshen and inquire of this matter, and afterwards make report of the truth to you. Then, if it seems to you that the People of Israel are unjustly dealt by, you may lighten their burden and bring the curse of their prophets to nothing. But if it seems to you that the tales they tell are idle then your words shall stand.'

Now, listening, I, Ana, thought that Pharaoh would once more be angry. But it was not so, for when he spoke again it was in the voice of one who is crushed by grief or weariness.

'Have your will, Son,' he said. 'Only take with you a great guard of soldiers lest these hook-nosed dogs should do you mischief. I trust them not, who, like the Hyksos whose blood runs in many of them, were ever the foes of Egypt. Did they not conspire with the Ninebow Barbarians whom I crushed in the great battle, and do they not now threaten us in the name of their outland god? Still, let the writing be prepared and I will seal it. And stay. I think, Seti, that you, who were ever gentle-natured, have some-what too soft a heart towards these shepherd slaves. Therefore I will not send you alone. Amenmeses your cousin shall go with you, but under your command. It is spoken.'

'Life! Blood! Strength!' said both Seti and Amenmeses, thus acknowledging the king's command.

Now I thought that all was finished. But it was not so, for presently Pharaoh said,

'Let the guards withdraw to the end of the hall and with them the servants. Let the King's councillors and the officers of the household remain.'

Instantly all saluted and withdrew out of hearing. I, too, made ready to go, but the Prince said to me,

'Stay, that you may take note of what passes.'

Pharaoh, watching, saw if he did not hear.

'Who is that man, Son?' he asked.

'He is Ana my private scribe and librarian, O Pharaoh, whom I trust. It was he who saved me from harm but last night.'

'You say it, Son. Let him remain in attendance on you, knowing that if he betrays our council he dies.'

THE COURT OF BETROTHAL

Userti looked up frowning as though she were about to speak. If so, she changed her mind and was silent, perhaps because Pharaoh's word once spoken could not be altered. Bakenkhonsu remained also as a Councillor of the King according to his right.

When all had gone Pharaoh, who had been brooding, lifted his head and spoke slowly but in the voice of one who gives a judgment that may not be questioned, saying,

'Prince Seti, you are my only son born of Queen Ast-Nefert, royal Sister, royal Mother, who sleeps in the bosom of Osiris. It is true that you are not my first-born son, since the Count Ramessu'—here he pointed to a stout mild-faced man of pleasing, rather foolish appearance—'is your elder by two years. But, as he knows well, his mother, who is still with us, is a Syrian by birth and of no royal blood, and therefore he can never sit upon the throne of Egypt. Is it not so, my son Ramessu?'

'It is so, O Pharaoh,' answered the Count in a pleasant voice, 'nor do I seek ever to sit upon that throne, who am well content with the offices and wealth that Pharaoh has been pleased to confer upon me, his first-born.'

'Let the words of the Count Ramessu be written down,' said Pharaoh, 'and placed in the temple of Ptah of this city, and in the temples of Ptah at Memphis and of Amon at Thebes, that hereafter they may never be questioned.'

The scribes in attendance wrote down the words and, at a sign from the Prince Seti, I also wrote them down, setting the papyrus I had with me on my knee. When this was finished Pharaoh went on.

'Therefore, O Prince Seti, you are the heir of Egypt and

perhaps, as those Hebrew prophets said, will ere long be called upon to sit in my place on its throne.'

'May the King live for ever!' exclaimed Seti, 'for well he knows that I do not seek his crown and dignities.'

'I do know it well, my son; so well that I wish you thought more of that crown and those dignities which, if the gods will, must come to you. If they will it not, next in the order of succession stands your cousin, the Count Amenmeses, who is also of royal blood both on his father's and his mother's side, and after him I know not who, unless it be my daughter and your half-sister, the royal Princess Userti, Lady of Egypt.'

Now Userti spoke, very earnestly, saying,

'O Pharaoh, surely my right in the succession, according to ancient precedent, precedes that of my cousin, the Count Amenmeses.'

Amenmeses was about to answer, but Pharaoh lifted his hand and he was silent.

'It is a matter for those learned in such lore to discuss,' Meneptah replied in a somewhat hesitating voice. 'I pray the gods that it may never be needful that this high question should be considered in the Council. Nevertheless, let the words of the royal Princess be written down. Now, Prince Seti,' he went on when this had been done, 'you are still unmarried, and if you have children they are not royal.'

'I have none, O Pharaoh,' said Seti.

'Is it so?' answered Meneptah indifferently. 'The Count Amenmeses has children I know, for I have seen them, but by his wife Unuri, who also is of the royal line, he has none.'

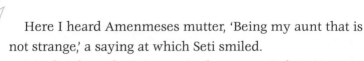

Here I heard Amenmeses mutter, 'Being my aunt that is not strange,' a saying at which Seti smiled.

'My daughter, the Princess, is also unmarried. So it seems that the fountain of the royal blood is running dry——'

'Now it is coming,' whispered Seti below his breath so that only I could hear.

'Therefore,' continued Pharaoh, 'as you know, Prince Seti, for the royal Princess of Egypt by my command went to speak to you of this matter last night, I make a decree——'

'Pardon, O Pharaoh,' interrupted the Prince, 'my sister spoke to me of no decree last night, save that I should attend at the court here to-day.'

'Because I could not, Seti, seeing that another was present with you whom you refused to dismiss,' and she let her eyes rest on me.

'It matters not,' said Pharaoh, 'since now I will utter it with my own lips which perhaps is better. It is my will, Prince, that you forthwith wed the royal Princess Userti, that children of the true blood of the Ramessides may be born. Hear and obey.'

Now Userti shifted her eyes from me to Seti, watching him very closely. Seated at his side upon the ground with my writing roll spread across my knee, I, too, watched him closely, and noted that his lips turned white and his face grew fixed and strange.

'I hear the command of Pharaoh,' he said in a low voice making obeisance, and hesitated.

'Have you aught to add?' asked Meneptah sharply.

'Only, O Pharaoh, that though this would be a marriage decreed for reasons of the State, still there is a lady who must be given in marriage, and she my half-sister who heretofore has only loved me as a relative. Therefore, I would know from her lips if it is her will to take me as a husband.'

Now all looked at Userti who replied in a cold voice,

'In this matter, Prince, as in all others I have no will but that of Pharaoh.'

'You have heard,' interrupted Meneptah impatiently, 'and as in our House it has always been the custom for kin to marry kin, why should it not be her will? Also, who else should she marry? Amenmeses is already wed. There remains only Saptah his brother who is younger than herself——'

'So am I,' murmured Seti, 'by two long years,' but happily Userti did not hear him.

'Nay, my father,' she said with decision, 'never will I take a deformed man to husband.'

Now from the shadow on the further side of the throne, where I could not see him, there hobbled forward a young noble, short in stature, light-haired like Seti, and with a sharp, clever face which put me in mind of that of a jackal (indeed for this reason he was named Thoth by the common people, after the jackal-headed god). He was very angry, for his cheeks were flushed and his small eyes flashed.

'Must I listen, Pharaoh,' he said in a little voice, 'while my cousin the Royal Princess reproaches me in public for my lame foot, which I have because my nurse let me fall when I was still in arms?'

'Then his nurse let his grandfather fall also, for he too

was club-footed, as I who have seen him naked in his cradle can bear witness,' whispered old Bakenkhonsu.

'It seems so, Count Saptah, unless you stop your ears,' replied Pharaoh.

'She says she will not marry me,' went on Saptah, 'me who from childhood have been a slave to her and to no other woman.'

'Not by my wish, Saptah. Indeed, I pray you to go and be a slave to any woman whom you will,' exclaimed Userti.

'But I say,' continued Saptah, 'that one day she shall marry me, for the Prince Seti will not live for ever.'

'How do you know that, Cousin?' asked Seti. 'The High-priest here will tell you a different story.'

Now certain of those present turned their heads away to hide the smile upon their faces. Yet on this day some god spoke with Saptah's voice making him a prophet, since in a year to come she did marry him, in order that she might stay upon the throne at a time of trouble when Egypt would not suffer that a woman should have sole rule over the land.

But Pharaoh did not smile like the courtiers; indeed he grew angry.

'Peace, Saptah!' he said. 'Who are you that wrangle before me, talking of the death of kings and saying that you will wed the Royal Princess? One more such word and you shall be driven into banishment. Hearken now. Almost am I minded to declare my daughter, the Royal Princess, sole heiress to the throne, seeing that in her there is more strength and wisdom than in any other of our House.'

'If such be Pharaoh's will, let Pharaoh's will be done,'

said Seti most humbly. 'Well I know my own unworthiness to fill so high a station, and by all the gods I swear that my beloved sister will find no more faithful subject than myself.'

'You mean, Seti,' interrupted Userti, 'that rather than marry me you would abandon your right to the double crown. Truly I am honoured. Seti, whether you reign or I, I will not marry you.'

'What words are these I hear?' cried Meneptah. 'Is there indeed one in this land of Egypt who dares to say that Pharaoh's decree shall be disobeyed? Write it down, Scribes, and you, O Officers, let it be proclaimed from Thebes to the sea, that on the third day from now at the hour of noon in the temple of Hathor in this city, the Prince, the Royal Heir, Seti Meneptah, Beloved of Ra, will wed the Royal Princess of Egypt, Lily of Love, Beloved of Hathor, Userti, Daughter of me, the god.'

'Life! Blood! Strength!' called all the Court.

Then, guided by some high officer, the Prince Seti was led before the throne and the Princess Userti was set beside him, or rather facing him. According to the ancient custom a great gold cup was brought and filled with red wine, to me it looked like blood. Userti took the cup and, kneeling, gave it to the Prince, who drank and gave it back to her that she might also drink in solemn token of their betrothal. Is not the scene graven on the broad bracelets of gold which in after days Seti wore when he sat upon the throne, those same bracelets that at a future time I with my own hands clasped about the wrists of dead Userti?

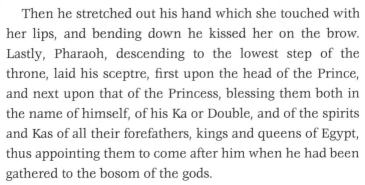

Then he stretched out his hand which she touched with her lips, and bending down he kissed her on the brow. Lastly, Pharaoh, descending to the lowest step of the throne, laid his sceptre, first upon the head of the Prince, and next upon that of the Princess, blessing them both in the name of himself, of his Ka or Double, and of the spirits and Kas of all their forefathers, kings and queens of Egypt, thus appointing them to come after him when he had been gathered to the bosom of the gods.

These things done, he departed in state, surrounded by his court, preceded and followed by his guards and leaning on the arm of the Princess Userti, whom he loved better than anyone in the world.

A while later I stood alone with the Prince in his private chamber, where I had first seen him.

'That is finished,' he said in a cheerful voice, 'and I tell you, Ana, that I feel quite, quite happy. Have you ever shivered upon the bank of a river of a winter morning, fearing to enter, and yet, when you did enter, have you not been pleased to find that the icy water refreshed you and made you not cold but hot?'

'Yes, Prince. It is when one comes out of the water, if the wind blows and no sun shines, that one feels colder than before.'

'True, Ana, and therefore one must not come out. One should stop there till one—drowns or is eaten by a croco-dile. But, say, did I do it well?'

'Old Bakenkhonsu told me, Prince, that he had been pres-ent at many royal betrothals, I think he said eleven, and had never seen one conducted with more grace. He added that the way in which you kissed the brow of her Highness was perfect, as was all your demeanour after the first argument.'

'And so it would remain, Ana, if I were never called upon to do more than kiss her brow, to which I have been accustomed from boyhood. Oh! Ana, Ana,' he added in a kind of cry, 'already you are becoming a courtier like the rest of them, a courtier who cannot speak the truth. Well, nor can I, so why should I blame you? Tell me again all about your marriage, Ana, of how it began and how it ended.'

5

THE
PROPHECY

Whether or no the Prince Seti saw Userti again before the hour of his marriage with her I cannot say, because he never told me. Indeed I was not present at the marriage, for the reason that I had been granted leave to return to Memphis, there to settle my affairs and sell my house on entering upon my appointment as private scribe to his Highness. Thus it came about that fourteen full days went by from that of the holding of the Court of Betrothal before I found myself standing once more at the gate of the Prince's palace, attended by a servant who led an ass on which were laden all my manuscripts and certain possessions that had descended to me from my ancestors with the title-deeds of their tombs. Different indeed was my reception on this my second coming. Even as I reached the steps the old chamberlain Pambasa appeared, running down them so fast that his white robes and beard streamed upon the air.

'Greeting, most learned scribe, most honourable Ana,'

he panted. 'Glad indeed am I to see you, since every hour his Highness asks if you have returned, and blames me because you have not come. Verily I believe that if you had stayed upon the road another day I should have been sent to look for you, who have had sharp words said to me because I did not arrange that you should be accompanied by a guard, as though the Vizier Nehesi would have paid the costs of a guard without the direct order of Pharaoh. O most excellent Ana, give me of the charm which you have doubtless used to win the love of our royal master, and I will pay you well for it who find it easier to earn his wrath.'

'I will, Pambasa. Here it is—write better stories than I do instead of telling them, and he will love you more than he does me. But say—how went the marriage? I have heard upon the way that it was very splendid.'

'Splendid! Oh! it was ten times more than splendid. It was as though the god Osiris were once more wed to the goddess Isis in the very halls of heaven. Indeed his Highness, the bridegroom, was dressed as a god, yes, he wore the robes and the holy ornaments of Amon. And the procession! And the feast that Pharaoh gave! I tell you that the Prince was so overcome with joy and all this weight of glory that, before it was over, looking at him I saw that his eyes were closed, being dazzled by the gleam of gold and jewels and the loveliness of his royal bride. He told me that it was so himself, fearing perhaps lest I should have thought that he was asleep. Then there were the presents, something to everyone of us according to his degree. I got—well it matters not. And, learned Ana, I did not forget you. Knowing well that everything would be gone before you returned I spoke your name in the ear of his Highness, offering to keep your gift.'

'Indeed, Pambasa, and what did he say?'

'He said that he was keeping it himself. When I stared wondering what it might be, for I saw nothing on him, he added, "It is here," and touched the private signet guard that he has always worn, an ancient ring of gold, but of no great value I should say, with "Beloved of Thoth and of the King" cut upon it. It seems that he must take it off to make room for another and much finer ring which her Highness has given him.'

Now, by this time, the ass having been unloaded by the slaves and led away, we had passed through the hall where many were idling as ever, and were come to the private apartments of the palace.

'This way,' said Pambasa. 'The orders are that I am to take you to the Prince wherever he may be, and just now he is seated in the great apartment with her Highness, where they have been receiving homage and deputations from distant cities. The last left about half an hour ago.'

'First I will prepare myself, worthy Pambasa,' I began.

'No, no, the orders are instant, I dare not disobey them. Enter,' and with a courtly flourish he drew a rich curtain.

'By Amon,' exclaimed a weary voice which I knew as that of the Prince, 'here come more councillors or priests. Prepare, my sister, prepare!'

'I pray you, Seti,' answered another voice, that of Userti, 'to learn to call me by my right name, which is no longer sister. Nor, indeed, am I your full sister.'

'I crave your pardon,' said Seti. 'Prepare, Royal Wife, prepare!'

By now the curtain was fully drawn and I stood, travel-stained, forlorn and, to tell the truth, trembling a little, for I feared her Highness, in the doorway, hesitating to pass the threshold. Beyond was a splendid chamber full of light, in the centre of which upon a carven and golden chair, one of two that were set there, sat her Highness magnificently apparelled, faultlessly beautiful and calm. She was engaged in studying a painted roll, left no doubt by the last deputation, for others similar to it were laid neatly side by side upon a table.

The second chair was empty, for the Prince was walking restlessly up and down the chamber, his ceremonial robe somewhat disarrayed and the uræus circlet of gold which he wore, tilted back upon his head, because of his habit of running his fingers through his brown hair. As I still stood in the dark shadow, for Pambasa had left me, and thus remained unseen, the talk went on.

'I am prepared, Husband. Pardon me, it is you who look otherwise. Why would you dismiss the scribes and household before the ceremony was ended?'

'Because they wearied me,' said Seti, 'with their continual bowing and praising and formalities.'

'In which I saw nothing unusual. Now they must be recalled.'

'Let whoever it is enter,' he exclaimed.

Then I stepped forward into the light, prostrating myself.

'Why,' he cried, 'it is Ana returned from Memphis! Draw near, Ana, and a thousand welcomes to you. Do you know

I thought that you were another high-priest, or governor of some Nome of which I had never heard.'

'Ana! Who is Ana?' asked the Princess. 'Oh! I remember that scribe——. Well, it is plain that he has returned from Memphis,' and she eyed my dusty robe.

'Royal One,' I murmured abashed, 'do not blame me that I enter your presence thus. Pambasa led me here against my will by the direct order of the Prince.'

'Is it so? Say, Seti, does this man bring tidings of import from Memphis that you needed his presence in such haste?'

'Yes, Userti, at least I think so. You have the writings safe, have you not, Ana?'

'Quite safe, your Highness,' I answered, though I knew not of what writings he spoke, unless they were the manuscripts of my stories.

'Then, my Lord, I will leave you to talk of the tidings from Memphis and these writings,' said the Princess.

'Yes, yes. We must talk of them, Userti. Also of the journey to the land of Goshen on which Ana starts with me tomorrow.'

'To-morrow! Why this morning you told me it was fixed for three days hence.'

'Did I, Sister—I mean Wife? If so, it was because I was not sure whether Ana, who is to be my chariot companion, would be back.'

'A scribe your chariot companion! Surely it would be more fitting that your cousin Amenmeses——'

'To Set with Amenmeses!' he exclaimed. 'You know well, Userti, that the man is hateful to me with his cunning yet empty talk.'

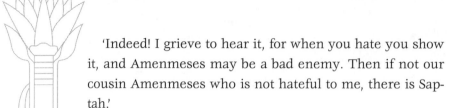

'Indeed! I grieve to hear it, for when you hate you show it, and Amenmeses may be a bad enemy. Then if not our cousin Amenmeses who is not hateful to me, there is Saptah.'

'I thank you; I will not travel in a cage with a jackal.'

'Jackal! I do not love Saptah, but one of the royal blood of Egypt a jackal! Then there is Nehesi the Vizier, or the General of the escort whose name I forget.'

'Do you think, Userti, that I wish to talk about state economies with that old money-sack, or to listen to boastings of deeds he never did in war from a half-bred Nubian butcher?'

'I do not know, Husband. Yet of what will you talk with this Ana? Of poems, I suppose, and silliness. Or will it be perchance of Merapi, Moon of Israel, whom I gather both of you think so beautiful. Well, have your way. You tell me that I am not to accompany you upon this journey, I your new-made wife, and now I find that it is because you wish my place to be filled by a writer of tales whom you picked up the other day—your "twin in Ra" forsooth! Fare you well, my Lord,' and she rose from her seat, gathering up her robes with both hands.

Then Seti grew angry.

'Userti,' he said, stamping upon the floor, 'you should not use such words. You know well that I do not take you with me because there may be danger yonder among the Hebrews. Moreover, it is not Pharaoh's wish.'

She turned and answered with cold courtesy,

'Then I crave your pardon and thank you for your kind thought for the safety of my person. I knew not this mission was so dangerous. Be careful, Seti, that the Scribe Ana comes to no harm.'

So saying she bowed and vanished through the curtains.

'Ana,' said Seti, 'tell me, for I never was quick at figures, how many minutes is it from now till the fourth hour to-morrow morning when I shall order my chariot to be ready? Also, do you know whether it is possible to travel from Goshen across the marshes and to return by Syria? Or, failing that, to travel across the desert to Thebes and sail down the Nile in the spring?'

'Oh! my Prince, my Prince,' I said, 'I pray you to dismiss me. Let me go anywhere out of the reach of her Highness's tongue.'

'It is strange how alike we think upon every matter, Ana, even of Merapi and the tongues of royal ladies. Hearken to my command. You are not to go. If it is a question of going, there are others who will go first. Moreover, you cannot go, but must stay and bear your burdens as I bear mine. Remember the broken cup, Ana.'

'I remember, my Prince, but sooner would I be scourged with rods than by such words as those to which I must listen.'

Yet that very night, when I had left the Prince, I was destined to hear more pleasant words from this same changeful, or perchance politic, royal lady. She sent for me and I went, much afraid. I found her in a small chamber alone, save for one old lady of honour who sat at the end of the room and appeared to be deaf, which perhaps was why she was chosen. Userti bade me be seated before her very courteously, and spoke to me thus, whether because of some talk she had held with the Prince or not, I do not know.

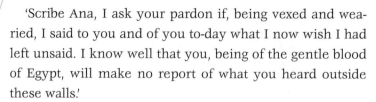

'Scribe Ana, I ask your pardon if, being vexed and wearied, I said to you and of you to-day what I now wish I had left unsaid. I know well that you, being of the gentle blood of Egypt, will make no report of what you heard outside these walls.'

'May my tongue be cut out first,' I answered.

'It seems, Scribe Ana, that my lord the Prince has taken a great love of you. How or why this came about so suddenly, you being a man, I do not understand, but I am sure that as it is so, it must be because there is much in you to love, since never did I know the Prince to show deep regard for one who was not most honourable and worthy. Now things being so, it is plain that you will become the favourite of his Highness, a man who does not change his mind in such matters, and that he will tell you all his secret thoughts, perhaps some that he hides from the Councillors of State, or even from me. In short you will grow into a power in the land and perhaps one day be the greatest in it—after Pharaoh— although you may still seem to be but a private scribe.

'I do not pretend to you that I should have wished this to be so, who would rather that my husband had but one real councillor—myself. Yet seeing that it is so, I bow my head, hoping that it may be decreed for the best. If ever any jealousy should overcome me in this matter and I should speak sharply to you, as I did to-day, I ask your pardon in advance for that which has not happened, as I have asked it for that which has happened. I pray of you, Scribe Ana, that you will do your best to influence the mind of the Prince for good, since he is easily led by any whom he loves. I pray you also being quick and thoughtful, as I see you are, that you will make a study of statecraft, and of the policies of our royal House, coming to me, if it be needful, for instruction therein, so that you may be able to guide the feet of the Prince aright, should he turn to you for counsel.'

'All of this I will do, your Highness, if by any chance it lies in my power, though who am I that I should hope to make a path for the feet of kings? Moreover, I would add this, although he is so gentle-natured, I think that in the end the Prince is one who will always choose his own path.'

'It may be so Ana. At the least I thank you. I pray you to be sure also that in me you will always have a friend and not an enemy, although at times the quickness of my nature, which has never been controlled, may lead you to think otherwise. Now I will say one more thing that shall be secret between us. I know that the Prince loves me as a friend and relative rather than as a wife, and that he would not have sought this marriage of himself, as is perhaps natural. I know, too, that other women will come into his life, though these may be fewer than in the case of most kings, because he is more hard to please. Of such I cannot complain, as this is according to the customs of our country. I fear only one thing—namely that some woman, ceasing to be his toy, may take Seti's heart and make him altogether hers. In this matter, Scribe Ana, as in others I ask your help, since I would be queen of Egypt in all ways, not in name only.'

'Your Highness, how can I say to the Prince—"So much shall you love this or that woman and no more?" Moreover,

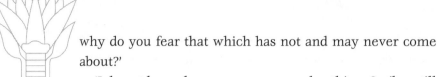

why do you fear that which has not and may never come about?'

'I do not know how you can say such a thing, Scribe, still I ask you to say it if you can. As to why I fear, it is because I seem to feel the near shadow of some woman lying cold upon me and building a wall of blackness between his Highness and myself.'

'It is but a dream, Princess.'

'Mayhap. I hope so. Yet I think otherwise. Oh! Ana, cannot you, who study the hearts of men and women, understand my case? I have married where I can never hope to be loved as other women are, I who am a wife, yet not a wife. I read your thought; it is—why then did you marry? Since I have told you so much I will tell you that also. First, it is because the Prince is different to other men and in his own fashion above them, yes, far above any with whom I could have wed as royal heiress of Egypt. Secondly, because being cut off from love, what remains to me but ambition? At least I would be a great queen, as was Hatshepu in her day, and lift my country out of the many troubles in which it is sunk and write my name large upon the books of history, which I could only do by taking Pharaoh's heir to husband, as is my duty.'

She brooded a while, then added, 'Now I have shown you all my thought. Whether I have been wise to do so the gods know alone and time will tell me.'

'Princess,' I said, 'I thank you for trusting me and I will help you if I may. Yet I am troubled. I, a humble man if of good blood, who a little while ago was but a scribe and a student, a dreamer who had known trouble also, have suddenly by chance, or some divine decree, been lifted high in the favour of the heir of Egypt, and it would seem have even won your trust. Now I wonder how I shall bear myself in this new place which in truth I never sought.'

'I do not know, who find the present and its troubles enough to carry. But, doubtless, the decree of which you speak that set you there has also written down what will be the end of all. Meanwhile, I have a gift for you. Say, Scribe, have you ever handled any weapon besides a pen?'

'Yes, your Highness, as a lad I was skilled in sword play. Moreover, though I do not love war and bloodshed, some years ago I fought in the great battle between the Ninebow Barbarians, when Pharaoh called upon the young men of Memphis to do their part. With my own hands I slew two in fair fight, though one nearly brought me to my end,' and I pointed to a scar which showed red through my grey hair where a spear had bitten deep.

'It is well, or so I think, who love soldiers better than stainers of papyrus pith.'

Then, going to a painted chest of reeds, she took from it a wonderful shirt of mail fashioned of bronze rings, and a short sword also of bronze, having a golden hilt of which the end was shaped to the likeness of the head of a lion, and with her own hands gave them to me, saying,

'These are spoils that my grandsire, the great Rameses, took in his youth from a prince of the Khitah, whom he smote with his own hands in Syria in that battle whereof your grandfather made the poem. Wear the shirt, which no spear will pierce, beneath your robe and gird the sword about you when you go down yonder among the Israelites,

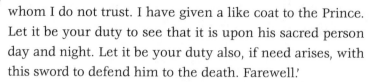

whom I do not trust. I have given a like coat to the Prince. Let it be your duty to see that it is upon his sacred person day and night. Let it be your duty also, if need arises, with this sword to defend him to the death. Farewell.'

'May all the gods reject me from the Fields of the Blessed if I fail in this trust,' I answered, and departed wondering, to seek sleep which, as it chanced, I was not to find for a while.

For as I went down the corridor, led by one of the ladies of the household, whom should I find waiting at the end of it but old Pambasa to inform me with many bows that the Prince needed my presence. I asked how that could be seeing he had dismissed me for the night. He replied that he did not know, but he was commanded to conduct me to the private chamber, the same room in which I had first seen his Highness. Thither I went and found him warming himself at the fire, for the night was cold. Looking up he bade Pambasa admit those who were waiting, then noting the shirt of mail and the sword I carried in my hand, said,

'You have been with the Princess, have you not, and she must have had much to say to you for your talk was long? Well, I think I can guess its purport who from a child have known her mind. She told you to watch me well, body and heart and all that comes from the heart—oh! and much else. Also she gave you that Syrian gear to wear among the Hebrews as she has given the like to me, being of a careful mind which foresees everything. Now, hearken, Ana; I grieve to keep you from your rest, who must be weary both with talk and travel. But old Bakenkhonsu, whom you know, waits without, and with him Ki the great magician, whom I think you have not seen. He is a man of wonderful lore and in some ways not altogether human. At least he does strange feats of magic, and at times both the past and the future seem to be open to his sight, though as we know neither the one nor the other, who can tell whether he reads them truly. Doubtless he has, or thinks he has, some message to me from the heavens, which I thought you might wish to hear.'

'I wish it much, Prince, if I am worthy, and you will protect me from the anger of this magician whom I fear.'

'Anger sometimes turns to trust, Ana. Did you not find it so just now in the case of her Highness, as I told you might very well happen? Hush! They come. Be seated and prepare your tablets to make record of what they say.'

The curtains were drawn and through them came the aged Bakenkhonsu leaning upon his staff, and with him another man, Ki himself, clad in a white robe and having his head shaven, for he was an hereditary priest of Amon of Thebes and an initiate of Isis, Mother of Mysteries. Also his office was that of Kherheb, or chief magician of Egypt. At first sight there was nothing strange about this man. Indeed, he might well have been a middle-aged merchant by his looks; in body he was short and stout; in face fat and smiling. But in this jovial countenance were set two very strange eyes, grey-hued rather than black. While the rest of the face seemed to smile these eyes looked straight into nothingness as do those of a statue. Indeed they were like to the eyes or rather the eye-places of a stone statue, so deeply were they set into the head. For my part I can only say I thought them awful, and by their look judged that whatever Ki might be he was no cheat.

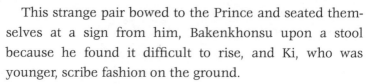

This strange pair bowed to the Prince and seated themselves at a sign from him, Bakenkhonsu upon a stool because he found it difficult to rise, and Ki, who was younger, scribe fashion on the ground.

'What did I tell you, Bakenkhonsu?' said Ki in a full, rich voice, ending the words with a curious chuckle.

'You told me, Magician, that we should find the Prince in this chamber of which you described every detail to me as I see it now, although neither of us have entered it before. You said also that seated therein on the ground would be the scribe Ana, whom I know but you do not, having in his hands waxen tablets and a stylus and by him a coat of curious mail and a lion-hilted sword.'

'That is strange,' interrupted the Prince, 'but forgive me, Bakenkhonsu sees these things. If you, O Ki, would tell us what is written upon Ana's tablets which neither of you can see, it would be stranger still, that is if anything is written.'

Ki smiled and stared upwards at the ceiling. Presently he said,

'The scribe Ana uses a shorthand of his own that is not easy to decipher. Yet I see written on the tablets the price he obtained for some house in a city that is not named—it is so much. Also I see the sums he disbursed for himself, a servant, and the food of an ass at two inns where he stopped upon a journey. They are so much and so much. Also there is a list of papyrus rolls and the words, "blue cloak," and then an erasure.'

'Is that right, Ana?' asked the Prince.

'Quite right,' I answered with awe, 'only the words "blue

cloak," which it is true I wrote upon the tablet, have also been erased.'

Ki chuckled and turned his eyes from the ceiling to my face.

'Would your Highness wish me to tell you anything of what is written upon the tablets of this scribe's memory as well as upon those of wax which he holds in his hand? They are easier to decipher than the others and I see on them many things of interest. For instance, secret words that seem to have been said to him by some Great One within an hour, matters of high policy, I think. For instance, a certain saying, I think of your Highness's, as to shivering upon the edge of water on a cold day, which when entered produced heat, and the answer thereto. For instance, words that were spoken in this palace when an alabaster cup was broke. By the way, Scribe, that was a very good place you chose in which to hide one half of the cup in the false bottom of a chest in your chamber, a chest that is fastened with a cord and sealed with a scarab of the time of the second Rameses. I think that the other half of the cup is somewhat nearer at hand' and turning, he stared at the wall where I could see nothing save slabs of alabaster.

Now I sat open-mouthed, for how could this man know these things, and the Prince laughed outright, saying,

'Ana, I begin to think you keep your counsel ill. At least I should think so, were it not that you have had no time to tell what the Princess yonder may have said to you, and can scarcely know the trick of the sliding panel in that wall which I have never shown to you.'

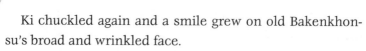

Ki chuckled again and a smile grew on old Bakenkhon-su's broad and wrinkled face.

'O Prince,' I began, 'I swear to you that never has one word passed my lips of aught——'

'I know it, friend,' broke in the Prince, 'but it seems there are some who do not wait for words but can read the Book of Thought. Therefore it is well not to meet them too often, since all have thoughts that should be known only to them and God. Magician, what is your business with me? Speak on as though we were alone.'

'This, Prince. You go upon a journey among the Hebrews, as all have heard. Now, Bakenkhonsu and I, also two seers of my College, seeing that we all love you and that your welfare is much to Egypt, have separately sought out the future as regards the issue of this journey. Although what we have learned differs in some matters, on others it is the same. Therefore we thought it our duty to tell you what we have learned.'

'Say on, Kherheb.'

'First, then, that your Highness's life will be in danger.'

'Life is always in danger, Ki. Shall I lose it? If so, do not fear to tell me.'

'We do not know, but we think not, because of the rest that is revealed to us. We learn that it is not your body only that will be in danger. Upon this journey you will see a woman whom you will come to love. This woman will, we think, bring you much sorrow and also much joy.'

'Then perhaps that journey is worth making, Ki, since many travel far before they find aught that they can love. Tell me, have I met this woman?'

'There we are troubled, Prince, for it would seem—unless we are deceived—that you have met her often and often; that you have known her for thousands of years, as you have known that man at your side for thousands of years.'

Seti's face grew very interested.

'What do you mean, Magician?' he asked, eyeing him keenly. 'How can I who am still young have known a woman and a man for thousands of years?'

Ki considered him with his strange eyes, and answered,

'You have many titles, Prince. Is not one of them "Lord of Re-births," and if so, how did you get it and what does it mean?'

'It is. What it means I do not know, but it was given to me because of some dream that my mother had the night before I was born. Do *you* tell *me* what it means, since you seem to know so much.'

'I cannot, Prince. The secret is not one that has been shown to me. Yet there was an aged man, a magician like myself from whom I learned much in my youth—Bak-enkhonsu here knew him well—who made a study of this matter. He told me he was sure, because it had been revealed to him, that men do not live once only and then depart hence for ever. He said that they live many times and in many shapes, though not always on this world, and that between each life there is a wall of darkness.'

'If so, of what use are lives which we do not remember after death has shut the door of each of them?'

'The doors may open again at last, Prince, and show us all the chambers through which our feet have wandered from the beginning.'

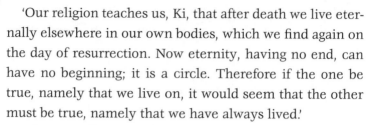

'Our religion teaches us, Ki, that after death we live eternally elsewhere in our own bodies, which we find again on the day of resurrection. Now eternity, having no end, can have no beginning; it is a circle. Therefore if the one be true, namely that we live on, it would seem that the other must be true, namely that we have always lived.'

'That is well reasoned, Prince. In the early days, before priests froze the thought of man into blocks of stone and built of them shrines to a thousand gods, many held that this reasoning was true, as then they held that there was but one god.'

'As do these Israelites whom I go to visit. What say you of their god, Ki?'

'That *he* is the same as our gods, Prince. To men's eyes God has many faces, and each swears that the one he sees is the only true god. Yet they are wrong, for all are true.'

'Or perchance false, Ki, unless even falsehood is a part of truth. Well, you have told me of two dangers, one to my body and one to my heart. Has any other been revealed to your wisdom?'

'Yes, Prince. The third is that this journey may in the end cost you your throne.'

'If I die certainly it will cost me my throne.'

'No, Prince, if you live.'

'Even so, Ki, I think that I could endure life seated more humbly than on a throne, though whether her Highness could endure it is another matter. Then you say that if I go upon this journey another will be Pharaoh in my place.'

'We do not say that, Prince. It is true that our arts have

shown us another filling your place in a time of wizardry and wonders and of the death of thousands. Yet when we look again we see not that other but you once more filling your own place.'

Here I, Ana, bethought me of my vision in Pharaoh's hall.

'The matter is even worse than I thought, Ki, since having once left the crown behind me, I think that I should have no wish to wear it any more,' said Seti. 'Who shows you all these things, and how?'

'Our *Kas*, which are our secret selves, show them to us, Prince, and in many ways. Sometimes it is by dreams or visions, sometimes by pictures on water, sometimes by writings in the desert sand. In all these fashions, and by others, our *Kas*, drawing from the infinite well of wisdom that is hidden in the being of every man, give us glimpses of the truth, as they give us who are instructed power to work marvels.'

'Of the truth. Then these things you tell me are true?'

'We believe so, Prince.'

'And being true must happen. So what is the use of your warning me against what must happen? There cannot be two truths. What would you have me do? Not go upon this journey? Why have you told me that I must go, since if I did not go the truth would become a lie, which it cannot? You say it is fated that I should go and because I go such and such things will come about. And yet you tell me not to go, for that is what you mean. Oh! Kherheb Ki and Bakenkhonsu, doubtless you are great magicians and strong in wisdom, but there are greater than you who rule the world, and there is a wisdom to which yours is but as a drop of water to the Nile. I thank you for your warnings, but to-morrow I go down to the land of Goshen to fulfil the commands of Pharaoh. If I come back again we will talk more of these matters here upon the earth. If I do not come back, perchance we will talk of them elsewhere. Farewell!'

6

THE
LAND OF
GOSHEN

The Prince Seti and all his train, a very great company, came in safety to the land of Goshen, I, Ana, travelling with him in his chariot. It was then as now a rich land, quite flat after the last line of desert hills through which we travelled by a narrow, tortuous path. Everywhere it was watered by canals, between which lay the grain fields wherein the seed had just been sown. Also there were other fields of green fodder whereon were tethered beasts by the hundred, and beyond these, upon the drier soil, grazed flocks of sheep. The town Goshen, if so it could be called, was but a poor place, numbers of mud huts, no more, in the centre of which stood a building, also of mud, with two brick pillars in front of it, that we were told was the temple of this people, into the inner parts of which none might enter save their High-priest. I laughed at the sight of it, but the Prince reproved me, saying that I should not judge of the spirit by the body, or of the god by his house.

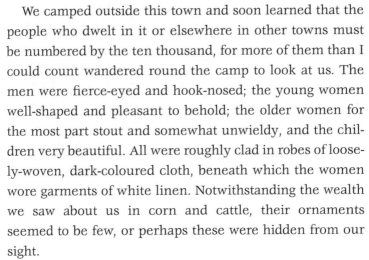

We camped outside this town and soon learned that the people who dwelt in it or elsewhere in other towns must be numbered by the ten thousand, for more of them than I could count wandered round the camp to look at us. The men were fierce-eyed and hook-nosed; the young women well-shaped and pleasant to behold; the older women for the most part stout and somewhat unwieldy, and the children very beautiful. All were roughly clad in robes of loosely-woven, dark-coloured cloth, beneath which the women wore garments of white linen. Notwithstanding the wealth we saw about us in corn and cattle, their ornaments seemed to be few, or perhaps these were hidden from our sight.

It was easy to see that they hated us Egyptians, and even dared to despise us. Hate shone in their glittering eyes, and I heard them calling us the 'idol-worshippers' one to the other and asking where was our god, the Bull, for being ignorant they thought that we worshipped Apis (as mayhap some of the common people do) instead of looking upon the sacred beast as a symbol of the powers of Nature. Indeed they did more, for on the first night after our coming they slaughtered a bull marked much as Apis is, and in the morning we found it lying near the gate of the camp, and pinned to its hide with sharp thorns great numbers of the scarabæus beetle still living. For again they did not know that among us Egyptians this beetle is no god but an emblem of the Creator, because it rolls a ball of mud between its feet and sets therein its eggs to hatch, as the Creator rolls the world that seems to be round, and causes it to produce life.

Now all were angry at these insults except the Prince, who laughed and said that he thought the jest coarse but clever. But worse was to happen. It seems that a soldier with wine in him had done insult to a Hebrew maiden who came alone to draw water at a canal. The news spread among the people and some thousands of them rushed to the camp, shouting and demanding vengeance in so threatening a manner that it was necessary to form up the regiments of guards.

The Prince being summoned commanded that the girl and her kin should be admitted and state their case. She came, weeping and wailing and tearing her garments, throwing dust on her head also, though it appeared that she had taken no great harm from the soldier from whom she ran away. The Prince bade her point out the man if she could see him, and she showed us one of the bodyguard of the Count Amenmeses, whose face was scratched as though by a woman's nails. On being questioned he said he could remember little of the matter, but confessed that he had seen the maiden by the canal at moonrise and jested with her.

The kin of this girl clamoured that he should be killed, because he had offered insult to a high-born lady of Israel. This Seti refused, saying that the offence was not one of death, but that he would order him to be publicly beaten. Thereupon Amenmeses, who was fond of the soldier, a good man enough when not in his cups, sprang up in a rage, saying that no servant of his should be touched because he had offered to caress some light Israelitish woman who had no business to be wandering about alone at night. He added that if the man were flogged he and all those under his command would leave the camp and march back to make report to Pharaoh.

Now the Prince, having consulted with the councillors, told the woman and her kin that as Pharaoh had been appealed to, he must judge of the matter, and commanded them to appear at his court within a month and state their case against the soldier. They went away very ill-satisfied, saying that Amenmeses had insulted their daughter even more than his servant had done. The end of the matter was that on the following night this soldier was discovered dead, pierced through and through with knife thrusts. The girl, her parents and brethren could not be found, having fled away into the desert, nor was there any evidence to show by whom the soldier had been murdered. Therefore nothing could be done in the business except bury the victim.

On the following morning the Inquiry began with due ceremony, the Prince Seti and the Count Amenmeses taking their seats at the head of a large pavilion with the councillors behind them and the scribes, among whom I was, seated at their feet. Then we learned that the two prophets whom I had seen at Pharaoh's Court were not in the land of Goshen, having left before we arrived 'to sacrifice to God in the wilderness,' nor did any know when they would return. Other elders and priests, however, appeared and began to set out their case, which they did at great length and in a fierce and turbulent fashion, speaking often all of them at once, thus making it difficult for the interpreters to render their words, since they pretended that they did not know the Egyptian tongue.

Moreover they told their story from the very beginning,

when they had entered Egypt hundreds of years before and were succoured by the vizier of the Pharaoh of that day, one Yusuf, a powerful and clever man of their race who stored corn in a time of famine and low Niles. This Pharaoh was of the Hyksos people, one of the Shepherd kings whom we Egyptians hated and after many wars drove out of Khem. Under these Shepherd kings, being joined by many of their own blood, the Israelites grew rich and powerful, so that the Pharaohs who came after and who loved them not, began to fear them.

This was as far as the story was taken on the first day.

On the second day began the tale of their oppression, under which, however, they still multiplied like gnats upon the Nile, and grew so strong and numerous that at length the great Rameses did a wicked thing, ordering that their male children should be put to death. This order was never carried out, because his daughter, she who found Moses among the reeds of the river, pleaded for them.

At this point the Prince, wearied with the noise and heat in that crowded place, broke off the sitting until the morrow. Commanding me to accompany him, he ordered a chariot, not his own, to be made ready, and, although I prayed him not to do so, set out unguarded save for myself and the charioteer, saying that he would see how these people laboured with his own eyes.

Taking a Hebrew lad to run before the horses as our guide, we drove to the banks of a canal where the Israelites made bricks of mud which, after drying in the sun, were laden into boats that waited for them on the canal and taken away to other parts of Egypt to be used on Pharaoh's

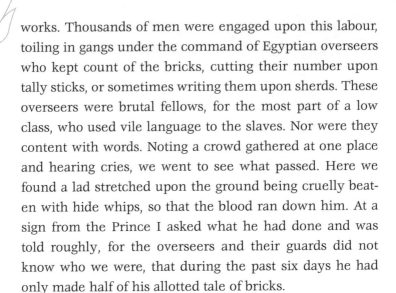

works. Thousands of men were engaged upon this labour, toiling in gangs under the command of Egyptian overseers who kept count of the bricks, cutting their number upon tally sticks, or sometimes writing them upon sherds. These overseers were brutal fellows, for the most part of a low class, who used vile language to the slaves. Nor were they content with words. Noting a crowd gathered at one place and hearing cries, we went to see what passed. Here we found a lad stretched upon the ground being cruelly beaten with hide whips, so that the blood ran down him. At a sign from the Prince I asked what he had done and was told roughly, for the overseers and their guards did not know who we were, that during the past six days he had only made half of his allotted tale of bricks.

'Loose him,' said the Prince quietly.

'Who are you that give me orders?' asked the head overseer, who was helping to hold the lad while the guards flogged him. 'Begone, lest I serve you as I serve this idle fellow.'

Seti looked at him, and as he looked his lips turned white.

'Tell him,' he said to me.

'You dog!' I gasped. 'Do you know who it is to whom you dare to speak thus?'

'No, nor care. Lay on, guard.'

The Prince, whose robes were hidden by a wide-sleeved cloak of common stuff and make, threw the cloak open revealing beneath it the pectoral he had worn in the Court, a beautiful thing of gold whereon were inscribed his royal names and titles in black and red enamel. Also he held up his right hand on which was a signet of Pharaoh's that he wore as his commissioner. The men stared, then one of them who was more learned than the rest cried,

'By the gods! this is his Highness the Prince of Egypt!' at which words all of them fell upon their faces.

'Rise,' said Seti to the lad who looked at him, forgetting his pain in his wonderment, 'and tell me why you have not delivered your tale of bricks.'

'Sir,' sobbed the boy in bad Egyptian, 'for two reasons. First, because I am a cripple, see,' and he held up his left arm which was withered and thin as a mummy's, 'and therefore cannot work quickly. Secondly, because my mother, whose only child I am, is a widow and lies sick in bed, so that there are no women or children in our home who can go out to gather straw for me, as Pharaoh has commanded that we should do. Therefore I must spend many hours in searching for straw, since I have no means wherewith to pay others to do this for me.'

'Ana,' said the Prince, 'write down this youth's name with the place of his abode, and if his tale prove true, see that his wants and those of his mother are relieved before we depart from Goshen. Write down also the names of this overseer and his fellows and command them to report themselves at my camp to-morrow at sunrise, when their case shall be considered. Say to the lad also that, being one afflicted by the gods, Pharaoh frees him from the making of bricks and all other labour of the State.'

Now while I did these things the overseer and his companions beat their heads upon the ground and prayed for mercy, being cowards as the cruel always are. His Highness answered them never a word, but only looked at them

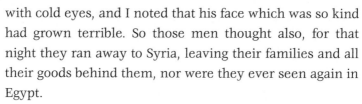

with cold eyes, and I noted that his face which was so kind had grown terrible. So those men thought also, for that night they ran away to Syria, leaving their families and all their goods behind them, nor were they ever seen again in Egypt.

When I had finished writing the Prince turned and, walking to where the chariot waited, bade the driver cross the canal by a bridge there was here. We drove on a while in silence, following a track which ran between the cultivated land and the desert. At length I pointed to the sinking sun and asked if it were not time to return.

'Why?' replied the Prince. 'The sun dies, but there rises the full moon to give us light, and what have we to fear with swords at our sides and her Highness Userti's mail beneath our robes? Oh! Ana, I am weary of men with their cruelties and shouts and strugglings, and I find this wilderness a place of rest, for in it I seem to draw nearer to my own soul and the Heaven whence it came, or so I hope.'

'Your Highness is fortunate to have a soul to which he cares to draw near; it is not so with all of us'; I answered laughing, for I sought to change the current of his thoughts by provoking argument of a sort that he loved.

Just then, however, the horses, which were not of the best, came to a halt on a slope of heavy sand. Nor would Seti allow the driver to flog them, but commanded him to let them rest a space. While they did so we descended from the chariot and walked up the desert rise, he leaning on my arm. As we reached its crest we heard sobs and a soft voice speaking on the further side. Who it was that spoke and sobbed we could not see, because of a line of tamarisk shrubs which once had been a fence.

'More cruelty, or at least more sorrow,' whispered Seti. 'Let us look.'

So we crept to the tamarisks, and peeping through their feathery tops, saw a very sweet sight in the pure rays of that desert moon. There, not five paces away, stood a woman clad in white, young and shapely in form. Her face we could not see because it was turned from us, also the long dark hair which streamed about her shoulders hid it. She was praying aloud, speaking now in Hebrew, of which both of us knew something, and now in Egyptian, as does one who is accustomed to think in either tongue, and stopping from time to time to sob.

'O God of my people,' she said, 'send me succour and bring me safe home, that Thy child may not be left alone in the wilderness to become the prey of wild beasts, or of men who are worse than beasts.'

Then she sobbed, knelt down on a great bundle which I saw was stubble straw, and again began to pray. This time it was in Egyptian, as though she feared lest the Hebrew should be overheard and understood.

'O God,' she said, 'O God of my fathers, help my poor heart, help my poor heart!'

We were about to withdraw, or rather to ask her what she ailed, when suddenly she turned her head, so that the light fell full upon her face. So lovely was it that I caught my breath and the Prince at my side started. Indeed it was more than lovely, for as a lamp shines through an alabaster vase or a shell of pearl so did the spirit within this woman

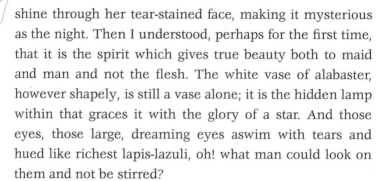

shine through her tear-stained face, making it mysterious as the night. Then I understood, perhaps for the first time, that it is the spirit which gives true beauty both to maid and man and not the flesh. The white vase of alabaster, however shapely, is still a vase alone; it is the hidden lamp within that graces it with the glory of a star. And those eyes, those large, dreaming eyes aswim with tears and hued like richest lapis-lazuli, oh! what man could look on them and not be stirred?

'Merapi!' I whispered.

'Moon of Israel!' murmured Seti, 'filled with the moon, lovely as the moon, mystic as the moon and worshipping the moon, her mother.'

'She is in trouble; let us help her,' I said.

'Nay, wait a while, Ana, for never again shall you and I see such a sight as this.'

Low as we spoke beneath our breath, I think the lady heard us. At least her face changed and grew frightened. Hastily she rose, lifted the great bundle of straw upon which she had been kneeling and placed it on her head. She ran a few steps, then stumbled and sank down with a little moan of pain. In an instant we were at her side. She stared at us affrighted, for who we were she could not see because of the wide hoods of our common cloaks that made us look like midnight thieves, or slave-dealing Bedouins.

'Oh! Sirs,' she babbled, 'harm me not. I have nothing of value on me save this amulet.'

'Who are you and what do you here?' asked the Prince disguising his voice.

'Sirs, I am Merapi, the daughter of Nathan the Levite, he

whom the accursed Egyptian captain, Khuaka, murdered at Tanis.'

'How do you dare to call the Egyptians accursed?' asked Seti in tones made gruff to hide his laughter.

'Oh! Sirs, because they are—I mean because I thought you were Arabs who hate them, as we do. At least this Egyptian was accursed, for the high Prince Seti, Pharaoh's heir, caused him to be beheaded for that crime.'

'And do you also hate the high Prince Seti, Pharaoh's heir, and call him accursed?'

She hesitated, then in a doubtful voice said,

'No, I do not hate him.'

'Why not, seeing that you hate the Egyptians of whom he is one of the first and therefore twice worthy of hatred, being the son of your oppressor, Pharaoh?'

'Because, although I have tried my best, I cannot. Also,' she added with the joy of one who has found a good reason, 'he avenged my father.'

'This is no cause, girl, seeing that he only did what the law forced him to do. They say that this dog of a Pharaoh's son is here in Goshen upon some mission. Is it true, and have you seen him? Answer, for we of the desert folk desire to know.'

'I believe it is true, Sir, but I have not seen him.'

'Why not, if he is here?'

'Because I did not wish to, Sir. Why should a daughter of Israel desire to look upon the face of a Prince of Egypt?'

'In truth I do not know,' replied Seti forgetting his feigned voice. Then, seeing that she glanced at him sharply, he added in gruff tones,

'Brother, either this woman lies or she is none other

than the maid they call Moon of Israel who dwells with old Jabez the Levite, her uncle. What think you?'

'I think, Brother, that she lies, and for three reasons,' I answered, falling into the jest. 'First, she is too fair to be of the black Hebrew blood.'

'Oh! Sir,' moaned Merapi, 'my mother was a Syrian lady of the mountains, with a skin as white as milk, and eyes blue as the heavens.'

'Secondly,' I went on without heeding her, 'if the great Prince Seti is really in Goshen and she dwells there, it is unnatural that she should not have gone to look upon him. Being a woman only two things would have kept her away, one—that she feared and hated him, which she denies, and the other—that she liked him too well, and, being prudent, thought it wisest not to look upon him more.'

When she heard the first of these words, Merapi glanced up with her lips parted as though to answer. Instead, she dropped her eyes and suddenly seemed to choke, while even in the moonlight I saw the red blood pour to her brow and along her white arms.

'Sir,' she gasped, 'why should you affront me? I swear that never till this moment did I think such a thing. Surely it would be treason.'

'Without doubt,' interrupted Seti, 'yet one of a sort that kings might pardon.'

'Thirdly,' I went on as though I heard neither of them, 'if this girl were what she declares, she would not be wandering alone in the desert at night, seeing that I have heard among the Arabs that Merapi, daughter of Nathan the Levite, is a lady of no mean blood among the Hebrews and that her family has wealth. Still, however much she lies, we can see for ourselves that she is beautiful.'

'Yes, Brother, in that we are fortunate, since without doubt she will sell for a high price among the slave traders beyond the desert.'

'Oh! Sir,' cried Merapi seizing the hem of his robe, 'surely you who I feel, I know not why, are no evil thief, you who have a mother and, perchance, sisters, would not doom a maiden to such a fate. Misjudge me not because I am alone. Pharaoh has commanded that we must find straw for the making of bricks. This morning I came far to search for it on behalf of a neighbour whose wife is ill in childbed. But towards sundown I slipped and cut myself upon the edge of a sharp stone. See,' and holding up her foot she showed a wound beneath the instep from which the blood still dropped, a sight that moved both of us not a little, 'and now I cannot walk and carry this heavy straw which I have been at such pains to gather.'

'Perchance she speaks truth, Brother,' said the Prince, 'and if we took her home we might earn no small reward from Jabez the Levite. But first tell me, Maiden, what was that prayer which you made to the moon, that Hathor should help your heart?'

'Sir,' she answered, 'only the idolatrous Egyptians pray to Hathor, the Lady of Love.'

'I thought that all the world prayed to the Lady of Love, Maiden. But what of the prayer? Is there some man whom you desire?'

'None,' she answered angrily.

'Then why does your heart need so much help that you

ask it of the air? Is there perchance someone whom you do *not* desire?'

She hung her head and made no answer.

'Come, Brother,' said the Prince, 'this lady is weary of us, and I think that if she were a true woman she would answer our questions more readily. Let us go and leave her. As she cannot walk we can take her later if we wish.'

'Sirs,' she said, 'I am glad that you are going, since the hyenas will be safer company than two men who can threaten to sell a helpless woman into slavery. Yet as we part to meet no more I will answer your question. In the prayer to which you were not ashamed to listen I did not pray for any lover, I prayed to be rid of one.'

'Now, Ana,' said the Prince bursting into laughter and throwing back his dark cloak, 'do you discover the name of that unhappy man of whom the lady Merapi wishes to be rid, for I dare not.'

She gazed into his face and uttered a little cry.

'Ah!' she said, 'I thought I knew the voice again when once you forgot your part. Prince Seti, does your Highness think that this was a kind jest to practise upon one alone and in fear?'

'Lady Merapi,' he answered smiling, 'be not wroth, for at least it was a good one and you have told us nothing that we did not know. You may remember that at Tanis you said that you were affianced and there was that in your voice——. Suffer me now to tend this wound of yours.'

Then he knelt down, tore a strip from his ceremonial robe of fine linen, and began to bind up her foot, not unskilfully, being a man full of strange and unexpected knowledge. As he worked at the task, watching them, I saw their eyes meet, saw too that rich flood of colour creep once more to Merapi's brow. Then I began to think it unseemly that the Prince of Egypt should play the leech to a woman's hurts in the desert, and to wonder why he had not left that humble task to me.

Presently the bandaging was done and made fast with a royal scarabæus mounted on a pin of gold, which the Prince wore in his garments. On it was cut the uræus crown and beneath it were the signs which read 'Lord of the Lower and the Upper Land,' being Pharaoh's style and title.

'See now, Lady,' he said, 'you have Egypt beneath your foot,' and when she asked him what he meant, he read her the writing upon the jewel, whereat for the third time she coloured to the eyes. Then he lifted her up, instructing her to rest her weight upon his shoulder, saying he feared lest the scarab, which he valued, should be broken.

Thus we started, I bearing the bundle of straw behind as he bade me, since, he said, having been gathered with such toil, it must not be lost. On reaching the chariot, where we found the guide gone and the driver asleep, he sat her in it upon his cloak, and wrapped her in mine which he borrowed, saying I should not need it who must carry the straw. Then he mounted also and they drove away at a foot's pace. As I walked after the chariot with the straw that fell about my ears, I heard nothing of their further talk, if indeed they talked at all which, the driver being present, perhaps they did not. Nor in truth did I listen who was engaged in thought as to the hard lot of these poor Hebrews, who must collect this dirty stuff and bear it so far, made heavy as it was by the clay that clung about the roots.

Even now, as it chanced, we did not reach Goshen without further trouble. Just as we had crossed the bridge over the canal I, toiling behind, saw in the clear moonlight a young man running towards us. He was a Hebrew, tall, well-made and very handsome in his fashion. His eyes were dark and fierce, his nose was hooked, his teeth were regular and white, and his long, black hair hung down in a mass upon his shoulders. He held a wooden staff in his hand and a naked knife was girded about his middle. Seeing the chariot he halted and peered at it, then asked in Hebrew if those who travelled had seen aught of a young Israelitish lady who was lost.

'If you seek me, Laban, I am here,' replied Merapi, speaking from the shadow of the cloak.

'What do you there alone with an Egyptian, Merapi?' he said fiercely.

What followed I do not know for they spoke so quickly in their unfamiliar tongue that I could not understand them. At length Merapi turned to the Prince, saying,

'Lord, this is Laban my affianced, who commands me to descend from the chariot and accompany him as best I can.'

'And I, Lady, command you to stay in it. Laban your affianced can accompany us.'

Now at this Laban grew angry, as I could see he was prone to do, and stretched out his hand as though to push Seti aside and seize Merapi.

'Have a care, man,' said the Prince, while I, throwing down the straw, drew my sword and sprang between them, crying,

'Slave, would you lay hands upon the Prince of Egypt?'

'Prince of Egypt!' he said, drawing back astonished, then added sullenly, 'Well what does the Prince of Egypt with my affianced?'

'He helps her who is hurt to her home, having found her helpless in the desert with this accursed straw,' I answered.

'Forward, driver,' said the Prince, and Merapi added, 'Peace, Laban, and bear the straw which his Highness's companion has carried such a weary way.'

He hesitated a moment, then snatched up the bundle and set it on his head.

As we walked side by side, his evil temper seemed to get the better of him. Without ceasing, he grumbled because Merapi was alone in the chariot with an Egyptian. At length I could bear it no longer.

'Be silent, fellow,' I said. 'Least of all men should you complain of what his Highness does, seeing that already he has avenged the killing of this lady's father, and now has saved her from lying out all night among the wild beasts and men of the wilderness.'

'Of the first I have heard more than enough,' he answered, 'and of the second doubtless I shall hear more than enough also. Ever since my affianced met this prince, she has looked on me with different eyes and spoken to me with another voice. Yes, and when I press for marriage, she says it cannot be for a long while yet, because she is mourning for her father; her father forsooth, whom she never forgave because he betrothed her to me according to the custom of our people.'

'Perhaps she loves some other man?' I queried, wishing to learn all I could about this lady.

'She loves no man, or did not a while ago. She loves herself alone.'

'One with so much beauty may look high in marriage.'

'High!' he replied furiously. 'How can she look higher than myself who am a lord of the line of Judah, and therefore greater far than an upstart prince or any other Egyptian, were he Pharaoh himself?'

'Surely you must be trumpeter to your tribe,' I mocked, for my temper was rising.

'Why?' he asked. 'Are not the Hebrews greater than the Egyptians, as those oppressors soon shall learn, and is not a lord of Israel more than any idol-worshipper among your people?'

I looked at the man clad in mean garments and foul from his labour in the brickfield, marvelling at his insolence. There was no doubt but that he believed what he said; I could see it in his proud eye and bearing. He thought that his tribe was of more import in the world than our great and ancient nation, and that he, an unknown youth, equalled or surpassed Pharaoh himself. Then, being enraged by these insults, I answered,

'You say so, but let us put it to the proof. I am but a scribe, yet I have seen war. Linger a little that we may learn whether a lord of Israel is better than a scribe of Egypt.'

'Gladly would I chastise you, Writer,' he answered, 'did I not see your plot. You wish to delay me here, and perhaps to murder me by some foul means, while your master basks in the smiles of the Moon of Israel. Therefore I will not stay, but another time it shall be as you wish, and perhaps ere long.'

Now I think that I should have struck him in the face, though I am not one of those who love brawling. But at this moment there appeared a company of Egyptian horse led by none other than the Count Amenmeses. Seeing the Prince in the Chariot, they halted and gave the salute. Amenmeses leapt to the ground.

'We are come out to search for your Highness,' he said, 'fearing lest some hurt had befallen you.'

'I thank you, Cousin,' answered the Prince, 'but the hurt has befallen another, not me.'

'That is well, your Highness,' said the Count, studying Merapi with a smile. 'Where is the lady wounded? Not in the breast, I trust.'

'No, Cousin, in the foot, which is why she travels with me in this chariot.'

'Your Highness was ever kind to the unfortunate. I pray you let me take your place, or suffer me to set this girl upon a horse.'

'Drive on,' said Seti.

So, escorted by the soldiers whom I heard making jests to each other about the Prince and the lady, as I think did the Hebrew Laban also, for he glared about him and ground his teeth, we came at last to the town. Here, guided by Merapi, the chariot was halted at the house of Jabez her uncle, a white-bearded old Hebrew with a cunning eye, who rushed from the door of his mud-roofed dwelling crying he had done no harm that soldiers should come to take him.

'It is not you whom the Egyptians wish to capture, it is your niece and my betrothed,' shouted Laban, whereat the soldiers laughed, as did some women who had gathered round. Meanwhile the Prince was helping Merapi to descend out of the chariot, from which indeed he lifted her. The sight seemed to madden Laban, who rushed forward to tear her from his arms, and in the attempt jostled his Highness. The captain of the soldiers—he was an officer of Pharaoh's bodyguard—lifted his sword in a fury and struck Laban such a blow upon the head with the flat of the blade that he fell upon his face and lay there groaning.

'Away with that Hebrew dog and scourge him!' cried the captain. 'Is the royal blood of Egypt to be handled by such as he?'

Soldiers sprang forward to do his bidding, but Seti said quietly,

'Let the fellow be, friends; he lacks manners, that is all. Is he hurt?'

As he spoke Laban leapt to his feet and, fearing worse things, fled away with a curse and a glare of hate at the Prince.

'Farewell, Lady,' said Seti. 'I wish you a quick recovery.'

'I thank your Highness,' she answered, looking about her confusedly. 'Be pleased to wait a little while that I may return to you your jewel.'

'Nay, keep it, Lady, and if ever you are in need or trouble of any sort, send it to me who know it well and you shall not lack succour.'

She glanced at him and burst into tears.

'Why do you weep?' he asked.

'Oh! your Highness, because I fear that trouble is near at hand. My affianced, Laban, has a revengeful heart. Help me to the house, my uncle.'

'Listen, Hebrew,' said Seti, raising his voice; 'if aught that is evil befalls this niece of yours, or if she is forced to walk whither she would not go, sorrow shall be your portion and that of all with whom you have to do. Do you hear?'

'O my Lord, I hear, I hear. Fear nothing. She shall be guarded carefully as—as she will doubtless guard that trinket on her foot.'

'Ana,' said the Prince to me that night, when I was talking with him before he went to rest, 'I know not why, but I fear that man Laban; he has an evil eye.'

'I too think it would have been better if your Highness had left him to be dealt with by the soldiers, after which there would have been nothing to fear from him in this world.'

'Well, I did not, so there's an end. Ana, she is a fair woman and a sweet.'

'The fairest and the sweetest that ever I saw, my Prince.'

'Be careful, Ana. I pray you be careful, lest you should fall in love with one who is already affianced.'

I only looked at him in answer, and as I looked I bethought me of the words of Ki the Magician. So, I think, did the Prince; at least he laughed not unhappily and turned away.

For my part I rested ill that night, and when at last I slept, it was to dream of Merapi making her prayer in the rays of the moon.

7

THE
AMBUSH

Eight full days went by before we left the land of Goshen. The story that the Israelites had to tell was long, sad also. Moreover, they gave evidence as to many cruel things that they had suffered, and when this was finished the testimony of the guards and others must be called, all of which it is necessary to write down. Lastly, the Prince seemed to be in no hurry to be gone, as he said because he hoped that the two prophets would return from the wilderness, which they never did. During all this time Seti saw no more of Merapi, nor indeed did he speak of her, even when the Count Amenmeses jested him as to his chariot companion and asked him if he had driven again in the desert by moonlight.

I, however, saw her once. When I was wandering in the town one day towards sunset, I met her walking with her uncle Jabez upon one side and her lover, Laban, on the other, like a prisoner between two guards. I thought she

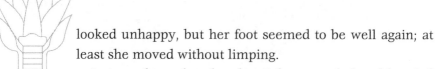

looked unhappy, but her foot seemed to be well again; at least she moved without limping.

I stopped to salute her, but Laban scowled and hurried her away. Jabez stayed behind and fell into talk with me. He told me that she was recovered of her hurt, but that there had been trouble between her and Laban because of all that happened on that evening when she came by it, ending in his encounter with the captain.

'This young man seems to be of a jealous nature,' I said, 'one who will make a harsh husband for any woman.'

'Yes, learned scribe, jealousy has been his curse from youth as it is with so many of our people, and I thank God that I am not the woman whom he is to marry.'

'Why, then, do you suffer her to marry him, Jabez?'

'Because her father affianced her to this lion's whelp when she was scarce more than a child, and among us that is a bond hard to break. For my own part,' he added, dropping his voice, and glancing round with his shifting eyes, 'I should like to see my niece in some different place to that of the wife of Laban. With her great beauty and wit, she might become anything—anything if she had opportunity. But under our laws, even if Laban died, as might happen to so violent a man, she could wed no one who is not a Hebrew.'

'I thought she told us that her mother was a Syrian.'

'That is so, Scribe Ana. She was a beautiful captive of war whom Nathan came to love and made his wife, and the daughter takes after her. Still she is Hebrew and of the Hebrew faith and congregation. Had it not been so, she might have shone like a star, nay, like the very moon after which she is named, perhaps in the court of Pharaoh himself.

'As the great queen Taia did, she who changed the religion of Egypt to the worship of one god in a bygone generation,' I suggested.

'I have heard of her, Scribe Ana. She was a wondrous woman, beautiful too by her statues. Would that you Egyptians could find such another to turn your hearts to a purer faith and to soften them towards us poor aliens. When does his Highness leave the land of Goshen?'

'At sunrise on the third day from this.'

'Provision will be needed for the journey, much provision for so large a train. I deal in sheep and other foodstuffs, Scribe Ana.'

'I will mention the matter to his Highness and to the Vizier, Jabez.'

'I thank you, Scribe, and will be in waiting at the camp to-morrow morning. See, Laban returns with Merapi. One word, let his Highness beware of Laban. He is very revengeful and has not forgotten that sword-blow on the head.'

'Let Laban be careful,' I answered. 'Had it not been for his Highness the soldiers would have killed him the other night because he dared to offer affront to the royal blood. A second time he will not escape. Moreover, Pharaoh would avenge aught he did upon the people of Israel.'

'I understand. It would be sad if Laban were killed, very sad. But the people of Israel have One who can protect them even against Pharaoh and all his hosts. Farewell, learned Scribe. If ever I come to Tanis, with your leave we will talk more together.'

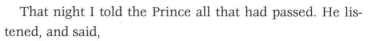

That night I told the Prince all that had passed. He listened, and said,

'I grieve for the lady Merapi, for hers is like to be a hard fate. Yet,' he added laughing, 'perhaps it is as well for you, friend, that you should see no more of her who is sure to bring trouble wherever she goes. That woman has a face which haunts the mind, as the Ka haunts the tomb, and for my part I do not wish to look upon it again.'

'I am glad to hear it, Prince, and for my part, I have done with women, however sweet. I will tell this Jabez that the provisions for the journey will be bought elsewhere.'

'Nay, buy them from him, and if Nehesi grumbles at the price, pay it on my account. The way to a Hebrew's heart is through his treasure bags. If Jabez is well treated, it may make him kinder to his niece, of whom I shall always have a pleasant memory, for which I am grateful among this sour folk who hate us, and with reason.'

So the sheep and all the foodstuffs for the journey were bought from Jabez at his own price, for which he thanked me much, and on the third day we started. At the last moment the Prince, whose mood seemed to be perverse that evening, refused to travel with the host upon the morrow because of the noise and dust. In vain did the Count Amenmeses reason with him, and Nehesi and the great officers implore him almost on their knees, saying that they must answer for his safety to Pharaoh and the Princess Userti. He bade them begone, replying that he would join them at their camp on the following night. I also prayed him to listen, but he told me sharply that what he had said he had said, and that he and I would journey in his chariot alone, with two armed runners and no more, adding that if I thought there was danger I could go forward with the troops. Then I bit my lip and was silent, whereon, seeing that he had hurt me, he turned and craved my pardon humbly enough as his kind heart taught him to do.

'I can bear no more of Amenmeses and those officers,' he said, 'and I love to be in the desert alone. Last time we journeyed there we met with adventures that were pleasant, Ana, and at Tanis doubtless I shall find others that are not pleasant. Admit that Hebrew priest who is waiting to instruct me in the mysteries of his faith which I desire to understand.'

So I bowed and left him to make report that I had failed to shake his will. Taking the risk of his wrath, however, I did this—for had I not sworn to the Princess that I would protect him? In place of the runners I chose two of the best and bravest soldiers to play their part. Moreover, I instructed that captain who smote down Laban to hide away with a score of picked men and enough chariots to carry them, and to follow after the Prince, keeping just out of sight.

So on the morrow the troops, nobles, and officers went on at daybreak, together with the baggage carriers; nor did we follow them till many hours had gone by. Some of this time the Prince spent in driving about the town, taking note of the condition of the people. These, as I saw, looked on us sullenly enough, more so than before, I thought, perhaps because we were unguarded. Indeed, turning round I caught sight of a man shaking his fist and of an old hag spitting after us, and wished that we were out of the land of

Goshen. But when I reported it to the Prince he only laughed and took no heed.

'All can see that they hate us Egyptians,' he said. 'Well, let it be our task to try to turn their hate to love.'

'That you will never do, Prince, it is too deep-rooted in their hearts; for generations they have drunk it in with their mother's milk. Moreover, this is a war of the gods of Egypt and of Israel, and men must go where their gods drive them.'

'Do you think so, Ana? Then are men nothing but dust blown by the winds of heaven, blown from the darkness that is before the dawn to be gathered at last and for ever into the darkness of the grave of night?'

He brooded a while, then went on,

'Yet if I were Pharaoh I would let these people go, for without doubt their god has much power and I tell you that I fear them.'

'Why will he not let them go?' I asked. 'They are a weakness, not a strength to Egypt, as was shown at the time of the invasion of the Barbarians with whom they sided. Moreover, the value of this rich land of theirs, which they cannot take with them, is greater than that of all their labour.'

'I do not know, friend. The matter is one upon which my father keeps his own counsel, even from the Princess Userti. Perhaps it is because he will not change the policy of his father, Rameses; perhaps because he is stiff-necked to those who cross his will. Or it may be that he is held in this path by a madness sent of some god to bring loss and shame on Egypt.'

'Then, Prince, all the priests and nobles are mad also, from Count Amenmeses down.'

'Where Pharaoh leads priests and nobles follow. The question is, who leads Pharaoh? Here is the temple of these Hebrews; let us enter.'

So we descended from the chariot, where, for my part, I would have remained, and walked through the gateway in the surrounding mud wall into the outer court of the temple, which on this the holy seventh day of the Hebrews was full of praying women, who feigned not to see us yet watched us out of the corners of their eyes. Passing through them we came to a doorway, by which we entered another court that was roofed over. Here were many men who murmured as we appeared. They were engaged in listening to a preacher in a white robe, who wore a strange shaped cap and some ornaments on his breast. I knew the man; he was the priest Kohath who had instructed the Prince in so much of the mysteries of the Hebrew faith as he chose to reveal. On seeing us he ceased suddenly in his discourse, uttered some hasty blessing and advanced to greet us.

I waited behind the Prince, thinking it well to watch his back among all those fierce men, and did not hear what the priest said to him, as he whispered in that holy place. Kohath led him forward, to free him from the throng, I thought, till they came to the head of the little temple that was marked by some steps, above which hung a thick and heavy curtain. The Prince, walking on, did not see the lowest of these steps in the gloom, which was deep. His foot caught on it; he fell forward, and to save himself grasped at the curtain where the two halves of it met, and dragged it open, revealing a chamber plain and small beyond, in which was an altar. That was all I had time to see, for next

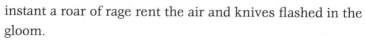

instant a roar of rage rent the air and knives flashed in the gloom.

'The Egyptian defiles the tabernacle!' shouted one. 'Drag him out and kill him!' screamed another.

'Friends,' said Seti, turning as they surged towards him, 'if I have done aught wrong it was by chance——'

He could add no more, seeing that they were on him, or rather on me who had leapt in front of him. Already they had grasped my robes and my hand was on my sword-hilt, when the priest Kohath cried out,

'Men of Israel, are you mad? Would you bring Pharaoh's vengeance on us?'

They halted a little and their spokesman shouted,

'We defy Pharaoh! Our God will protect us from Pharaoh. Drag him forth and kill him beyond the wall!'

Again they began to move, when a man, in whom I recognised Jabez, the uncle of Merapi, called aloud,

'Cease! If this Prince of Egypt has done insult to Jahveh by will and not by chance, it is certain that he will avenge himself upon him. Shall men take the judgment of God into their own hands? Stand back and wait awhile. If Jahveh is affronted, the Egyptian will fall dead. If he does not fall dead, let him pass hence unharmed, for such is Jahveh's will. Stand back, I say, while I count threescore.'

They withdrew a space and slowly Jabez began to count.

Although at that time I knew nothing of the power of the god of Israel, I will say that I was filled with fear as one by one he counted, pausing at each ten. The scene was very strange. There by the steps stood the Prince against the

background of the curtain, his arms folded and a little

smile of wonder mixed with contempt upon his face, but not a sign of fear. On one side of him was I, who knew well that I should share his fate whatever it might be, and indeed desired no other; and on the other the priest Kohath, whose hands shook and whose eyes started from his head. In front of us old Jabez counted, watching the fierce-faced congregation that in a dead silence waited for the issue. The count went on. Thirty. Forty. Fifty—oh! it seemed an age.

At length sixty fell from his lips. He waited a while and all watched the Prince, not doubting but that he would fall dead. But instead he turned to Kohath and asked quietly if this ordeal was now finished, as he desired to make an offering to the temple, which he had been invited to visit, and begone.

'Our God has given his answer,' said Jabez. 'Accept it, men of Israel. What this Prince did he did by chance, not of design.'

They turned and went without a word, and after I had laid the offering, no mean one, in the appointed place, we followed them.

'It would seem that yours is no gentle god,' said the Prince to Kohath, when at length we were outside the temple.

'At least he is just, your Highness. Had it been otherwise, you who had violated his sanctuary, although by chance, would ere now be dead.'

'Then you hold, Priest, that Jahveh has power to slay us when he is angry?'

'Without a doubt, your Highness—as, if our Prophets speak truth, I think that Egypt will learn ere all be done,' he added grimly.

Seti looked at him and answered.

'It may be so, but all gods, or their priests, claim the power to torment and slay those who worship other gods. It is not only women who are jealous, Kohath, or so it seems. Yet I think that you do your god injustice, seeing that even if this strength is his, he proved more merciful than his worshippers who knew well that I only grasped the veil to save myself from falling. If ever I visit your temple again it shall be in the company of those who can match might against might, whether of the spirit or the sword. Farewell!'

So we reached the chariot, near to which stood Jabez, he who had saved us.

'Prince,' he whispered, glancing at the crowd who lingered not far away, silent and glowering, 'I pray you leave this land swiftly for here your life is not safe. I know it was by chance, but you have defiled the sanctuary and seen that upon which eyes may not look save those of the highest priests, an offence no Israelite can forgive.'

'And you, or your people, Jabez, would have defiled this sanctuary of my life, spilling my heart's blood and *not* by chance. Surely you are a strange folk who seek to make an enemy of one who has tried to be your friend.'

'I do not seek it,' exclaimed Jabez. 'I would that we might have Pharaoh's mouth and ear who soon will himself be Pharaoh upon our side. O Prince of Egypt, be not wroth with all the children of Israel because their wrongs have made some few of them stubborn and hard-hearted. Begone now, and of your goodness remember my words.'

'I will remember,' said Seti, signing to the charioteer to drive on.

Yet still the Prince lingered in the town, saying that he feared nothing and would learn all he could of this people and their ways that he might report the better of them to Pharaoh. For my part I believed that there was one face which he wished to see again before he left, but of this I thought it wise to say nothing.

At length about midday we did depart, and drove eastwards on the track of Amenmeses and our company. All the afternoon we drove thus, preceded by the two soldiers disguised as runners and followed, as a distant cloud of dust told me, by the captain and his chariots, whom I had secretly commanded to keep us in sight.

Towards evening we came to the pass in the stony hills which bounded the land of Goshen. Here Seti descended from the chariot, and we climbed, accompanied by the two soldiers whom I signed to follow us, to the crest of one of these hills that was strewn with huge boulders and lined with ridges of sandstone, between which gullies had been cut by the winds of thousands of years.

Leaning against one of these ridges we looked back upon a wondrous sight. Far away across the fertile plain appeared the town that we had left, and behind it the sun sank. It would seem as though some storm had broken there, although the firmament above us was clear and blue. At least in front of the town two huge pillars of cloud stretched from earth to heaven like the columns of some mighty gateway. One of these pillars was as though it were made of black marble, and the other like to molten gold. Between them ran a road of light ending in a glory, and in the midst of the glory the round ball of Ra, the Sun, burned

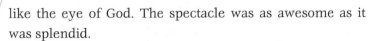

like the eye of God. The spectacle was as awesome as it was splendid.

'Have you ever seen such a sky in Egypt, Prince?' I asked.

'Never,' he answered, and although he spoke low, in that great stillness his voice sounded loud to me.

For a while longer we watched, till suddenly the sun sank, and only the glory about it and above remained, which took shapes like to the palaces and temples of a city in the heavens, a far city that no mortal could reach except in dreams.

'I know not why, Ana,' said Seti, 'but for the first time since I was a man I feel afraid. It seems to me that there are omens in that sky and I cannot read them. Would that Ki were here to tell us what is signified by the pillar of blackness to the right and the pillar of fire to the left, and what god has his home in the city of glory behind, and how man's feet may walk along the shining road which reaches to its pylon gates. I tell you that I am afraid; it is as though Death were very near to me and all his wonders open to my mortal sight.'

'I too am afraid,' I whispered. 'Look! The pillars move. That of fire goes before; that of black cloud follows after, and between them I seem to see a countless multitude marching in unending companies. See how the light glitters on their spears! Surely the god of the Hebrews is afoot.'

'He, or some other god, or no god at all, who knows? Come, Ana, let us be going if we would reach that camp ere dark.'

So we descended from the ridge, and re-entering the chariot, drove on towards the neck of the pass. Now this neck was very narrow, not more than four paces wide for a certain distance, and, on either side of the roadway were tumbled sandstone boulders, between which grew desert plants, and gullies that had been cut by storm-water, while beyond these rose the sides of the mountain. Here the horses went at a walk towards a turn in the path, at which point the land began to fall again.

When we were about half a spear's throw from this turn of a sudden I heard a sound and, glancing to the right, perceived a woman leaping down the hillside towards us. The charioteer saw also and halted the horses, and the two runner guards turned and drew their swords. In less than half a minute the woman had reached us, coming out of the shadow so that the light fell upon her face.

'Merapi!' exclaimed the Prince and I, speaking as though with one breath.

Merapi it was indeed, but in evil case. Her long hair had broken loose and fell about her, the cloak she wore was torn, and there were blood and foam upon her lips. She stood gasping, since speak she could not for breathlessness, supporting herself with one hand upon the side of the chariot and with the other pointing to the bend in the road. At last a word came, one only. It was:

'Murder!'

'She means that she is going to be murdered,' said the Prince to me.

'No,' she panted, 'you—you! The Hebrews. Go back!'

'Turn the horses!' I cried to the charioteer.

He began to obey helped by the two guards, but because of the narrowness of the road and the steepness of the banks this was not easy. Indeed they were but half round in such fashion that they blocked the pathway from side to

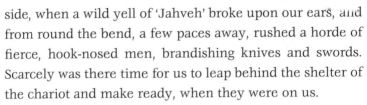

side, when a wild yell of 'Jahveh' broke upon our ears, and from round the bend, a few paces away, rushed a horde of fierce, hook-nosed men, brandishing knives and swords. Scarcely was there time for us to leap behind the shelter of the chariot and make ready, when they were on us.

'Hearken,' I said to the charioteer as they came, 'run as you never ran before, and bring up the guard behind!'

He sprang away like an arrow.

'Get back, Lady,' cried Seti. 'This is no woman's work, and see here comes Laban to seek you,' and he pointed with his sword to the leader of the murderers.

She obeyed, staggering a few paces to a stone at the roadside, behind which she crouched. Afterwards she told me that she had no strength to go further, and indeed no will, since if we were killed, it were better that she who had warned us should be killed also.

Now they had reached us, the whole flood of them, thirty or forty men. The first who came stabbed the frightened horses, and down they went against the bank, struggling. On to the chariot leapt the Hebrews, seeking to come at us, and we met them as best we might, tearing off our cloaks and throwing them over our left arms to serve as shields.

Oh! what a fight was that. In the open, or had we not been prepared, we must have been slain at once, but, as it was, the place and the barrier of the chariot gave us some advantage. So narrow was the roadway, the walls of which were here too steep to climb, that not more than four of the Hebrews could strike at us at once, which four must first surmount the chariot or the still living horses.

But we also were four, and thanks to Userti, two of us

were clad in mail beneath our robes—four strong men fighting for their lives. Against us came four of the Hebrews. One leapt from the chariot straight at Seti, who received him upon the point of his iron sword, whereof I heard the hilt ring against his breast-bone, that same famous iron sword which to-day lies buried with him in his grave.

Down he came dead, throwing the Prince to the ground by the weight of his body. The Hebrew who attacked me caught his foot on the chariot pole and fell forward, so I killed him easily with a blow upon the head, which gave me time to drag the Prince to his feet again before another followed. The two guards also, sturdy fighters both of them, killed or mortally wounded their men. But others were pressing behind so thick and fast that I could keep no count of all that happened afterwards.

Presently I saw one of the guards fall, slain by Laban. A stab on the breast sent me reeling backwards; had it not been for that mail I was sped. The other guard killed him who would have killed me, and then himself was killed by two who came on him at once.

Now only the Prince and I were left, fighting back to back. He closed with one man, a very great fellow, and wounded him on the hand, so that he dropped his sword. This man gripped him round the middle and they rolled together on the ground. Laban appeared and stabbed the Prince in the back, but the curved knife he was using snapped on the Syrian mail. I struck at Laban and wounded him on the head, dazing him so that he staggered back and seemed to fall over the chariot. Then others rushed at

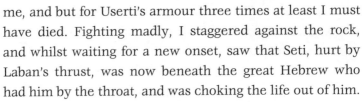

me, and but for Userti's armour three times at least I must have died. Fighting madly, I staggered against the rock, and whilst waiting for a new onset, saw that Seti, hurt by Laban's thrust, was now beneath the great Hebrew who had him by the throat, and was choking the life out of him.

I saw something else also—a woman holding a sword with both hands and stabbing downward, after which the grip of the Hebrew loosened from Seti's throat.

'Traitress!' cried one, and struck at her, so that she reeled back hurt. Then when all seemed finished, and beneath the rain of blows my senses were failing, I heard the thunder of horses' hoofs and the shout of '*Egypt! Egypt!*' from the throats of soldiers. The flash of bronze caught my dazed eyes, and with the roar of battle in my ears I seemed to fall asleep just as the light of day departed.

8

SETI
COUNSELS
PHARAOH

Dream upon dream. Dreams of voices, dreams of faces, dreams of sunlight and of moonlight and of myself being borne forward, always forward; dreams of shouting crowds, and, above all, dreams of Merapi's eyes looking down on me like two watching stars from heaven. Then at last the awakening, and with it throbs of pain and qualms of sickness.

At first I thought that I was dead and lying in a tomb. Then by degrees I saw that I was in no tomb but in a darkened room that was familiar to me, my own room in Seti's palace at Tanis. It must be so, for there, near to the bed on which I lay, was my own chest filled with the manuscripts that I had brought from Memphis. I tried to lift my left hand, but could not, and looking down saw that the arm was bandaged like to that of a mummy, which made me think again that I must be dead, if the dead could suffer so much pain. I closed my eyes and thought or slept a while.

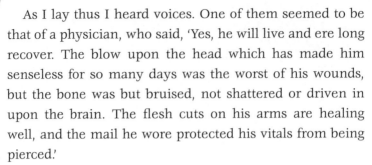

As I lay thus I heard voices. One of them seemed to be that of a physician, who said, 'Yes, he will live and ere long recover. The blow upon the head which has made him senseless for so many days was the worst of his wounds, but the bone was but bruised, not shattered or driven in upon the brain. The flesh cuts on his arms are healing well, and the mail he wore protected his vitals from being pierced.'

'I am glad, physician,' answered a voice that I knew to be that of Userti, 'since without doubt, had it not been for Ana, his Highness would have perished. It is strange that one whom I thought to be nothing but a dreaming scribe should have shown himself so brave a warrior. The Prince says that this Ana killed three of those dogs with his own hands, and wounded others.'

'It was well done, your Highness,' answered the physician, 'but still better was his forethought in providing a rear-guard and in despatching the charioteer to call it up. It seems to have been the Hebrew lady who really saved the life of his Highness, when, forgetting her sex, she stabbed the murderer who had him by the throat.'

'That is the Prince's tale, or so I understand,' she answered coldly. 'Yet it seems strange that a weak and worn-out girl could have pierced a giant through from back to breast.'

'At least she warned him of the ambush, your Highness.'

'So they say. Perhaps Ana here will soon tell us the truth about these matters. Tend him well, physician, and you shall not lack for your reward.'

Then they went away, still talking, and I lay quiet, filled

with thankfulness and wonder, for now everything came back to me.

A while later, as I lay with my eyes still shut, for even that low light seemed to hurt them, I became aware of a woman's soft step stealing round my bed and of a fragrance such as comes from a woman's robes and hair. I looked and saw Merapi's star-like eyes gazing down on me just as I had seen them in my dreams.

'Greeting, Moon of Israel,' I said. 'Of a truth we meet again in strange case.'

'Oh!' she whispered, 'are you awake at last? I thank God, Scribe Ana, who for three days thought that you must die.'

'As, had it not been for you, Lady, surely I should have done—I and another. Now it seems that all three of us will live.'

'Would that but two lived, the Prince and you, Ana. Would that I had died,' she answered, sighing heavily.

'Why?'

'Cannot you guess? Because I am an outcast who has betrayed my people. Because their blood flows between me and them. For I killed that man, and he was my own kinsman, for the sake of an Egyptian—I mean, Egyptians. Therefore the curse of Jahveh is on me, and as my kinsman died doubtless I shall die in a day to come, and afterwards—what?'

'Afterwards peace and great reward, if there be justice in earth or heaven, O most noble among women.'

'Would that I could think so! Hush, I hear steps. Drink this; I am the chief of your nurses, Scribe Ana, an honourable post, since to-day all Egypt loves and praises you.'

'Surely it is you, lady Merapi, whom all Egypt should love and praise,' I answered.

Then the Prince Seti entered. I strove to salute him by lifting my less injured arm, but he caught my hand and pressed it tenderly.

'Hail to you, beloved of Menthu, god of war,' he said, with his pleasant laugh. 'I thought I had hired a scribe, and lo! in this scribe I find a soldier who might be an army's boast.'

At this moment he caught sight of Merapi, who had moved back into the shadow.

'Hail to you also, Moon of Israel,' he said bowing. 'If I name Ana here a warrior of the best, what name can both of us find for you to whom we owe our lives? Nay, look not down, but answer.'

'Prince of Egypt,' she replied confusedly, 'I did but little. The plot came to my ears through Jabez my uncle, and I fled away and, knowing the short paths from childhood, was just in time. Had I stayed to think perchance I should not have dared.'

'And what of the rest, Lady? What of the Hebrew who was choking me and of a certain sword thrust that loosed his hands for ever?'

'Of that, your Highness, I can recall nothing, or very little,' then, doubtless remembering what she had just said to me, she made obeisance and passed from the chamber.

'She can tell falsehoods as sweetly as she does all else,' said Seti, when he had watched her go. 'Oh! what a woman have we here, Ana. Perfect in beauty, perfect in courage, perfect in mind. Where are her faults, I wonder? Let it be your part to search them out, since I find none.'

'Ask them of Ki, O Prince. He is a very great magician, so great that perhaps his art may even avail to discover what a woman seeks to hide. Also you may remember that he gave you certain warnings before we journeyed to Goshen.'

'Yes—he told me that my life would be in danger, as certainly it was. There he was right. He told me also that I should see a woman whom I should come to love. There he was wrong. I have seen no such woman. Oh! I know well what is passing in your mind. Because I hold the lady Merapi to be beautiful and brave, you think that I love her. But it is not so. I love no woman, except, of course, her Highness. Ana, you judge me by yourself.'

'Ki said "come to love," Prince. There is yet time.'

'Not so, Ana. If one loves, one loves at once. Soon I shall be old and she will be fat and ugly, and how can one love then? Get well quickly, Ana, for I wish you to help me with my report to Pharaoh. I shall tell him that I think these Israelites are much oppressed and that he should make them amends and let them go.'

'What will Pharaoh say to that after they have just tried to kill his heir?'

'I think Pharaoh will be angry, and so will the people of Egypt, who do not reason well. He will not see that, believing what they do, Laban and his band were right to try to kill me who, however unwittingly, had desecrated the sanctuary of their god. Had they done otherwise they would have been no good Hebrews, and for my part I cannot bear them malice. Yet all Egypt is afire about this business and cries out that the Israelites should be destroyed.'

'It seems to me, Prince, that whatever may be the case

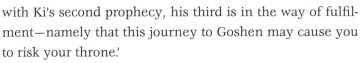

with Ki's second prophecy, his third is in the way of fulfil-
ment—namely that this journey to Goshen may cause you
to risk your throne.'

He shrugged his shoulders and answered,

'Not even for that, Ana, will I say to Pharaoh what is not
in my mind. But let that matter be till you are stronger.'

'What chanced at the end of the fight, Prince, and how
came I here?'

'The guard killed most of the Hebrews who remained
alive. Some few fled and escaped in the darkness, among
them Laban their leader, although you had wounded him,
and six were taken alive. They await their trial. I was but
little hurt and you, whom we thought dead, were but
senseless, and senseless or wandering you have remained
till this hour. We carried you in a litter, and here you have
been these three days.'

'And the lady Merapi?'

'We set her in a chariot and brought her to the city, since
had we left her she would certainly have been murdered
by her people. When Pharaoh heard what she had done, as
I did not think it well that she should dwell here, he gave
her the small house in this garden that she might be guarded, and with it slave women to attend upon her. So there
she dwells, having the freedom of the palace, and all the
while has filled the office of your nurse.'

At this moment I grew faint and shut my eyes. When I
opened them again, the Prince had gone. Six more days
went by before I was allowed to leave my bed, and during
this time I saw much of Merapi. She was very sad and lived
in fear of being killed by the Hebrews. Also she was trou-

bled in her heart because she thought she had betrayed her faith and people.

'At least you are rid of Laban,' I said.

'Never shall I be rid of him while we both live,' she answered. 'I belong to him and he will not loose my bond, because his heart is set on me.'

'And is your heart set on him?' I asked.

Her beautiful eyes filled with tears.

'A woman may not have a heart. Oh! Ana, I am unhappy,' she answered, and went away.

Also I saw others. The Princess came to visit me. She thanked me much because I had fulfilled my promise to her and guarded the Prince. Moreover she brought me a gift of gold from Pharaoh, and other gifts of fine raiment from herself. She questioned me closely about Merapi, of whom I could see she was already jealous, and was glad when she learned that she was affianced to a Hebrew. Old Bakenkhonsu came too, and asked me many things about the Prince, the Hebrews and Merapi, especially Merapi, of whose deeds, he said, all Egypt was talking, questions that I answered as best I could.

'Here we have that woman of whom Ki told us,' he said, 'she who shall bring so much joy and so much sorrow to the Prince of Egypt.'

'Why so?' I asked. 'He has not taken her into his house, nor do I think that he means to do so.'

'Yet he will, Ana, whether he means it or not. For his sake she betrayed her people, which among the Israelites is a deadly crime. Twice she saved his life, once by warning him of the ambush, and again by stabbing with her own

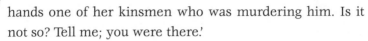

hands one of her kinsmen who was murdering him. Is it not so? Tell me; you were there.'

'It is so, but what then?'

'This: that whatever she may say, she loves him; unless indeed, it is you whom she loves,' and he looked at me shrewdly.

'When a woman has a prince, and such a prince to her hand, would she trouble herself to set snares to catch a scribe?' I asked, with some bitterness.

'Oho!' he said, with one of his great laughs, 'so things stand thus, do they? Well, I thought it, but, friend Ana, be warned in time. Do not try to conjure down the Moon to be your household lamp lest she should set, and the Sun, her lord, should grow wroth and burn you up. Well, she loves him, and therefore soon or late she will make him love her, being what she is.'

'How, Bakenkhonsu?'

'With most men, Ana, it would be simple. A sigh, some half-hidden tears at the right moment, and the thing is done, as I have known it done a thousand times. But this prince being what he is, it may be otherwise. She may show him that her name is gone for him; that because of him she is hated by her people, and rejected by her god, and thus stir his pity, which is Love's own sister. Or mayhap, being also, as I am told, wise, she will give him counsel as to all these matters of the Israelites, and thus creep into his heart under the guise of friendship, and then her sweetness and her beauty will do the rest in Nature's way. At least by this road or by that, upstream or downstream, thither she will come.'

'If so, what of it? It is the custom of the kings of Egypt to have more wives than one.'

'This, Ana; Seti, I think, is a man who in truth will have but one, and that one will be this Hebrew. Yes, a Hebrew woman will rule Egypt, and turn him to the worship of her god, for never will she worship ours. Indeed, when they see that she is lost to them, her people will use her thus. Or perchance her god himself will use her to fulfil his purpose, as already he may have used her.'

'And afterwards, Bakenkhonsu?'

'Afterwards—who knows? I am not a magician, at least not one of any account, ask it of Ki. But I am very, very old and I have watched the world, and I tell you that these things will happen, unless——' and he paused.

'Unless what?'

He dropped his voice.

'Unless Userti is bolder than I think, and kills her first or, better still, procures some Hebrew to kill her—say, that cast-off lover of hers. If you would be a friend to Pharaoh and to Egypt, you might whisper it in her ear, Ana.'

'Never!' I answered angrily.

'I did not think you would, Ana, who also struggle in this net of moonbeams that is stronger and more real than any twisted out of palm or flax. Well, nor will I, who in my age love to watch such human sport and, being so near to them, fear to thwart the schemes of gods. Let this scroll unroll itself as it will, and when it is open, read it, Ana, and remember what I said to you this day. It will be a pretty tale, written at the end with blood for ink. Oho! O-ho-ho!'

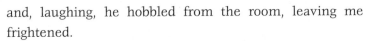

and, laughing, he hobbled from the room, leaving me frightened.

Moreover the Prince visited me every day, and even before I left my bed began to dictate to me his report to Pharaoh, since he would employ no other scribe. The substance of it was what he had foreshadowed, namely that the people of Israel, having suffered much for generations at the hands of the Egyptians, should now be allowed to depart as their prophets demanded, and go whither they would unharmed. Of the attack upon us in the pass he made light, saying that it was the evil work of a few zealots wrought on by fancied insult to their god, a deed for which the whole people should not be called upon to suffer. The last words of the report were:

'Remember, O Pharaoh, I pray thee, that Amon, god of the Egyptians, and Jahveh, the god of the Israelites, cannot rule together in the same land. If both abide in Egypt there will be a war of the gods wherein mortals may be ground to dust. Therefore, I pray thee, let Israel go.'

After I had risen and was recovered, I copied out this report in my fairest writing, refusing to tell any of its purport, although all asked, among them the Vizier Nehesi, who offered me a bribe to disclose its secret. This came to the ears of Seti, I know not how, and he was much pleased with me about the matter, saying he rejoiced to find that there was one scribe in Egypt who could not be bought. Userti also questioned me, and when I refused to answer, strange to say, was not angry, because, she declared, I only did my duty.

At last the roll was finished and sealed, and the Prince with his own hand, but without speaking, laid it on the knees of Pharaoh at a public Court, for this he would trust no one else to do. Amenmeses also brought up his report, as did Nehesi the Vizier, and the Captain of the guard which saved us from death. Eight days later the Prince was summoned to a great Council of State, as were all others of the royal House, together with the high officers. I too received a summons, as one who had been concerned in these matters.

The Prince, accompanied by the Princess, drove to the palace in Pharaoh's golden chariot, drawn by two milk-white horses of the blood of those famous steeds that had saved the life of the great Rameses in the Syrian war. All down the streets, that were filled with thousands of the people, they were received with shouts of welcome.

'See,' said the old councillor Bakenkhonsu, who was my companion in a second chariot, 'Egypt is proud and glad. It thought that its Prince was but a dreamer of dreams. But now it has heard the tale of the ambush in the pass and learned that he is a man of war, a warrior who can fight with the best. Therefore it loves him and rejoices.'

'Then, by the same rule, Bakenkhonsu, a butcher should be more great than the wisest of scribes.'

'So he is, Ana, especially if the butcher be one of men. The writer creates, but the slayer kills, and in a world ruled of death he who kills has more honour than he who creates. Hearken, now they are shouting out your name. Is that because you are the author of certain writings? I tell you, No. It is because you killed three men yonder in the pass. If you would become famous and beloved, Ana, cease from the writing of books and take to the cutting of throats.'

'Yet the writer still lives when he is dead.'

'Oho!' laughed Bakenkhonsu, 'you are even more foolish than I thought. How is a man advantaged by what happens when he is dead? Why, to-day that blind beggar whining on the temple steps means more to Egypt than all the mummies of all the Pharaohs, unless they can be robbed. Take what life can give you, Ana, and do not trouble about the offerings which are laid in the tombs for time to crumble.'

'That is a mean faith, Bakenkhonsu.'

'Very mean, Ana, like all else that we can taste and handle. A mean faith suited to mean hearts, among whom should be reckoned all save one in every thousand. Yet, if you would prosper, follow it, and when you are dead I will come and laugh upon your grave, and say, "Here lies one of whom I had hoped higher things, as I hope them of your master." '

'And not in vain, Bakenkhonsu, whatever may happen to the servant.'

'That we shall learn, and ere long, I think. I wonder who will ride at his side before the next Nile flood. By then, per-chance, he will have changed Pharaoh's golden chariot for an ox-cart, and you will goad the oxen and talk to him of the stars—or, mayhap of the moon. Well, you might both be happier thus, and she of the moon is a jealous goddess who loves worship. Oho-ho! Here are the palace steps. Help me to descend, Priest of the Lady of the Moon.'

We entered the palace and were led through the great hall to a smaller chamber where Pharaoh, who did not wear his robes of state, awaited us, seated in a cedar chair. Glancing at him I saw that his face was stern and troubled; also it seemed to me that he had grown older. The Prince and Princess made obeisance to him, as did we lesser folk, but he took no heed. When all were present and the doors had been shut, Pharaoh said,

'I have read your report, Son Seti, concerning your visit to the Israelites, and all that chanced to you; and also the reports of you, nephew Amenmeses, and of you, Officers, who accompanied the Prince of Egypt. Before I speak of them, let the Scribe Ana, who was the chariot companion of his Highness when the Hebrews attacked him, stand forward and tell me all that passed.'

So I advanced, and with bowed head repeated that tale, only leaving out so far as was possible any mention of myself. When I had finished, Pharaoh said,

'He who speaks but half the truth is sometimes more mischievous than a liar. Did you then sit in the chariot, Scribe, doing nothing while the Prince battled for his life? Or did you run away? Speak, Seti, and say what part this man played for good or ill.'

Then the Prince told of my share in the fight, with words that brought the blood to my brow. He told also how that it was I who, taking the risk of his wrath, had ordered the guard of twenty men to follow us unseen, had disguised two seasoned soldiers as chariot runners, and had thought to send back the driver to summon help at the commencement of the fray; how I had been hurt also, and was but lately recovered. When he had finished, Pharaoh said,

'That this story is true I know from others. Scribe, you have done well. But for you to-day his Highness would lie upon the table of the embalmers, as indeed for his folly he

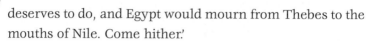

deserves to do, and Egypt would mourn from Thebes to the mouths of Nile. Come hither.'

I came with trembling steps, and knelt before his Majesty. Around his neck hung a beauteous chain of wrought gold. He took it, and cast it over my head, saying,

'Because you have shown yourself both brave and wise, with this gold I give you the title of Councillor and King's Companion, and the right to inscribe the same upon your funeral stele. Let it be noted. Retire, Scribe Ana, Councillor and King's Companion.'

So I withdrew confused, and as I passed Seti, he whispered in my ear,

'I pray you, my lord, do not cease to be Prince's Companion, because you have become that of the King.'

Then Pharaoh ordered that the Captain of the guard should be advanced in rank, and that gifts should be given to each of the soldiers, and provision be made for the children of those who had been killed, with double allowance to the families of the two men whom I had disguised as runners.

This done, once more Pharaoh spoke, slowly and with much meaning, having first ordered that all attendants and guards should leave the chamber. I was about to go also, but old Bakenkhonsu caught me by the robe, saying that in my new rank of Councillor I had the right to remain.

'Prince Seti,' he said, 'after all that I have heard, I find this report of yours strange reading. Moreover, the tenor of it is different indeed to that of those of the Count Amenmeses and the officers. You counsel me to let these Israelites go where they will, because of certain hardships that they have suffered in the past, which hardships, how-ever, have left them many and rich. That counsel I am not minded to take. Rather am I minded to send an army to the land of Goshen with orders to despatch this people, who conspired to murder the Prince of Egypt, through the Gate-way of the West, there to worship their god in heaven or in hell. Aye, to slay them all from the greybeard down to the suckling at the breast.'

'I hear Pharaoh,' said Seti, quietly.

'Such is my will,' went on Meneptah, 'and those who accompanied you upon your business, and all my council-lors think as I do, for truly Egypt cannot bear so hideous a treason. Yet, according to our law and custom it is needful, before such great acts of war and policy are undertaken, that he who stands next to the throne, and is destined to fill it, should give consent thereto. Do you consent, Prince of Egypt?'

'I do not consent, Pharaoh. I think it would be a wicked deed that tens of thousands should be massacred for the reason that a few fools waylaid a man who chanced to be of royal blood, because by inadvertence, he had desecrated their sanctuary.'

Now I saw that this answer made Pharaoh wroth, for never before had his will been crossed in such a fashion. Still he controlled himself, and asked,

'Do you then consent, Prince, to a gentler sentence, namely that the Hebrew people should be broken up; that the more dangerous of them should be sent to labour in the desert mines and quarries, and the rest distributed throughout Egypt, there to live as slaves?'

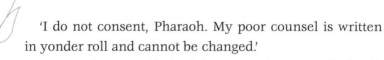

'I do not consent, Pharaoh. My poor counsel is written in yonder roll and cannot be changed.'

Meneptah's eyes flashed, but again he controlled self, and asked,

'If you should come to fill this place of mine, Prince Seti, tell us, here assembled, what policy will you pursue towards these Hebrews?'

'That policy, O Pharaoh, which I have counselled in the roll. If ever I fill the throne, I shall let them go whither they will, taking their goods with them.'

Now all those present stared at him and murmured. But Pharaoh rose, shaking with wrath. Seizing his robe where it was fastened at the breast, he rent it, and cried in a terrible voice,

'Hear him, ye gods of Egypt! Hear this son of mine who defies me to my face and would set your necks beneath the heel of a stranger god. Prince Seti, in the presence of these royal ones, and these my councillors, I—'

He said no more, for the Princess Userti, who till now had sat silent, ran to him, and throwing her arms about him, began to whisper in his ear. He hearkened to her, then sat himself down, and spoke again,

'The Princess brings it to my mind that this is a great matter, one not to be dealt with hastily. It may happen that when the Prince has taken counsel with her, and with his own heart, and perchance has sought the wisdom of the gods, he will change the words which have passed his lips. I command you, Prince, to wait upon me here at the same hour on the third day from this. Meanwhile, I command all present, upon pain of death, to say nothing of what has passed within these walls.'

'I hear Pharaoh,' said the Prince, bowing.

Meneptah rose to show that the Council was discharged, when the Vizier Nehesi approached him, and asked,

'What of the Hebrew prisoners, O Pharaoh, those murderers who were captured in the pass?'

'Their guilt is proved. Let them be beaten with rods till they die, and if they have wives or children, let them be seized and sold as slaves.'

'Pharaoh's will be done!' said the Vizier.

9

THE
SMITING
OF AMON

That evening I sat ill at ease in my work-chamber in Seti's palace, making pretence to write, I who felt that great evils threatened my lord the Prince, and knew not what to do to turn them from him. The door opened, and old Pambasa the chamberlain appeared and addressed me by my new titles, saying that the Hebrew lady Merapi, who had been my nurse in sickness, wished to speak with me. Presently she came and stood before me.

'Scribe Ana,' she said, 'I have but just seen my uncle Jabez, who has come, or been sent, with a message to me,' and she hesitated.

'Why was he sent, Lady? To bring you news of Laban?'

'Not so. Laban has fled away and none know where he is, and Jabez has only escaped much trouble as the uncle of a traitress by undertaking this mission.'

'What is the mission?'

'To pray me, if I would save myself from death and the

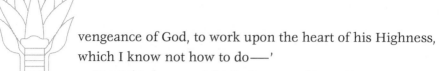

vengeance of God, to work upon the heart of his Highness, which I know not how to do——'

'Yet I think you might find means, Merapi.'

'——save through you, his friend and counsellor,' she went on, turning away her face. 'Jabez has learned that it is in the mind of Pharaoh utterly to destroy the people of Israel.'

'How does he know that, Merapi?'

'I cannot say, but I think all the Hebrews know. I knew it myself though none had told me. He has learned also that this cannot be done under the law of Egypt unless the Prince who is heir to the throne and of full age consents. Now I am come to pray you to pray the Prince not to consent.'

'Why not pray to the Prince yourself, Merapi—' I began, when from the shadows behind me I heard the voice of Seti, who had entered by the private door bearing some writings in his hand, saying,

'And what prayer has the lady Merapi to make to me? Nay, rise and speak, Moon of Israel.'

'O Prince,' she pleaded, 'my prayer is that you will save the Hebrews from death by the sword, as you alone have the power to do.'

At that moment the doors opened and in swept the royal Userti.

'What does this woman here?' she asked.

'I think that she came to see Ana, wife, as I did, and as doubtless you do. Also being here she prays me to save her people from the sword.'

'And I pray you, husband, to give her people to the sword, which they have earned, who would have murdered you.'

'And been paid, everyone of them, Userti, unless some still linger beneath the rods,' he added with a shudder. 'The rest are innocent—why should they die?'

'Because your throne hangs upon it, Seti. I say that if you continue to thwart the will of Pharaoh, as by the law of Egypt you can do, he will disinherit you and set your cousin Amenmeses in your place, as by the law of Egypt he can do.'

'I thought it, Userti. Yet why should I turn my back upon the right over a matter of my private fortunes? The question is—is it the right?'

She stared at him in amazement, she who never understood Seti and could not dream that he would throw away the greatest throne in all the world to save a subject people, merely because he thought that they should not die. Still, warned by some instinct, she left the first question unanswered, dealing only with the second.

'It is the right,' she said, 'for many reasons whereof I need give but one, for in it lie all the others. The gods of Egypt are the true gods whom we must serve and obey, or perish here and hereafter. The god of the Israelites is a false god and those who worship him are heretics and by their heresy under sentence of death. Therefore it is most right that those whom the true gods have condemned should die by the swords of their servants.'

'That is well argued, Userti, and if it be so, mayhap my mind will become as yours in this matter, so that I shall no longer stand between Pharaoh and his desire. But is it so? There's the problem. I will not ask you why you say that the gods of the Egyptians are the true gods, because I know what you would answer, or rather that you could give no

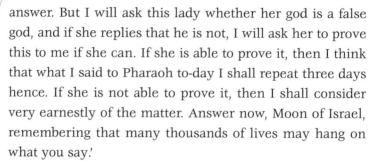

answer. But I will ask this lady whether her god is a false god, and if she replies that he is not, I will ask her to prove this to me if she can. If she is able to prove it, then I think that what I said to Pharaoh to-day I shall repeat three days hence. If she is not able to prove it, then I shall consider very earnestly of the matter. Answer now, Moon of Israel, remembering that many thousands of lives may hang on what you say.'

'O your Highness,' began Merapi. Then she paused, clasped her hands and looked upwards. I think that she was praying, for her lips moved. As she stood thus I saw, and I think Seti saw also, a very wonderful light grow on her face and gather in her eyes, a kind of divine fire of inspiration and resolve.

'How can I, a poor Hebrew maiden, prove to your Highness that my God is the true God and that the gods of Egypt are false gods? I know not, and yet, is there any one god among all the many whom you worship, whom you are prepared to set up against him?'

'Of a surety, Israelite,' answered Userti. 'There is Amon-Ra, Father of the gods, of whom all other gods have their being, and from whom they draw their strength. Yonder his statue sits in the sanctuary of his ancient temple. Let your god stir him from his place! But what will you bring forward against the majesty of Amon-Ra?'

'My God has no statues, Princess, and his place is in the hearts of men, or so I have been taught by his prophets. I have nothing to bring forward in this war save that which must be offered in all wars—my life.'

'What do you mean?' asked Seti, astounded.

'I mean that I, unfriended and alone, will enter the presence of Amon-Ra in his chosen sanctuary, and in the name of my God will challenge him to kill me, if he can.'

We stared at her, and Userti exclaimed,

'If he can! Hearken now to this blasphemer, and do you, Seti, accept her challenge as hereditary high-priest of the god Amon? Let her life pay forfeit for her sacrilege.'

'And if the great god Amon cannot, or does not deign to kill you, Lady, how will that prove that your god is greater than he?' asked the Prince. 'Perchance he might smile and in his pity, let the insult pass, as your god did by me.'

'Thus it shall be proved, your Highness. If naught happens to me, or if I am protected from anything that does happen, then I will dare to call upon my god to work a sign and a wonder, and to humble Amon-Ra before your eyes.'

'And if your god should also smile and let the matter pass, Lady, as he did by me the other day when his priests called upon him, what shall we have learned as to his strength, or as to that of Amon-Ra?'

'O Prince, you will have learned nothing. Yet if I escape from the wrath of Amon and my God is deaf to my prayer, then I am ready to be delivered over into the hands of the priests of Amon that they may avenge my sacrilege upon me.'

'There speaks a great heart,' said Seti; 'yet I am not minded that this lady should set her life upon such an issue. I do not believe that either the high-god of Egypt or the god of the Israelites will stir, but I am quite sure that the priests of Amon will avenge the sacrilege, and that cru-

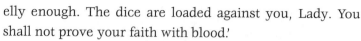

elly enough. The dice are loaded against you, Lady. You shall not prove your faith with blood.'

'Why not?' asked Userti. 'What is this girl to you, Seti, that you should stand between her and the fruit of her wickedness, you who at least in name are the high-priest of the god whom she blasphemes and who wear his robes at temple feasts? She believes in her god, leave it to her god to help her as she has dared to say he will.'

'You believe in Amon, Userti. Are you prepared to stake your life against hers in this contest?'

'I am not so mad and vain, Seti, as to believe that the god of all the world will descend from heaven to save me at my prayer, as this impious girl pretends that she believes.'

'You refuse. Then, Ana, what say you, who are a loyal worshipper of Amon?'

'I say, O Prince, that it would be presumptuous of me to take precedence of his high-priest in such a matter.'

Seti smiled and answered,

'And the high-priest says that it would be presumptuous of him to push so far the prerogative of a high office which he never sought.'

'Your Highness,' broke in Merapi in her honeyed, pleading voice, 'I pray you to be gracious to me, and to suffer me to make this trial, which I have sought, I know not why. Words such as I have spoken cannot be recalled. Already they are registered in the books of Eternity, and soon or late, in this way or in that, must be fulfilled. My life is staked, and I desire to learn at once if it be forfeit.'

Now even Userti looked on her with admiration, but answered only,

'Of a truth, Israelite, I trust that this courage will not forsake you when you are handed over to the mercies of Ki, the Sacrificer of Amon, and the priests, in the vaults of the temple you would profane.'

'I also trust that it will not, your Highness, if such should be my fate. Your word, Prince of Egypt.'

Seti looked at her standing before him so calmly with bowed head, and hands crossed upon her breast. Then he looked at Userti, who wore a mocking smile upon her face. He read the meaning of that smile as I did. It was that she did not believe that he would allow this beautiful woman, who had saved his life, to risk her life for the sake of any or all the powers of heaven or hell. For a little while he walked to and fro about the chamber, then he stopped and said suddenly addressing, not Merapi, but Userti,

'Have your will, remembering that if this brave woman fails and dies, her blood is on your hands, and that if she triumphs and lives, I shall hold her to be one of the noblest of her sex, and shall make study of all this matter of religion. Moon of Israel, as titular high-priest of Amon-Ra, I accept your challenge on behalf of the god, though whether he will take note of it I do not know. The trial shall be made to-morrow night in the sanctuary of the temple, at an hour that will be communicated to you. I shall be present to make sure that you meet with justice, as will some others. Register my commands, Scribe Ana, and let the head-priest of Amon, Roi, and the sacrificer to Amon, Ki the Magician, be summoned, that I may speak with them. Farewell, Lady.'

She went, but at the door turned and said,

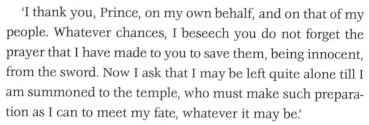

'I thank you, Prince, on my own behalf, and on that of my people. Whatever chances, I beseech you do not forget the prayer that I have made to you to save them, being innocent, from the sword. Now I ask that I may be left quite alone till I am summoned to the temple, who must make such preparation as I can to meet my fate, whatever it may be.'

Userti departed also without a word.

'Oh! friend, what have I done?' said Seti. 'Are there any gods? Tell me, are there any gods?'

'Perhaps we shall learn to-morrow night, Prince,' I answered. 'At least Merapi thinks that there is a god, and doubtless has been commanded to put her faith to proof. This, as I believe, was the real message that Jabez her uncle has brought to her.'

It was the hour before the dawn, just when the night is darkest. We stood in the sanctuary of the ancient temple of Amon-Ra, that was lit with many lamps. It was an awful place. On either side the great columns towered to the massive roof. At the head of the sanctuary sat the statue of Amon-Ra, thrice the size of a man. On his brow, rising from the crown, were two tall feathers of stone, and in his hands he held the Scourge of Rule and the symbols of Power and Ever-lastingness. The lamplight flickered upon his stern and terrible face staring towards the east. To his right was the statue of Mut, the Mother of all things. On her head was the double crown of Egypt and the uræus crest, and in her hand the looped cross, the sign of Life eternal. To his left sat Khonsu, the hawk-headed god of the moon. On his head was the crescent of the young moon carrying the disc of the full moon; in his right hand he also held the looped cross, the sign of Life eternal, and in his left the Staff of Strength. Such was this mighty triad, but of these the greatest was Amon-Ra, to whom the shrine was dedicated. Fearful they looked towering above us against the background of blackness.

Gathered there were Seti the Prince, clothed in a priest's white robe, and wearing a linen headdress, but no ornaments, and Userti the Princess, high-priestess of Hathor, Lady of the West, Goddess of Love and Nature. She wore Hathor's vulture headdress, and on it the disc of the moon fashioned of silver. Also were present Roi the head-priest, clad in his sacerdotal robes, an old and wizened man with a strong, fierce face, Ki the Sacrificer and Magician, Bakenkhonsu the ancient, myself, and a company of the priests of Amon-Ra, Mut, and Khonsu. From behind the statues came the sound of solemn singing, though who sang we could not see.

Presently from out of the darkness that lay beyond the lamps appeared a woman, led by two priestesses and wrapped in a long cloak. They brought her to an open place in front of the statue of Amon, took from her the cloak and departed, glancing back at her with eyes of hate and fear. There before us stood Merapi, clad in white, with a white wimple about her head made fast beneath her chin with that scarabæus clasp which Seti had given to her in the city of Goshen, one spot of brightest blue amid a cloud of white. She looked neither to right nor left of her. Once only she glanced at the towering statue of the god that frowned above, then with a little shiver, fixed her eyes upon the pattern of the floor.

'What does she look like?' whispered Bakenkhonsu to me.

'A corpse made ready for the embalmers,' I answered.

He shook his great head.

'Then a bride made ready for her husband.'

Again he shook his head.

'Then a priestess about to read from the roll of Mysteries.'

'Now you have it, Ana, and to understand what she reads, which few priestesses ever do. Also all three answers were right, for in this woman I seem to see doom that is Death, life that is Love, and spirit that is Power. She has a soul which both Heaven and Earth have kissed.'

'Aye, but which of them will claim her in the end?'

'That we may learn before the dawn, Ana. Hush! the fight begins.'

The head-priest, Roi, advanced and, standing before the god, sprinkled his feet with water and with perfume. Then he stretched out his hands, whereon all present prostrated themselves, save Merapi only, who stood alone in that great place like the survivor of a battle.

'Hail to thee, Amon-Ra,' he began, 'Lord of Heaven, Establisher of all things, Maker of the gods, who unrolled the skies and built the foundations of the Earth. O god of gods, appears before thee this woman Merapi, daughter of Nathan, a child of the Hebrew race that owns thee not. This woman blasphemes thy might; this woman defies thee; this woman sets up her god above thee. Is it not so, woman?'

'It is so,' answered Merapi in a low voice.

'Thus does she defy thee, thou Only One of many Forms, saying "if the god Amon of the Egyptians be a greater god than my god, let him snatch me out of the arms of my god and here in this the shrine of Amon take the breath from out my lips and leave me a thing of clay." Are these thy words, O woman?'

'They are my words,' she said in the same low voice, and oh! I shivered as I heard.

The priest went on.

'O Lord of Time, Lord of Life, Lord of Spirits and the Divinities of Heaven, Lord of Terror, come forth now in thy majesty and smite this blasphemer to the dust.'

Roi withdrew and Seti stood forward.

'Know, O god Amon,' he said, addressing the statue as though he were speaking to a living man, 'from the lips of me, thy high-priest, by birth the Prince and Heir of Egypt, that great things hang upon this matter here in the Land of Egypt, mayhap even who shall sit upon the throne that thou givest to its kings. This woman of Israel dares thee to thy face, saying that there is a greater god than thou art and that thou canst not harm her through the buckler of his strength. She says, moreover, that she will call upon her god to work a sign and a wonder upon thee. Lastly, she says that if thou dost not harm her and if her god works no sign upon thee, then she is ready to be handed over to thy priests and die the death of a blasphemer. Thy honour is set against her life, O great God of Egypt, and we, thy worshippers, watch to see the balance turn.'

'Well and justly put,' muttered Bakenkhonsu to me. 'Now if Amon fails us, what will you think of Amon, Ana?'

'I shall learn the high-priest's mind and think what the high-priest thinks,' I answered darkly, though in my heart I

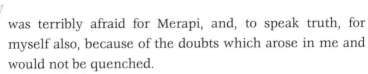

was terribly afraid for Merapi, and, to speak truth, for myself also, because of the doubts which arose in me and would not be quenched.

Seti withdrew, taking his stand by Userti, and Ki stood forward and said,

'O Amon, I thy Sacrificer, I thy Magician, to whom thou givest power, I the priest and servant of Isis, Mother of Mysteries, Queen of the company of the gods, call upon thee. She who stands before thee is but a Hebrew woman. Yet, as thou knowest well, O Father, in this house she is more than woman, inasmuch as she is the Voice and Sword of thine enemy, Jahveh, god of the Israelites. She thinks, mayhap, that she has come here of her own will, but thou knowest, Father Amon, as I know, that she is sent by the great prophets of her people, those magicians who guide her soul with spells to work thee evil and to set thee, Amon, beneath the heel of Jahveh. The stake seems small, the life of this one maid, no more; yet it is very great. This is the stake, O Father: Shall Amon rule the world, or Jahveh. If thou fallest to-night, thou fallest for ever; if thou dost triumph to-night, thou dost triumph for ever. In yonder shape of stone hides thy spirit; in yonder shape of woman's flesh hides the spirit of thy foe. Smite her, O Amon, smite her to small dust; let not the strength that is in her prevail against thy strength, lest thy name should be defiled and sorrows and loss should come upon the land which is thy throne; lest, too, the wizards of the Israelites should overcome us thy servants. Thus prayeth Ki thy Magician, on whose soul it has pleased thee to pour strength and wisdom.'

Then followed a great silence.

Watching the statue of the god, presently I thought that it moved, and as I could see by the stir among them, so did the others. I thought that its stone eyes rolled, I thought that it lifted the Scourge of Power in its granite hand, though whether these things were done by some spirit or by some priest, or by the magic of Ki, I do not know. At the least, a great wind began to blow about the temple, stirring our robes and causing the lamps to flicker. Only the robes of Merapi did not stir. Yet she saw what I could not see, for suddenly her eyes grew frightened.

'The god is awake,' whispered Bakenkhonsu. 'Now good-bye to your fair Israelite. See, the Prince trembles, Ki smiles, and the face of Userti glows with triumph.'

As he spoke the blue scarabæus was snatched from Merapi's breast as though by a hand. It fell to the floor as did her wimple, so that now she appeared with her rich hair flowing down her robe. Then the eyes of the statue seemed to cease to roll, the wind ceased to blow, and again there was silence.

Merapi stooped, lifted the wimple, replaced it on her head, found the scarabæus clasp, and very quietly, as a woman who was tiring herself might do, made it fast in its place again, a sight at which I heard Userti gasp.

For a long while we waited. Watching the faces of the congregation, I saw amazement and doubt on those of the priests, rage on that of Ki, and on Seti's the flicker of a little smile. Merapi's eyes were closed as though she were asleep. At length she opened them, and turning her head towards the Prince said,

'O high-priest of Amon-Ra, has your god worked his will on me, or must I wait longer before I call upon my God?'

'Do what you will or can, woman, and make an end, for almost it is the moment of dawn when the temple worship opens.'

Then Merapi clasped her hands, and looking upwards, prayed aloud very sweetly and simply, saying,

'O God of my fathers, trusting in Thee, I, a poor maid of Thy people Israel, have set the life Thou gavest me in Thy Hand. If, as I believe, Thou art the God of gods, I pray Thee show a sign and a wonder upon this god of the Egyptians, and thereby declare Thine Honour and keep my breath within my breast. If it pleases Thee not, then let me die, as doubtless for my many sins I deserve to do. O God of my fathers, I have made my prayer. Hear it or reject it according to Thy Will.'

So she ended, and listening to her, I felt the tears rising in my eyes, because she was so much alone, and I feared that this god of hers would never come to save her from the torments of the priests. Seti also turned his head away, and stared down the sanctuary at the sky over the open court where the lights of dawn were gathering.

Once more there was silence. Then again that wind blew, very strongly, extinguishing the lamps, and, as it seemed to me, whirling away Merapi from where she was, so that now she stood to one side of the statue. The sanctuary was filled with gloom, till presently the first rays of the rising sun struck upon the roof. They fell down, down, as minute followed minute, till at length they rested like a sword of flame upon the statue of Amon-Ra. Once more that statue seemed to move. I thought that it lifted its stone arms to protect its head. Then in a moment with a rending noise, its mighty mass burst asunder, and fell in small dust about the throne, almost hiding it from sight.

'Behold my God has answered me, the most humble of His servants,' said Merapi in the same sweet and gentle voice. 'Behold the sign and the wonder!'

'Witch!' screamed the head-priest Roi, and fled away, followed by his fellows.

'Sorceress!' hissed Userti, and fled also, as did all the others, save the Prince, Bakenkhonsu, I Ana, and Ki the Magician.

We stood amazed, and while we did so, Ki turned to Merapi and spoke. His face was terrible with mingled fear and fury, and his eyes shone like lamps. Although he did but whisper, I who was nearest to them heard all that was said, which the others could not do.

'Your magic is good, Israelite,' he muttered, 'so good that it has overcome mine here in the temple where I serve.'

'I have no magic,' she answered very low. 'I obeyed a command, no more.'

He laughed bitterly, and asked,

'Should two of a trade waste time on foolishness? Listen now. Teach me your secrets, and I will teach you mine, and together we will drive Egypt like a chariot.'

'I have no secrets, I have only faith,' said Merapi again.

'Woman,' he went on, 'woman or devil, will you take me for friend or foe? Here I have been shamed, since it was to me and not to their gods that the priests trusted to destroy you. Yet I can still forgive. Choose now, knowing that as

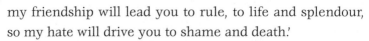

my friendship will lead you to rule, to life and splendour, so my hate will drive you to shame and death.'

'You are beside yourself, and know not what you say. I tell you that I have no magic to give or to withhold,' she answered, as one who did not understand or was indifferent, and turned away from him.

Thereon he muttered some curse which I could not catch, bowed to the heap of dust that had been the statue of the god, and vanished away among the pillars of the sanctuary.

'Oho-ho!' laughed Bakenkhonsu. 'Not in vain have I lived to be so very old, for now it seems we have a new god in Egypt, and there stands his prophetess.'

Merapi came to the prince.

'O high-priest of Amon,' she said, 'does it please you to let me go, for I am very weary?'

10

THE DEATH OF
PHARAOH

It was the appointed day and hour. By command of the
Prince I drove with him to the palace of Pharaoh, whither her Highness the Princess refused to be his companion,
and for the first time we talked together of that which had
passed in the temple.

'Have you seen the lady Merapi?' he asked of me.

I answered No, as I was told that she was sick within her
house and lay abed suffering from weariness, or I knew
not what.

'She does well to keep there,' said Seti, 'I think that if she
came out those priests would murder her if they could. Also
there are others,' and he glanced back at the chariot that bore
Userti in state. 'Say, Ana, can you interpret all this matter?'

'Not I, Prince. I thought that perhaps your Highness, the
high-priest of Amon, could give me light.'

'The high-priest of Amon wanders in thick darkness. Ki
and the rest swear that this Israelite is a sorceress who has

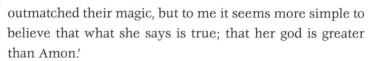

outmatched their magic, but to me it seems more simple to believe that what she says is true; that her god is greater than Amon.'

'And if this be so, Prince, what are we to do who are sworn to the gods of Egypt?'

'Bow our heads and fall with them, I suppose, Ana, since honour will not suffer us to desert them.'

'Even if they be false, Prince?'

'I do not think that they are false, Ana, though mayhap they be less true. At least they are the gods of the Egyptians and we are Egyptians.' He paused and glanced at the crowded streets, then added, 'See, when I passed this way three days ago I was received with shouts of welcome by the people. Now they are silent, every one.'

'Perhaps they have heard of what passed in the temple.'

'Doubtless, but it is not that which troubles them who think that the gods can guard themselves. They have heard also that I would befriend the Hebrews whom they hate, and therefore they begin to hate me. Why should I complain when Pharaoh shows them the way?'

'Prince,' I whispered, 'what will you say to Pharaoh?'

'That depends on what Pharaoh says to me. Ana, if I will not desert our gods because they seem to be the weaker, though it should prove to my advantage, do you think that I would desert these Hebrews because they seem to be weaker, even to gain a throne?'

'There greatness speaks,' I murmured, and as we descended from the chariot he thanked me with a look.

We passed through the great hall to that same chamber where Pharaoh had given me the chain of gold. Already he was there seated at the head of the chamber and wearing on his head the double crown. About him were gathered all those of royal blood and the great officers of state. We made our obeisances, but of these he seemed to take no note. His eyes were almost closed, and to me he looked like a man who is very ill. The Princess Userti entered after us and to her he spoke some words of welcome, giving her his hand to kiss. Then he ordered the doors to be closed. As he did so, an officer of the household entered and said that a messenger had come from the Hebrews who desired speech with Pharaoh.

'Let him enter,' said Meneptah, and presently he appeared.

He was a wild-eyed man of middle age, with long hair that fell over his sheepskin robe. To me he looked like a soothsayer. He stood before Pharaoh, making no salutation.

'Deliver your message and be gone,' said Nehesi the Vizier.

'These are the words of the Fathers of Israel, spoken by my lips,' cried the man in a voice that rang all round the vaulted chamber. 'It has come to our ears, O Pharaoh, that the woman Merapi, daughter of Nathan, who has refuged in your city, she who is named Moon of Israel, has shown herself to be a prophetess of power, one to whom our God has given strength, in that, standing alone amidst the priests and magicians of Amon of the Egyptians, she took no harm from their sorceries and was able with the sword of prayer to smite the idol of Amon to the dust. We demand that this prophetess be restored to us, making oath on our part that she shall be given over safely to her betrothed husband and that no harm shall come to her for any crimes or treasons she may have committed against her people.'

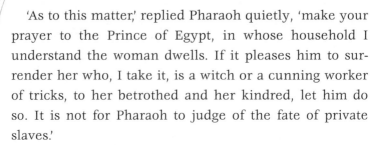

'As to this matter,' replied Pharaoh quietly, 'make your prayer to the Prince of Egypt, in whose household I understand the woman dwells. If it pleases him to surrender her who, I take it, is a witch or a cunning worker of tricks, to her betrothed and her kindred, let him do so. It is not for Pharaoh to judge of the fate of private slaves.'

The man wheeled round and addressed Seti, saying,

'You have heard, Son of the King. Will you deliver up this woman?'

'Neither do I promise to deliver her up nor not to deliver her up,' answered Seti, 'since the lady Merapi is no member of my household, nor have I any authority over her. She who saved my life dwells within my walls for safety's sake. If it pleases her to go, she can go; if it pleases her to remain, she can remain. When this Court is finished I give you safe-conduct to appear and in my presence learn her pleasure from her lips.'

'You have your answer; now be gone,' said Nehesi.

'Nay,' cried the man, 'I have more words to speak. Thus say the Fathers of Israel: We know the black counsel of your heart, O Pharaoh. It has been revealed to us that it is in your mind to put the Hebrews to the sword, as it is in the mind of the Prince of Egypt to save them from the sword. Change that mind of yours, O Pharaoh, and swiftly, lest death fall upon you from heaven above.'

'Cease!' thundered Meneptah in a voice that stilled the murmurs of the Court. 'Dog of a Hebrew, do you dare to threaten Pharaoh on his own throne? I tell you that were you not a messenger, and therefore according to our ancient law safe till the sun sets, you should be hewn limb from limb. Away with him, and if he is found in this city after nightfall let him be slain!'

Then certain of the councillors sprang upon the man and thrust him forth roughly. At the door he wrenched himself free and shouted,

'Think upon my words, Pharaoh, before this sun has set. And you, great ones of Egypt, think on them also before it appears again.'

They drove him out with blows and the doors were shut. Once more Meneptah began to speak, saying,

'Now that this brawler is gone, what have you to say to me, Prince of Egypt? Do you still give me the counsel that you wrote in the roll? Do you still refuse, as heir to the Throne, to assent to my decree that these accursed Hebrews be destroyed with the sword of my justice?'

Now all turned their eyes on Seti, who thought a while, and answered,

'Let Pharaoh pardon me, but the counsel that I gave I still give; the assent that I refused I still refuse, because my heart tells me that so it is right to do, and so I think will Egypt be saved from many troubles.'

When the scribes had finished writing down these words Pharaoh asked again,

'Prince of Egypt, if in a day to come you should fill my place, is it still your intent to let this people of the Hebrews go unharmed, taking with them the wealth that they have gathered here?'

'Let Pharaoh pardon me, that is still my intent.'

Now at these fateful words there arose a sigh of aston-

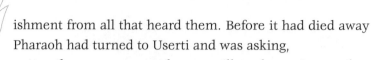

ishment from all that heard them. Before it had died away Pharaoh had turned to Userti and was asking,

'Are these your counsel, your will, and your intent also, O Princess of Egypt?'

'Let Pharaoh hear me,' answered Userti in a cold, clear voice, 'they are not. In this great matter my lord the Prince walks one road and I walk another. My counsel, will, and intent are those of Pharaoh.'

'Seti my son,' said Meneptah, more kindly than I had ever heard him speak before, 'for the last time, not as your king but as your father, I pray you to consider. Remember that as it lies in your power, being of full age and having been joined with me in many matters of government, to refuse your assent to a great act of state, so it lies in my power with the assent of the high-priests and of my ministers to remove you from my path. Seti, I can disinherit you and set another in your place, and if you persist, that and no less I shall do. Consider, therefore, my son.'

In the midst of an intense silence Seti answered,

'I have considered, O my Father, and whatever be the cost to me I cannot go back upon my words.'

Then Pharaoh rose and cried,

'Take note all you assembled here, and let it be proclaimed to the people of Egypt without the gates, that they take note also, that I depose Seti my son from his place as Prince of Egypt and declare that he is removed from the succession to the double Crown. Take note that my daughter Userti, Princess of Egypt, wife of the Prince Seti, I do not depose. Whatever rights and heritages are hers as heiress of Egypt let those rights and heritages remain to her, and if a child be born of her and Prince Seti, who lives, let that child be heir to the Throne of Egypt. Take note that, if no such child is born or until it is born, I name my nephew, the Count Amenmeses, son of my brother Khaemuas, now gathered to Osiris, to fill the Throne of Egypt when I am no more. Come hither, Count Amenmeses.'

He advanced and stood before him. Then Pharaoh lifted from his head the double crown he wore and for a moment set it on the brow of Amenmeses, saying as he replaced it on his own head,

'By this act and token do I name and constitute you, Amenmeses, to be Royal Prince of Egypt in place of my son, Prince Seti, deposed. Withdraw, Royal Prince of Egypt. I have spoken.'

'Life! Blood! Strength!' cried all the company bowing before Pharaoh, all save the Prince Seti who neither bowed nor stirred. Only he cried,

'And I have heard. Will Pharaoh be pleased to declare whether with my royal heritage he takes my life? If so, let it be here and now. My cousin Amenmeses wears a sword.'

'Nay, Son,' answered Meneptah sadly, 'your life is left to you and with it all your private rank and your possessions whatsoever and wherever they may be.'

'Let Pharaoh's will be done,' replied Seti indifferently, 'in this as in all things. Pharaoh spares my life until such time as Amenmeses his successor shall fill his place, when it will be taken.'

Meneptah started; this thought was new to him.

'Stand forth, Amenmeses,' he cried, 'and swear now the

threefold oath that may not be broken. Swear by Amon, by Ptah, and by Osiris, god of death, that never will you attempt to harm the Prince Seti, your cousin, either in body or in such state and prerogative as remain to him. Let Roi, the head-priest of Amon, administer the oath now before us all.'

So Roi spoke the oath in the ancient form, which was terrible even to hear, and Amenmeses, unwillingly enough as I thought, repeated it after him, adding however these words at the end, 'All these things I swear and all these penalties in this world and the world to be I invoke upon my head, provided only that when the time comes the Prince Seti leaves me in peace upon the throne which it has pleased Pharaoh to decree to me.'

Now some there murmured that this was not enough, since in their hearts there were few who did not love Seti and grieve to see him thus stripped of his royal heritage because his judgment differed from that of Pharaoh over a matter of State policy. But Seti only laughed and said scornfully,

'Let be, for of what value are such oaths? Pharaoh on the throne is above all oaths who must make answer to the gods only and from the hearts of some the gods are far away. Let Amenmeses not fear that I shall quarrel with him over this matter of a crown, I who in truth have never longed for the pomp and cares of royalty and who, deprived of these, still possess all that I can desire. I go my way henceforward as one of many, a noble of Egypt—no more, and if in a day to come it pleases the Pharaoh to be to shorten my wanderings, I am not sure that even then I shall grieve so very much, who am content to accept the judgment of the gods, as in the end he must do also. Yet, Pharaoh my father, before we part I ask leave to speak the thoughts that rise in me.'

'Say on,' muttered Meneptah.

'Pharaoh, having your leave, I tell you that I think you have done a very evil work this day, one that is unpleasing to those Powers which rule the world, whoever and whatsoever they may be, one too that will bring upon Egypt sorrows countless as the sand. I believe that these Hebrews whom you unjustly seek to slay worship a god as great or greater than our own, and that they and he will triumph over Egypt. I believe also that the mighty heritage which you have taken from me will bring neither joy nor honour to him by whom it has been received.'

Here Amenmeses started forward, but Meneptah held up his hand, and he was silent.

'I believe, Pharaoh—alas! that I must say it—that your days on earth are few and that for the last time we look on each other living. Farewell, Pharaoh my father, whom still I love mayhap more in this hour of parting than ever I did before. Farewell, Amenmeses, Prince of Egypt. Take from me this ornament which henceforth should be worn by you only,' and lifting from his headdress that royal circlet which marks the heir to the throne, he held it to Amenmeses, who took it and, with a smile of triumph, set it on his brow.

'Farewell, Lords and Councillors; it is my hope that in yonder prince you will find a master more to your liking than ever I could have been. Come, Ana, my friend, if it still pleases you to cling to me for a little while, now that I have nothing left to give.'

For a few moments he stood still looking very earnestly at his father, who looked back at him with tears in his deep-set, faded eyes.

Then, though whether this was by chance I cannot say, taking no note of the Princess Userti, who gazed at him perplexed and wrathful, Seti drew himself up and cried in the ancient form,

'Life! Blood! Strength! Pharaoh! Pharaoh! Pharaoh!' and bowed almost to the ground.

Meneptah heard. Muttering beneath his breath, 'Oh! Seti, my son, my most beloved son!' he stretched out his arms as though to call him back or perhaps to clasp him. As he did so I saw his face change. Next instant he fell forward to the ground and there lay still. All the company stood struck with horror, only the royal physician ran to him, while Roi and others who were priests began to mutter prayers.

'Has the good god been gathered to Osiris?' asked Amenmeses presently in a hoarse voice, 'because if it be so, I am Pharaoh.'

'Nay, Amenmeses,' exclaimed Userti, 'the decrees have not yet been sealed or promulgated. They have neither strength nor weight.'

Before he could answer the physician cried,

'Peace! Pharaoh still lives, his heart beats. This is but a fit which may pass. Begone, every one, he must have quiet.'

So we went, but first Seti knelt down and kissed his father on the brow.

* * *

An hour later the Princess Userti broke into the room of his palace where the Prince and I were talking.

'Seti,' she said, 'Pharaoh still lives, but the physicians say he will be dead by dawn. There is yet time. Here I have a writing, sealed with his signet and witnessed, wherein he recalls all that he decreed in the Court to-day, and declares you, his son, to be the true and only heir of the throne of Egypt.'

'Is it so, wife? Tell me now how did a dying man in a swoon command and seal this writing?' and he touched the scroll she held in her hand.

'He recovered for a little while; Nehesi will tell you how,' she replied, looking him in the face with cold eyes. Then before he could speak, she added, 'Waste no more breath in questions, but act and at once. The General of the guards waits below; he is your faithful servant. Through him I have promised a gift to every soldier on the day that you are crowned. Nehesi and most of the officers are on our side. Only the priests are against us because of that Hebrew witch whom you shelter, and of her tribe whom you befriend; but they have not had time to stir up the people nor will they attempt revolt. Act, Seti, act, for none will move without your express command. Moreover, no question will be raised afterwards, since from Thebes to the sea and throughout the world you are known to be the heir of Egypt.'

'What would you have me do, wife?' asked Seti, when she paused for lack of breath.

'Cannot you guess? Must I put statecraft into your head as well as a sword into your hand? Why that scribe of yours, who follows your heels like a favoured dog, would be more apt a pupil. Hearken then. Amenmeses has sent out to gather strength, but as yet there are not fifty men about him whom he can trust.' She leant forward and whispered fiercely, 'Kill the traitor Amenmeses—all will hold it a righteous act, and the General waits your word. Shall I summon him?'

'I think not,' answered Seti. 'Because Pharaoh, as he has a right to do, is pleased to name a certain man of royal blood to succeed him, how does this make that man a traitor to Pharaoh who still lives? But, traitor or none, I will not murder my cousin Amenmeses.'

'Then he will murder you.'

'Maybe. That is a matter between him and the gods which I leave them to settle. The oath he swore to-day is not one to be lightly broken. But whether he breaks it or not, I also swore an oath, at least in my heart, namely that I would not attempt to dispute the will of Pharaoh whom, after all, I love as my father and honour as my king, Pharaoh who still lives and may, as I hope, recover. What should I say to him if he recovered or, at the worst, when at last we meet elsewhere?'

'Pharaoh never will recover; I have spoken to the physician and he told me so. Already they pierce his skull to let out the evil spirit of sickness, after which none of our family have lived for very long.'

'Because, as I hold, thereby, whatever priests and physicians may say, they let in the good spirit of death. Ana, I pray you if I—'

'Man,' she broke in, striking her hand upon the table by

which she stood, 'do you understand that while you muse and moralise your crown is passing from you?'

'It has already passed, Lady. Did you not see me give it to Amenmeses?'

'Do you understand that you who should be the greatest king in all the world, in some few hours if indeed you are allowed to live, will be nothing but a private citizen of Egypt, one at whom the very beggars may spit and take no harm?'

'Surely, Wife. Moreover, there is little virtue in what I do, since on the whole I prefer that prospect and am willing to take the risk of being hurried from an evil world. Hearken,' he added, with a change of tone and gesture. 'You think me a fool and a weakling; a dreamer also, you, the clear-eyed, hard-brained states-woman who look to the glittering gain of the moment for which you are ready to pay in blood, and guess nothing of what lies beyond. I am none of these things, except, perchance, the last. I am only a man who strives to be just and to do right, as right seems to me, and if I dream, it is of good, not evil, as I understand good and evil. You are sure that this dreaming of mine will lead me to worldly loss and shame. Even of that *I* am not sure. The thought comes to me that it may lead me to those very baubles on which you set your heart, but by a path strewn with spices and with flowers, not by one paved with the bones of men and reeking with their gore. Crowns that are bought with the promise of blood and held with cruelty are apt to be lost in blood, Userti.'

She waved her hand. 'I pray you keep the rest, Seti, till I have more time to listen. Moreover if I need prophecies, I think it better to turn to Ki and those who make them their

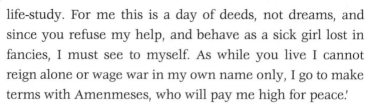

life-study. For me this is a day of deeds, not dreams, and since you refuse my help, and behave as a sick girl lost in fancies, I must see to myself. As while you live I cannot reign alone or wage war in my own name only, I go to make terms with Amenmeses, who will pay me high for peace.'

'You go—and do you return, Userti?'

She drew herself to her full height, looking very royal, and answered slowly,

'I do not return. I, the Princess of Egypt, cannot live as the wife of a common man who falls from a throne to set himself upon the earth, and smears his own brow with mud for an uræus crown. When your prophecies come true, Seti, and you crawl from your dust, then perhaps we may speak again.'

'Aye, Userti, but the question is, what shall we say?'

'Meanwhile,' she added, as she turned, 'I leave you to your chosen counsellors—yonder scribe, whom foolishness, not wisdom, has whitened before his time, and perchance the Hebrew sorceress, who can give you moonbeams to drink from those false lips of hers. Farewell, Seti, once a prince and my husband.'

'Farewell, Userti, who, I fear, must still remain my sister.'

Then he watched her go, and turning to me, said,

'To-day, Ana, I have lost both a crown and a wife, yet strange to tell I do not know which of these calamities grieves me least. Yet it is time that fortune turned. Or mayhap all the evils are not done. Would you not go also, Ana? Although she gibes at you in her anger, the Princess thinks well of you, and would keep you in her service. Remember, whoever falls in Egypt, she will be great till the last.'

'Oh! Prince,' I answered, 'have I not borne enough to-day that you must add insult to my load, you with whom I broke the cup and swore the oath?'

'What!' he laughed. 'Is there one left in Egypt who remembers oaths to his own loss? I thank you, Ana,' and taking my hand he pressed it.

At that moment the door opened, and old Pambasa entered, saying,

'The Hebrew woman, Merapi, would see you; also two Hebrew men.'

'Admit them,' said Seti. 'Note, Ana, how yonder old time-server turns his face from the setting sun. This morning even it would have been "to see your Highness," uttered with bows so low that his beard swept the floor. Now it is "to see you" and not so much as an inclination of the head in common courtesy. This, moreover, from one who has robbed me year by year and grown fat on bribes. It is the first of many bitter lessons, or rather the second—that of her Highness was the first; I pray that I may learn them with humility.'

While he mused thus and, having no comfort to offer, I listened sad at heart, Merapi entered, and a moment after her the wild-eyed messenger whom we had seen in Pharaoh's Court, and her uncle Jabez the cunning merchant. She bowed low to Seti, and smiled at me. Then the other two appeared, and with small salutation the messenger began to speak.

'You know my demand, Prince,' he said. 'It is that this woman should be returned to her people. Jabez, her uncle, will lead her away.'

'And you know my answer, Israelite,' answered Seti. 'It is that I have no power over the coming or the going of the lady Merapi, or at least wish to claim none. Address yourself to her.'

'What is it you wish with me, Priest?' asked Merapi quickly.

'That you should return to the town of Goshen, Daughter of Nathan. Have you no ears to hear?'

'I hear, but if I return, what will you of me?'

'That you who have proved yourself a prophetess by your deeds in yonder temple should dedicate your powers to the service of your people, receiving in return full forgiveness for the evils you have wrought against them, which we swear to you in the name of God.'

'I am no prophetess, and I have wrought no evils against my people, Priest. I have only saved them from the evil of murdering one who has shown himself their friend, even as I hear to the laying down of his crown for their sake.'

'That is for the Fathers of Israel and not for you to judge, woman. Your answer?'

'It is neither for them nor for me, but for God only.' She paused, then added, 'Is this all you ask of me?'

'It is all the Fathers ask, but Laban asks his affianced wife.'

'And am I to be given in marriage to—this assassin?'

'Without doubt you are to be given to this brave soldier, being already his.'

'And if I refuse?'

'Then, Daughter of Nathan, it is my part to curse you in the name of God, and to declare you cut off and outcast from the people of God. It is my part to announce to you further that your life is forfeit, and that any Hebrew may kill you when and how he can, and take no blame.'

Merapi paled a little, then turning to Jabez, asked,

'You have heard, my uncle. What say you?'

Jabez looked round shiftily, and said in his unctuous voice,

'My niece, surely you must obey the commands of the Elders of Israel who speak the will of Heaven, as you obeyed them when you matched yourself against the might of Amon.'

'You gave me a different counsel yesterday, my uncle. Then you said I had better bide where I was.'

The messenger turned and glared at him.

'There is a great difference between yesterday and to-day,' went on Jabez hurriedly. 'Yesterday you were protect-ed by one who would soon be Pharaoh, and might have been able to move his mind in favour of your folk. To-day his greatness is stripped from him, and his will has no more weight in Egypt. A dead lion is not to be feared, my niece.'

Seti smiled at this insult, but Merapi's face, like my own, grew red, as though with anger.

'Sleeping lions have been taken for dead ere now, my uncle, as those who would spurn them have discovered to their cost. Prince Seti, have you no word to help me in this strait?'

'What is the strait, Lady? If you wish to go to your people and—to Laban, who, I understand, is recovered from his hurts, there is naught between you and me save my grati-tude to you which gives me the right to say you shall not

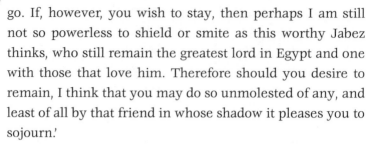

go. If, however, you wish to stay, then perhaps I am still not so powerless to shield or smite as this worthy Jabez thinks, who still remain the greatest lord in Egypt and one with those that love him. Therefore should you desire to remain, I think that you may do so unmolested of any, and least of all by that friend in whose shadow it pleases you to sojourn.'

'Those are very gentle words,' murmured Merapi, 'words that few would speak to a maid from whom naught is asked and who has naught to give.'

'A truce to this talk,' snarled the messenger. 'Do you obey or do you rebel? Your answer.'

She turned and looked him full in the face, saying,

'I do not return to Goshen and to Laban, of whose sword I have seen enough.'

'Mayhap you will see more of it before all is done. For the last time, think ere the curse of your God and your people falls upon you, and after it, death. For fall I say it shall, I who, as Pharaoh knows to-day, am no false prophet, and as that Prince knows also.'

'I do not think that my God, who sees the hearts of those that he has made, will avenge himself upon a woman because she refuses to be wedded to a murderer whom of her own will she never chose, which, Priest, is the fate you offer me. Therefore I am content to leave judgment in the hands of the great Judge of all. For the rest I defy you and your commands. If I must be slaughtered, let me die, but at least let me die mistress of myself and free, who am no man's love, or wife, or slave.'

'Well spoken!' whispered Seti to me.

Then this priest became terrible. Waving his arms and rolling his wild eyes, he poured out some hideous curse upon the head of this poor maid, much of which, as it was spoken rapidly in an ancient form of Hebrew, we did not understand. He cursed her living, dying, and after death. He cursed her in her love and hate, wedded or alone. He cursed her in child-bearing or in barrenness, and he cursed her children after her to all generations. Lastly, he declared her cut off from and rejected by the god she worshipped, and sentenced her to death at the hands of any who could slay her. So horrible was that curse that she shrank away from him, while Jabez crouched upon the ground hiding his eyes with his hands, and even I felt my blood turn cold.

At length he paused, foaming at the lips. Then, suddenly shouting, 'After judgment, doom!' he drew a knife from his robe and sprang at her.

She fled behind us. He followed, but Seti, crying, 'Ah, I thought it,' leapt between them, as he did so drawing the iron sword which he wore with his ceremonial dress. At him he sprang and the next thing I saw was the red point of the sword standing out beyond the priest's shoulders.

Down he fell, babbling,

'Is this how you show your love for Israel, Prince?'

'It is how I show my hate of murderers,' answered Seti.

Then the man died.

'Oh!' cried Merapi wringing her hands, 'once more I have caused Hebrew blood to flow and now all this curse will fall on me.'

'Nay, on me, Lady, if there is anything in curses, which I

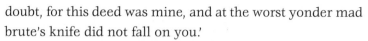

doubt, for this deed was mine, and at the worst yonder mad brute's knife did not fall on you.'

'Yes, life is left if only for a little while. Had it not been for you, Prince, by now, I——' and she shuddered.

'And had it not been for you, Moon of Israel, by now I——' and he smiled, adding, 'Surely Fate weaves a strange web round you and me. First you save me from the sword; then I save you. I think, Lady, that in the end we ought to die together and give Ana here stuff for the best of all his stories. Friend Jabez,' he went on to the Israelite who was still crouching in the corner with the eyes starting from his head, 'get you back to your gentle-hearted people and make it clear to them why the Lady Merapi cannot companion you, taking with you that carrion to prove your tale. Tell them that if they send more men to molest your niece a like fate awaits them, but that now as before I do not turn my back upon them because of the deeds of a few madmen or evil-doers, as I have given them proof to-day. Ana, make ready, since soon I leave for Memphis. See that the Lady Merapi, who will travel alone, has fit escort for her journey, that is if it pleases her to depart from Tanis.'

11
THE CROWNING
OF AMENMESES

Now, notwithstanding all the woes that fell on Egypt and a certain secret sorrow of my own, began the happiest of the days which the gods have given me. We went to Mennefer or Memphis, the white-walled city where I was born, the city that I loved. Now no longer did I dwell in a little house near to the enclosure of the temple of Ptah, which is vaster and more splendid than all those of Thebes or Tanis. My home was in the beautiful palace of Seti, which he had inherited from his mother, the Great Royal Wife. It stood, and indeed still stands, on a piled-up mound without the walls near to the temple of the goddess Neit, who always has her habitation to the north of the wall, why I do not know, because even her priests cannot tell me. In front of this palace, facing to the north, is a great portico, whereof the roof is borne upon palm-headed, painted columns whence may be seen the most lovely prospect in Egypt. First the gardens, then the palm-groves,

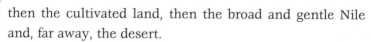

then the cultivated land, then the broad and gentle Nile and, far away, the desert.

Here, then, we dwelt, keeping small state and almost unguarded, but in wealth and comfort, spending our time in the library of the palace, or in those of the temples, and when we wearied of work, in the lovely gardens or, perchance, sailing upon the bosom of the Nile. The lady Merapi dwelt there also, but in a separate wing of the palace, with certain slaves and servants whom Seti had given to her. Sometimes we met her in the gardens, where it pleased her to walk at the same hours that we did, namely before the sun grew hot, or in the cool of the evening, and now and again when the moon shone at night. Then the three of us would talk together, for Seti never sought her company alone or within walls.

Those talks were very pleasant. Moreover they grew more frequent as time went on, since Merapi had a thirst for learning, and the Prince would bring her rolls to read in a little summer-house there was. Here we would sit, or if the heat was great, outside beneath the shadow of two spreading trees that stretched above the roof of the little pleasure-house, while Seti discoursed of the contents of the rolls and instructed her in the secrets of our writing. Sometimes, too, I read them stories of my making, to which it pleased them both to listen, or so they said, and I, in my vanity, believed. Also we would talk of the mystery and the wonder of the world and of the Hebrews and their fate, or of what passed in Egypt and the neighbouring lands.

Nor was Merapi altogether lonesome, seeing that there dwelt in Memphis certain ladies who had Hebrew blood in their veins, or were born of the Israelites and had married Egyptians against their law. Among these she made friends, and together they worshipped in their own fashion with none to say them nay, since here no priests were allowed to trouble them.

For our part we held intercourse with as many as we pleased, since few forgot that Seti was by blood the Prince of Egypt, that is, a man almost half divine, and all were eager to visit him. Also he was much beloved for his own sake and more particularly by the poor, whose wants it was his delight to relieve to the full limit of his wealth. Thus it came about that whenever he went abroad, although against his will, he was received with honours and homage that were almost royal, for though Pharaoh could rob him of the Crown he could not empty his veins of the blood of kings.

It was on this account that I feared for his safety, since I was sure that through his spies Amenmeses knew all and would grow jealous of a dethroned prince who was still so much adored by those over whom of right he should have ruled. I told Seti of my doubts and that when he travelled the streets he should be guarded by armed men. But he only laughed and answered that, as the Hebrews had failed to kill him, he did not think that any others would succeed. Moreover he believed there were no Egyptians in the land who would lift a sword against him, or put poison in his drink, whoever bade them. Also he added these words,

'The best way to escape death is to have no fear of death, for then Osiris shuns us.'

*   *   *

Now I must tell of the happenings at Tanis. Pharaoh Meneptah lingered but a few hours and never found his mind again before his spirit flew to Heaven. Then there was great mourning in the land, for, if he was not loved, Meneptah was honoured and feared. Only among the Israelites there was open rejoicing, because he had been their enemy and their prophets had foretold that death was near to him. They gave it out that he had been smitten of their God, which caused the Egyptians to hate them more than ever. There was doubt, too, and bewilderment in Egypt, for though his proclamation disinheriting the Prince Seti had been published abroad, the people, and especially those who dwelt in the south, could not understand why this should have been done over a matter of the shepherd slaves who dwelt in Goshen. Indeed, had the Prince but held up his hand, tens of thousands would have rallied to his standard. Yet this he refused to do, which astonished all the world, who thought it marvellous that any man should refuse a throne which would have lifted him almost to the level of the gods. Indeed, to avoid their importunities he had set out at once for Memphis, and there remained hidden away during the period of mourning for his father. So it came about that Amenmeses succeeded with none to say him nay, since without her husband Userti could not or would not act.

After the days of embalmment were accomplished the body of Pharaoh Meneptah was carried up the Nile to be laid in his eternal house, the splendid tomb that he had made ready for himself in the Valley of Dead Kings at Thebes. To this great ceremony the Prince Seti was not bidden, lest, as Bakenkhonsu told me afterwards, his presence should cause some rising in his favour, with or without his will. For this reason also the dead god, as he was named, was not suffered to rest at Memphis on his last journey up the Nile. Disguised as a man of the people the Prince watched his father's body pass in the funeral barge guarded by shaven, white-robed priests, the centre of a splendid procession. In front went other barges filled with soldiers and officers of state, behind came the new Pharaoh and all the great ones of Egypt, while the sounds of lamentation floated far over the face of the waters. They appeared, they passed, they disappeared, and when they had vanished Seti wept a little, for in his own fashion he loved his father.

'Of what use is it to be a king and named half-divine, Ana,' he said to me, 'seeing that the end of such gods as these is the same as that of the beggar at the gate?'

'This, Prince,' I answered, 'that a king can do more good than a beggar while the breath is in his nostrils, and leave behind him a great example to others.'

'Or more harm, Ana. Also the beggar can leave a great example, that of patience in affliction. Still, if I were sure that I should do nothing but good, then perhaps I would be a king. But I have noted that those who desire to do the most good often work the greatest harm.'

'Which, if followed out, would be an argument for wishing to do evil, Prince.'

'Not so,' he answered, 'because good triumphs at the last. For good is truth and truth rules earth and heaven.'

'Then it is clear, Prince, that you should seek to be a king.'

'I will remember the argument, Ana, if ever time brings me an opportunity unstained by blood,' he answered.

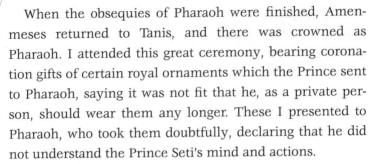

When the obsequies of Pharaoh were finished, Amen-meses returned to Tanis, and there was crowned as Pharaoh. I attended this great ceremony, bearing corona-tion gifts of certain royal ornaments which the Prince sent to Pharaoh, saying it was not fit that he, as a private per-son, should wear them any longer. These I presented to Pharaoh, who took them doubtfully, declaring that he did not understand the Prince Seti's mind and actions.

'They hide no snare, O Pharaoh,' I said. 'As you rejoice in the glory that the gods have sent you, so the Prince my master rejoices in the rest and peace which the gods have given him, asking no more.'

'It may be so, Scribe, but I find this so strange a thing, that sometimes I fear lest the rich flowers of this glory of mine should hide some deadly snake, whereof the Prince knows, if he did not set it there.'

'I cannot say, O Pharaoh, but without doubt, although he could work no guile, the Prince is not as are other men. His mind is both wide and deep.'

'Too deep for me,' muttered Amenmeses. 'Nevertheless, say to my royal cousin that I thank him for his gifts, espe-cially as some of them were worn, when he was heir to Egypt, by my father Khaemuas, who I would had left me his wisdom as well as his blood. Say to him also that while he refrains from working me harm upon the throne, as I know he has done up to the present, he may be sure that I will work him none in the station which he has chosen.'

Also I saw the Princess Userti who questioned me close-ly concerning her lord. I told her everything, keeping naught back. She listened and asked,

'What of that Hebrew woman, Moon of Israel? Without doubt she fills my place.'

'Not so, Princess,' I answered. 'The Prince lives alone. Neither she nor any other woman fills your place. She is a friend to him, no more.'

'A friend! Well, at least we know the end of such friendships. Oh! surely the Prince must be stricken with madness from the gods!'

'It may be so, your Highness, but I think that if the gods smote more men with such madness, the world would be better than it is.'

'The world is the world, and the business of those who are born to greatness is to rule it as it is, not to hide away amongst books and flowers, and to talk folly with a beautiful outland woman, and a scribe however learned,' she answered bitterly, adding, 'Oh! if the Prince is not mad, certainly he drives others to madness, and me, his spouse, among them. That throne is his, his; yet he suffers a cross-grained dolt to take his place, and sends him gifts and blessings.'

'I think your Highness should wait till the end of the story before you judge of it.'

She looked at me sharply, and asked,

'Why do you say that? Is the Prince no fool after all? Do he and you, who both seem to be so simple, perchance play a great and hidden game, as I have known men feign folly in order to do with safety? Or has that witch of an Israelite some secret knowledge in which she instructs you, such as a woman who can shatter the statue of Amon to fine dust might well possess? You make believe not to

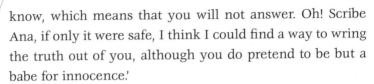

know, which means that you will not answer. Oh! Scribe Ana, if only it were safe, I think I could find a way to wring the truth out of you, although you do pretend to be but a babe for innocence.'

'It pleases your Highness to threaten and without cause.'

'No,' she answered, changing her voice and manner, 'I do not threaten; it is only the madness that I have caught from Seti. Would you not be mad if you knew that another woman was to be crowned to-morrow in your place, because—because——' and she began to weep, which frightened me more than all her rough words.

Presently she dried her tears, and said,

'Say to my lord that I rejoice to hear that he is well and send him greetings, but that never of my own wish will I look upon his living face again unless indeed he takes another counsel, and sets himself to win that which is his own. Say to him that though he has so little care for me, and pays no heed to my desires, still I watch over his welfare and his safety, as best I may.'

'His safety, Princess! Pharaoh assured me not an hour ago that he had naught to fear, as indeed he fears naught.'

'Oh! which of you is the more foolish,' she exclaimed stamping her foot, 'the man or his master? You believe that the Prince has naught to fear because that usurper tells you so, and he believes it—well, because he fears naught. For a little while he may sleep in peace. But let him wait until troubles of this sort or of that arise in Egypt and, understanding that the gods send them on account of the great wickedness that my father wrought when death had him by the throat and his mind was clouded, the people begin to turn their eyes towards their lawful king. Then the usurper will grow jealous, and if he has his way, the Prince will sleep in peace—for ever. If his throat remains uncut, it will be for one reason only, that I hold back the murderer's hand. Farewell, I can talk no more, for I say to you that my brain is afire—and to-morrow he should have been crowned, and I with him,' and she swept away, royal as ever, leaving me wondering what she meant when she spoke of troubles arising in Egypt, or if the words were but uttered at hazard.

Afterwards Bakenkhonsu and I supped together at the college of the temple of Ptah, of which because of his age he was called the father, when I heard more of this matter.

'Ana,' he said, 'I tell you that such gloom hangs over Egypt as I have never known even when it was thought that the Ninebow Barbarians would conquer and enslave the land. Amenmeses will be the fifth Pharaoh whom I have seen crowned, the first of them when I was but a little child hanging to my mother's robe, and not once have I known such joylessness.'

'That may be because the crown passes to one who should not wear it, Bakenkhonsu.'

He shook his head. 'Not altogether. I think this darkness comes from the heavens as light does. Men are afraid they know not of what.'

'The Israelites,' I suggested.

'Now you are near to it, Ana, for doubtless they have much to do with the matter. Had it not been for them Seti and not Amenmeses would be crowned to-morrow. Also the tale of the marvel which the beautiful Hebrew woman

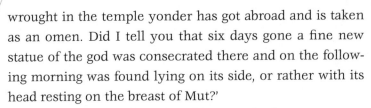

wrought in the temple yonder has got abroad and is taken as an omen. Did I tell you that six days gone a fine new statue of the god was consecrated there and on the following morning was found lying on its side, or rather with its head resting on the breast of Mut?'

'If so, Merapi is blameless, because she has gone away from this city.'

'Of course she has gone away, for has not Seti gone also? But I think she left something behind her. However that may be, even our new divine lord is afraid. He dreams ill, Ana,' he added, dropping his voice, 'so ill that he has called in Ki, the Kherheb,* to interpret his visions.'

'And what said Ki?'

'Ki could say nothing or, rather, that the only answer vouchsafed to him and his company, when they made inquiry of their Kas, was that this god's reign would be very short and that it and his life would end together.'

'Which perhaps did not please the god Amenmeses, Bakenkhonsu?'

'Which did not please the god at all. He threatened Ki. It is a foolish thing to threaten a great magician, Ana, as the Kherheb Ki, himself indeed told him, looking him in the eyes. Then he prayed his pardon and asked who would succeed him on the throne, but Ki said he did not know, as a Kherheb who had been threatened could never remember anything, which indeed he never can—except to pay back the threatener.'

'And did he know, Bakenkhonsu?'

---

*"Kherheb" was the title of the chief official magician in ancient Egypt.

By way of answer the old Councillor crumbled some bread fine upon the table, then with his finger traced among the crumbs the rough likeness of a jackal-headed god and of two feathers, after which with a swift movement he swept the crumbs onto the floor.

'Seti!' I whispered, reading the hieroglyphs of the Prince's name, and he nodded and laughed in his great fashion.

'Men come to their own sometimes, Ana, especially if they do not seek their own,' he said. 'But if so, much must happen first that is terrible. The new Pharaoh is not the only man who dreams, Ana. Of late years my sleep has been light and sometimes I dream, though I have no magic like to that of Ki.'

'What did you dream?'

'I dreamed of a great multitude marching like locusts over Egypt. Before them went a column of fire in which were two hands. One of these held Amon by the throat and one held the new Pharaoh by the throat. After them came a column of cloud, and in it a shape like to that of an unwrapped mummy, a shape of death standing upon water that was full of countless dead.'

Now I bethought me of the picture that the Prince and I had seen in the skies yonder in the land of Goshen, but of it I said nothing. Yet I think that Bakenkhonsu saw into my mind, for he asked,

'Do *you* never dream, Friend? You see visions that come true—Amenmeses on the throne, for instance. Do you not also dream at times? No? Well, then, the Prince? You look like men who might, and the time is ripe and pregnant. Oh! I remember. You are both of you dreaming, not of the pictures that pass across the terrible eyes of Ki, but of those that the moon reflects upon the waters of Memphis, the Moon of Israel. Ana, be advised by me, put away the flesh and increase the spirit, for in it alone is happiness, whereof woman and all our joys are but earthly symbols, shadows thrown by that mortal cloud which lies between us and the Light Above. I see that you understand, because some of that light has struggled to your heart. Do you remember that you saw it shining in the hour when your little daughter died? Ah! I thought so. It was the gift she left you, a gift that will grow and grow in such a breast as yours, if only you will put away the flesh and make room for it, Ana. Man, do not weep—laugh as I do, Oho-ho! Give me my staff, and good-night. Forget not that we sit together at the crowning to-morrow, for you are a King's Companion and that rank once conferred is one which no new Pharaoh can take away. It is like the gift of the spirit, Ana, which is hard to win, but once won more eternal than the stars. Oh! why do I live so long who would bathe in it, as when a child I used to bathe in Nile?'

On the following day at the appointed hour I went to the great hall of the palace, that in which I had first seen Meneptah, and took my stand in the place allotted to me. It was somewhat far back, perhaps because it was not wished that I, who was known to be the private scribe of Seti, should remind Egypt of him by appearing where all could see me.

Great as was the hall the crowd filled it to its furthest corners. Moreover no common man was present there, but rather every noble and head-priest in Egypt, and with them their wives and daughters, so that all the dim courts shone with gold and precious gems set upon festal garments. While I was waiting old Bakenkhonsu hobbled towards me, the crowd making way for him, and I could see that there was laughter in his sunken eyes.

'We are ill-placed, Ana,' he said. 'Still if any of the many gods there are in Egypt should chance to rain fires on Pharaoh, we shall be the safer. Talking of gods,' he went on in a whisper, 'have you heard what happened an hour ago in the temple of Ptah of Tanis whence I have just come? Pharaoh and all the Blood-royal—save one—walked according to custom before the statue of the god which, as you know, should bow its head to show that he chooses and accepts the king. In front of Amenmeses went the Princess Userti, and as she passed the head of the god bowed, for I saw it, though all pretended that they did not see. Then came Pharaoh and stood waiting, but it would not bow, though the priests called in the old formula, "The god greets the king."

'At length he went on, looking as black as night, and others of the blood of Rameses followed in their order. Last of all limped Siptah and, behold! the god bowed again.'

'How and why does it do these things,' I asked, 'and at the wrong time?'

'Ask the priests, Ana, or Userti, or Siptah. Perhaps the divine neck has not been oiled of late, or too much oiled, or too little oiled, or prayers—or strings—may have gone wrong. Or Pharaoh may have been niggard in his gifts to that college of the great god of his House. Who am I that I should know the ways of gods? That in the temple where I served at Thebes fifty years ago did not pretend to bow or

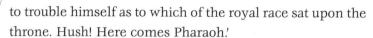

to trouble himself as to which of the royal race sat upon the throne. Hush! Here comes Pharaoh.'

Then in a splendid procession, surrounded by princes, councillors, ladies, priests, and guards, Amenmeses and the Royal Wife, Urnure, a large woman who walked awkwardly, entered the hall, a glittering band. The high-priest, Roi, and the chancellor, Nehesi, received Pharaoh and led him to his throne. The multitude prostrated itself, trumpets blew and thrice the old salute of 'Life! Blood! Strength! Pharaoh! Pharaoh! Pharaoh!' was cried aloud.

Amenmeses rose and bowed, and I saw that his heavy face was troubled and looked older. Then he swore some oath to gods and men which Roi dictated to him, and before all the company put on the double crown and the other emblems, and took in his hands the scourge and golden sickle. Next homage was paid. The Princess Userti came first and kissed Pharaoh's hand, but bent no knee. Indeed first she spoke with him a while. We could not hear what was said, but afterwards learned that she demanded that he should publicly repeat all the promises which her father Meneptah had made to her before him, confirming her in her place and rights. This in the end he did, though it seemed to me unwillingly enough.

So with many forms and ancient celebrations the ceremony went on, till all grew weary waiting for that time when Pharaoh should make his speech to the people. That speech, however, was never made, for presently, thrusting past us, I saw those two prophets of the Israelites who had visited Meneptah in this same hall. Men shrank from them, so that they walked straight up to the throne, nor did even the guards strive to bar their way. What they said there I could not hear, but I believe that they demanded that their people should be allowed to go to worship their god in their own fashion, and that Amenmeses refused as Meneptah had done.

Then one of them cast down a rod and it turned to a snake which hissed at Pharaoh, whereon the Kherheb Ki and his company also cast down rods that turned to snakes, though I could only hear the hissing. After this a great gloom fell upon the hall, so that men could not see each other's faces and everyone began to call aloud till the company broke up in confusion. Bakenkhonsu and I were borne together to the doorway by the pressure of the people, whence we were glad enough to see the sky again.

Thus ended the crowning of Amenmeses.

12

THE MESSAGE
OF JABEZ

That night there were none who rejoiced in the streets of the city, and save in the palace and houses of those of the Court, none who feasted. I walked abroad in the market-place and noted the people going to and fro gloomily, or talking together in whispers. Presently a man whose face was hidden in a hood began to speak with me, saying that he had a message for my master, the Prince Seti. I answered that I took no messages from veiled strangers, whereon he threw back his hood, and I saw that it was Jabez, the uncle of Merapi. I asked him whether he had obeyed the Prince, and borne the body of that prophet back to Goshen and told the elders of the manner of the man's death.

'Yes,' he answered, 'nor were the Elders angry with the Prince over this matter. They said that their messenger had exceeded his authority, since they had never told him to curse Merapi, and much less to attempt to kill her, and that the Prince did right to slay one who would have done

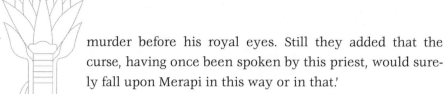

murder before his royal eyes. Still they added that the curse, having once been spoken by this priest, would surely fall upon Merapi in this way or in that.'

'What then should she do, Jabez?'

'I do not know, Scribe. If she returns to her people, perchance she will be absolved, but then she must surely marry Laban. It is for her to judge.'

'And what would you do if you were in her place, Jabez?'

'I think that I should stay where I was, and make myself very dear to Seti, taking the chance that the curse may pass her by, since it was not lawfully decreed upon her. Whichever way she looks, trouble waits, and at the worst, a woman might wish to satisfy her heart before it falls, especially if that heart should happen to turn to one who will be Pharaoh.'

'Why do you say "who will be Pharaoh," Jabez?' I asked, for we were standing in an empty place alone.

'That I may not tell you,' he replied cunningly, 'yet it will come about as I say. He who sits upon the throne is mad as Meneptah was mad, and will fight against a strength that is more than his until it overwhelms him. In the Prince's heart alone does the light of wisdom shine. That which you saw to-day is only the first of many miracles, Scribe Ana. I can say no more.'

'What then is your message, Jabez?'

'This: Because the Prince has striven to deal well with the people of Israel and for their sake has cast aside a crown, whatever may chance to others, let him fear nothing. No harm shall come to him, or to those about him, such as yourself, Scribe Ana, who also would deal justly by us. Yet it may happen that through my niece Merapi, on whose head the evil word has fallen, a great sorrow may come to both him and her. Therefore, perhaps, although setting this against that, she may be wise to stay in the house of Seti, he, on the balance, may be wise to turn her from his doors.'

'What sorrow?' I asked, who grew bewildered with his dark talk, but there was no answer, for he had gone.

Near to my lodging another man met me, and the moonlight shining on his face showed me the terrible eyes of Ki.

'Scribe Ana,' he said, 'you leave for Memphis tomorrow at the dawn, and not two days hence as you purposed.'

'How do you know that, Magician Ki?' I answered, for I had told my change of plan to none, not even to Bakenkhonsu, having indeed only determined upon it since Jabez left me.

'I know nothing, Ana, save that a faithful servant who has learned all you have learned to-day will hurry to make report of it to his master, especially if there is some other to whom he would also wish to make report, as Bakenkhonsu thinks.'

'Bakenkhonsu talks too much, whatever he may think,' I exclaimed testily.

'The aged grow garrulous. You were at the crowning to-day, were you not?'

'Yes, and if I saw aright from far away, those Hebrew prophets seemed to worst you at your own trade there, Kherheb, which must grieve you, as you were grieved in the temple when Amon fell.'

'It does not grieve me, Ana. If I have powers, there may be others who have greater powers, as I learned in the temple of Amon. Why therefore should I feel ashamed?'

'Powers!' I replied with a laugh, for the strings of my mind seemed torn that night, 'would not craft be a better word? How do you turn a stick into a snake, a thing which is impossible to man?'

'Craft might be a better word, since craft means knowledge as well as trickery. "Impossible to man!" After what you saw a while ago in the temple of Amon, do you hold that there is anything impossible to man or woman? Perhaps you could do as much yourself.'

'Why do you mock me, Ki? I study books, not snake-charming.'

He looked at me in his calm fashion, as though he were reading, not my face, but the thoughts behind it. Then he looked at the cedar wand in his hand and gave it to me, saying,

'Study this, Ana, and tell me, what is it.'

'Am I a child,' I answered angrily, 'that I should not know a priest's rod when I see one?'

'I think that you are something of a child, Ana,' he murmured, all the while keeping those eyes of his fixed upon my face.

Then a horror came about. For the rod began to twist in my hand and when I stared at it, lo! it was a long, yellow snake which I held by the tail. I threw the reptile down with a scream, for it was turning its head as though to strike me, and there in the dust it twisted and writhed away from me and towards Ki. Yet an instant later it was only a stick of yellow cedar-wood, though between me and Ki there was a snake's track in the sand.

'It is somewhat shameless of you, Ana,' said Ki, as he lifted the wand, 'to reproach me with trickery while you yourself try to confound a poor juggler with such arts as these.'

Then I know not what I said to him, save the end of it was that I supposed he would tell me next that I could fill a hall with darkness at noonday and cover a multitude with terror.

Suddenly his face and voice changed.

'Let us have done with jests,' he said, 'though these are well enough in their place. Will you take this rod again and point it to the moon? You refuse and you do well, for neither you nor I can cover up her face. Ana, because you are wise in your way and consort with one who is wiser, and were present in the temple when the statue of Amon was shattered by a certain witch who matched her strength against mine and conquered me, I, the great magician, have come to ask *you*—whence came that darkness in the hall to-day?'

'From God, I think,' I answered in an awed whisper.

'So I think also, Ana. But tell me, or ask Merapi, Moon of Israel, to tell me—from what god? Oh! I say to you that a terrible power is afoot in this land and that the Prince Seti did well to refuse the throne of Egypt and to fly to Memphis. Repeat it to him, Ana.'

Then he too was gone.

Now I returned in safety to Memphis and told all these tidings to the Prince, who listened to them eagerly. Once only was he greatly stirred; it was when I repeated to him the words of Userti, that never would she look upon his face again unless it pleased him to turn it towards the throne. On hearing this tears came into his eyes, and rising, he walked up and down the chamber.

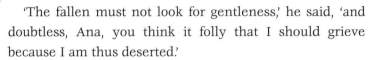

'The fallen must not look for gentleness,' he said, 'and doubtless, Ana, you think it folly that I should grieve because I am thus deserted.'

'Nay, Prince, for I too have been abandoned by a wife and the pain is unforgotten.'

'It is not of the wife I think, Ana, since in truth her Highness is no wife to me. For whatever may be the ancient laws of Egypt, how could it happen otherwise, at any rate in my case and hers? It is of the sister. For though my mother was not hers, she and I were brought up together and in our way loved each other, though always it was her pleasure to lord it over me, as it was mine to submit and pay her back in jests. That is why she is so angry because now of a sudden I have thrown off her rule to follow my own will whereby she has lost the throne.'

'It has always been the duty of the royal heiress of Egypt to marry the Pharaoh of Egypt, Prince, and having wed one who would be Pharaoh according to that duty, the blow cuts deep.'

'Then she had best thrust aside that foolish wife of his and wed him who is Pharaoh. But that she will never do; Amenmeses she has always hated, so much that she loathed to be in the same place with him. Nor indeed would he wed her, who wishes to rule for himself, not through a woman whose title to the crown is better than his own. Well, she has put me away and there's an end. Henceforth I must go lonely, unless—unless——Continue your story, friend. It is kind of her in her greatness to promise to protect one so humble. I should remember that, although it is true that fallen heads sometimes rise again,' he added bitterly.

'So at least Jabez thinks, Prince,' and I told him how the Israelites were sure that he would be Pharaoh, whereat he laughed and said,

'Perhaps, for they are good prophets. For my part I neither know or care. Or maybe Jabez sees advantage in talking thus, for as you know he is a clever trader.'

'I do not think so,' I answered and stopped.

'Had Jabez more to say of any other matter, Ana? Of the Lady Merapi, for instance?'

Now feeling it to be my duty, I told him every word that had passed between Jabez and myself, though somewhat shamefacedly.

'This Hebrew takes much for granted, Ana, even as to whom the Moon of Israel would wish to shine upon. Why, friend, it might be you whom she desires to touch with her light, or some youth in Goshen—not Laban—or no one.'

'Me, Prince, me!' I exclaimed.

'Well, Ana, I am sure you would have it so. Be advised by me and ask her mind upon the matter. Look not so confused, man, for one who has been married you are too modest. Come tell me of this Crowning.'

So glad enough to escape from the matter of Merapi, I spoke at length of all that had happened when Pharaoh Amenmeses took his seat upon the throne. When I described how the rod of the Hebrew prophet had been turned to a snake and how Ki and his company had done likewise, the Prince laughed and said that these were mere jugglers' tricks. But when I told of the darkness that had

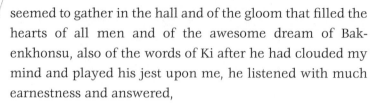

seemed to gather in the hall and of the gloom that filled the hearts of all men and of the awesome dream of Bak- enkhonsu, also of the words of Ki after he had clouded my mind and played his jest upon me, he listened with much earnestness and answered,

'My mind is as Ki's in this matter. I too think that a terri- ble power is afoot in Egypt, one that has its home in the land of Goshen, and that I did well to refuse the throne. But from what god these fortunes come I do not know. Perhaps time will tell us. Meanwhile if there is aught in the prophe- cies of these Hebrews, as interpreted by Jabez, at least you and I may sleep in peace, which is more than will chance to Pharaoh on the throne that Userti covets. If so, this play will be worth the watching. You have done your mission well, Ana. Go rest you while I think over all that you have said.'

It was evening and as the palace was very hot I went into the garden and making my way to that little pleasure- house where Seti and I were wont to study, I sat myself down there and, being weary, fell asleep. When I awoke from a dream about some woman who was weeping, night had fallen and the full moon shone in the sky, so that its rays fell on the garden before me.

Now in front of this little house, as I have said, grew trees that at this season of the year were covered with white and cup-like blossoms, and between these trees was a seat built up of sun-dried bricks. On this seat sat a woman whom I knew from her shape to be Merapi. Also she was sad, for although her head was bowed and her long hair hid her face I could hear her gentle sighs.

The sight of her moved me very much and I remembered what the Prince had said to me, telling me that I should do well to ask this lady whether she had any mind my way. Therefore if I did so, surely I could not be blamed. Yet I was certain that it was not to me that her heart turned, though to speak the truth, much I wished it otherwise. Who would look at the ibis in the swamp when the wide-winged eagle floated in heaven above?

An evil thought came into my mind, sent by Set. Suppose that this watcher's eyes were fixed upon the eagle, lord of the air. Suppose that she worshipped this eagle; that she loved it because its home was heaven, because to her it was the king of all the birds. And suppose one told her that if she lured it down to earth from the glorious safety of the skies, she would bring it to captivity or death at the hand of the snarer. Then would not that loving watcher say: 'Let it go free and happy, however much I long to look upon it,' and when it had sailed from sight, perhaps turn her eyes to the humble ibis in the mud?

Jabez had told me that if this woman and the Prince grew dear to each other she would bring great sorrow on his head. If I repeated his words to her, she who had faith in the prophecies of her people would certainly believe them. Moreover, whatever her heart might prompt, being so high-natured, never would she consent to do what might bring trouble on Seti's head, even if to refuse him should sink her soul in sorrow. Nor would she return to the Hebrews there to fall into the hands of one she hated. Then perhaps I——. Should I tell her? If Jabez had not meant that the matter must be brought to her ears, would

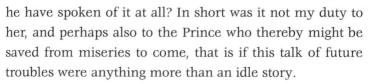

he have spoken of it at all? In short was it not my duty to her, and perhaps also to the Prince who thereby might be saved from miseries to come, that is if this talk of future troubles were anything more than an idle story.

Such was the evil reasoning with which Set assailed my spirit. How I beat it down I do not know. Not by my own goodness, I am sure, since at the moment I was aflame with love for the sweet and beautiful lady who sat before me and in my foolishness would, I think, have given my life to kiss her hand. Not altogether for her sake either, since passion is very selfish. No, I believe it was because the love that I bore the Prince was more deep and real than that which I could feel for any woman, and I knew well that were she not in my sight no such treachery would have overcome my heart. For I was sure, although he had never said so to me, that Seti loved Merapi and above all earthly things desired her as his companion, while if once I spoke those words, whatever my own gain or loss and whatever her secret wish, that she would never be.

So I conquered, though the victory left me trembling like a child, and wishing that I had not been born to know the pangs of love denied. My reward was very swift, for just then Merapi unfastened a gem from the breast of her white robe and held it towards the moon, as though to study it. In an instant I knew it again. It was that royal scarab of lapis-lazuli with which in Goshen the Prince had made fast the bandage on her wounded foot, which also had been snatched from her breast by some power on that night when the statue of Amon was shattered in the temple.

Long and earnestly she looked at it, then having glanced

round to make sure she was alone, she pressed it to her lips and kissed it thrice with passion, muttering I know not what between the kisses. Now the scales fell from my eyes and I knew that she loved Seti, and oh! how I thanked my guardian god who had saved me from such useless shame.

I wiped the cold damp from my brow and was about to flee away, discovering myself with as few words as might be, when, looking up, I saw standing behind Merapi the figure of a man, who was watching her replace the ornament in her robe. While I hesitated a moment the man spoke and I knew the voice for that of Seti. Then again I thought of flight, but being somewhat timid by nature, feared to show myself until it was too late, thinking that afterward the Prince would make me the target of his wit. So I sat close and still, hearing and seeing all despite myself.

'What gem is that, Lady, which you admire and cherish so tenderly?' asked Seti in his slow voice that so often hid a hint of laughter.

She uttered a little scream and springing up, saw him.

'Oh! my lord,' she exclaimed, 'pardon your servant. I was sitting here in the cool, as you gave me leave to do, and the moon was so bright—that—I wished to see if by it I could read the writing on this scarab.'

Never before, thought I to myself, did I know one who read with her lips, though it is true that first she used her eyes.

'And could you, Lady? Will you suffer me to try?'

Very slowly and colouring, so that even the moonlight showed her blushes, she withdrew the ornament again and held it towards him.

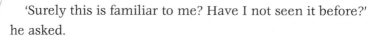

'Surely this is familiar to me? Have I not seen it before?' he asked.

'Perhaps. I wore it that night in the temple, your Highness.'

'You must not name me Highness, Lady. I have no longer any rank in Egypt.'

'I know—because of—my people. Oh! it was noble.'

'But about the scarabæus——' he broke in, with a wave of his hand. 'Surely it is the same with which the bandage was made fast upon your hurt—oh! years ago?'

'Yes, it is the same,' she answered, looking down.

'I thought it. And when I gave it to you, I said some words that seemed to me well spoken at the time. What were they? I cannot remember. Have you also forgotten?'

'Yes—I mean—no. You said that now I had all Egypt beneath my foot, speaking of the royal cartouche upon the scarab.'

'Ah! I recall. How true, and yet how false the jest, or prophecy.'

'How can anything be both true and false, Prince?'

'That I could prove to you very easily, but it would take an hour or more, so it shall be for another time. This scarab is a poor thing, give it back to me and you shall have a better. Or would you choose this signet? As I am no longer Prince of Egypt it is useless to me.'

'Keep the scarab, Prince. It is your own. But I will not take the ring because it is——'

'——useless to me, and you would not have that which is without value to the giver. Oh! I string words ill, but they were not what I meant.'

'No, Prince, because your royal ring is too large for one so small.'

'How can you tell until you have tried? Also that is a fault which might perhaps be mended.'

Then he laughed, and she laughed also, but as yet she did not take the ring.

'Have you seen Ana?' he went on. 'I believe he set out to search for you, in such a hurry indeed that he could scarcely finish his report to me.'

'Did he say that?'

'No, he only looked it. So much so that I suggested he should seek you at once. He answered that he was going to rest after his long journey, or perhaps I said that he ought to do so. I forget, as often one does, on so beauteous a night when other thoughts seem nearer.'

'Why did Ana wish to see me, Prince?'

'How can I tell? Why does a man who is still young— want to see a sweet and beautiful lady? Oh! I remember. He had met your uncle at Tanis who inquired as to your health. Perhaps that is why he wanted to see you.'

'I do not wish to hear about my uncle at Tanis. He reminds me of too many things that give pain, and there are nights when one wishes to escape pain, which is sure to be found again on the morrow.'

'Are you still of the same mind about returning to your people?' he asked, more earnestly.

'Surely. Oh! do not say that you will send me hence to——'

'Laban, Lady?'

'Laban amongst others. Remember, Prince, that I am

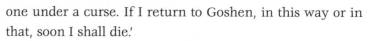

one under a curse. If I return to Goshen, in this way or in that, soon I shall die.'

'Ana says that your uncle Jabez declares that the mad fellow who tried to murder you had no authority to curse and much less to kill you. You must ask him to tell you all.'

'Yet the curse will cling and crush me at the last. How can I, one lonely woman, stand against the might of the people of Israel and their priests?'

'Are you then lonely?'

'How can it be otherwise with an outcast, Prince?'

'No, it cannot be otherwise. I know it who am also an outcast.'

'At least there is her Highness your wife, who doubtless will come to comfort you,' she said, looking down.

'Her Highness will not come. If you had seen Ana, he would perhaps have told you that she has sworn not to look upon my face again, unless above it shines a crown.'

'Oh! how can a woman be so cruel? Surely, Prince, such a stab must cut you to the heart,' she exclaimed, with a little cry of pity.

'Her Highness is not only a woman; she is a Princess of Egypt which is different. For the rest it does cut me to the heart that my royal sister should have deserted me, for that which she loves better—power and pomp. But so it is, unless Ana dreams. It seems therefore that we are in the same case, both outcasts, you and I, is it not so?'

She made no answer but continued to look upon the ground, and he went on very slowly,

'A thought comes into my mind on which I would ask

your judgment. If two who are forlorn came together they would be less forlorn by half, would they not?'

'It would seem so, Prince—that is if they remained forlorn at all. But I do not understand the riddle.'

'Yet you have answered it. If you are lonely and I am lonely apart, we should, you say, be less lonely together.'

'Prince,' she murmured, shrinking away from him, 'I spoke no such words.'

'No, I spoke them for you. Hearken to me, Merapi. They think me a strange man in Egypt because I have held no woman dear, never having seen one whom I could hold dear.' Here she looked at him searchingly, and he went on, 'A while ago, before I visited your land of Goshen—Ana can tell you about the matter, for I think he wrote it down—Ki and old Bakenkhonsu came to see me. Now, as you know, Ki is without doubt a great magician, though it would seem not so great as some of your prophets. He told me that he and others had been searching out my future and that in Goshen I should find a woman whom it was fated I must love. He added that this woman would bring me much joy.' Here Seti paused, doubtless remembering this was not all that Ki had said, or Jabez either. 'Ki told me also,' he went on slowly, 'that I had already known this woman for thousands of years.'

She started and a strange look came into her face.

'How can that be, Prince?'

'That is what I asked him and got no good answer. Still he said it, not only of the woman but of my friend Ana as well, which indeed would explain much, and it would appear that the other magicians said it also. Then I went to the land of Goshen and there I saw a woman——'

'For the first time, Prince?'

'No, for the third time.'

Here she sank upon the bench and covered her eyes with her hands.

'——and loved her, and felt as though I had loved her for "thousands of years."

'It is not true. You mock me, it is not true!' she whispered.

'It is true for if I did not know it then, I knew it afterwards, though never perhaps completely until to-day, when I learned that Userti had deserted me indeed. Moon of Israel, you are that woman. I will not tell you,' he went on passionately, 'that you are fairer than all other women, or sweeter, or more wise, though these things you seem to me. I will only tell you that I love you, yes, love you, whatever you may be. I cannot offer you the Throne of Egypt, even if the law would suffer it, but I can offer you the throne of this heart of mine. Now, Lady Merapi, what have you to say? Before you speak, remember that although you seem to be my prisoner here at Memphis, you have naught to fear from me. Whatever you may answer, such shelter and such friendship as I can give will be yours while I live, and never shall I attempt to force myself upon you, however much it may pain me to pass you by. I know not the future. It may happen that I shall give you great place and power, it may happen that I shall give you nothing but poverty and exile, or even perhaps a share in my own death, but with either will go the worship of my body and my spirit. Now, speak.'

She dropped her hands from her face, looking up at him, and there were tears shining in her beautiful eyes.

'It cannot be, Prince,' she murmured.

'You mean you do not wish it to be?'

'I said that it cannot be. Such ties between an Egyptian and an Israelite are not lawful.'

'Some in this city and elsewhere seem to find them so.'

'And I am married, I mean perhaps I am married—at least in name.'

'And I too am married, I mean—'

'That is different. Also there is another reason, the greatest of all, I am under a curse, and should bring you, not joy as Ki said, but sorrow, or, at the least, sorrow with the joy.'

He looked at her searchingly.

'Has Ana—' he began, then continued, 'if so what lives have you known that are not compounded of mingled joy and sorrow?'

'None. But the woe I should bring would outweigh the joy—to you. The curse of my God rests upon me and I cannot learn to worship yours. The curse of my people rests upon me, the law of my people divides me from you as with a sword, and should I draw close to you these will be increased upon my head, which matters not, but also upon yours,' and she began to sob.

'Tell me,' he said, taking her by the hand, 'but one thing, and if the answer is No, I will trouble you no more. Is your heart mine?'

'It is,' she sighed, 'and has been ever since my eyes fell upon you yonder in the streets of Tanis. Oh! then a change came into me and I hated Laban, whom before I had only misliked. Moreover, I too felt that of which Ki spoke, as though I had known you for thousands of years. My heart

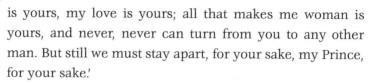

is yours, my love is yours; all that makes me woman is yours, and never, never can turn from you to any other man. But still we must stay apart, for your sake, my Prince, for your sake.'

'Then, were it not for me, you would be ready to run these hazards?'

'Surely! Am I not a woman who loves?'

'If that be so,' he said with a little laugh, 'being of full age and of an understanding which some have thought good, by your leave I think I will run them also. Oh! foolish woman, do you not understand that there is but one good thing in the world, one thing in which self and its miseries can be forgot, and that thing is love? Mayhap troubles will come. Well, let them come, for what do they matter if only the love or its memory remains, if once we have picked that beauteous flower and for an hour worn it on our breasts. You talk of the difference between the gods we worship and maybe it exists, but all gods send their gift of love upon the earth, without which it would cease to be. Moreover, my faith teaches me more clearly perhaps than yours, that life does not end with death and therefore that love, being life's soul, must endure while it endures. Last of all, I think, as you think, that in some dim way there is truth in what the magicians said, and that long ago in the past we have been what once more we are about to be, and that the strength of this invisible tie has drawn us together out of the whole world and will bind us together long after the world is dead. It is not a matter of what we wish to do, Merapi, it is a matter of what Fate has decreed we shall do. Now, answer again!'

But she made no answer, and when I looked up after a little moment she was in his arms and her lips were upon his lips.

Thus did Prince Seti of Egypt and Merapi, Moon of Israel, come together at Memphis in Egypt.

13
THE RED NILE

On the morrow of this night I found the Prince alone for a little while, and put him in mind of certain ancient manuscripts that he wished to read, which could only be consulted at Thebes where I might copy them; also of others that were said to be for sale there. He answered that they could wait, but I replied that the latter might find some other purchaser if I did not go at once.

'You are over fond of long journeys upon my business, Ana,' he said. Then he considered me curiously for a while, and since he could read my mind, as indeed I could his, saw that I knew all, and added in a gentle voice,

'You should have done as I told you, and spoken first. If so, who knows—'

'You do, Prince,' I answered, 'you and another.'

'Go, and the gods be with you, friend, but stay not too long copying those rolls, which any scribe can do. I think there is trouble at hand in Egypt, and I shall need you at my side. Another who holds you dear will need you also.'

'I thank my lord and that other,' I said, bowing, and went.

Moreover, while I was making some humble provision for my journey, I found that this was needless, since a slave came to tell me that the Prince's barge was waiting to sail with the wind. So in that barge I travelled to Thebes like a great noble, or a royal mummy being borne to burial. Only instead of wailing priests, until I sent them back to Memphis, musicians sat upon the prow, and when I willed, dancing girls came to amuse my leisure and, veiled in golden nets, to serve at my table.

So I journeyed as though I were the Prince himself, and as one who was known to have his ear was made much of by the governors of the Nomes, the chief men of the towns, and the high priests of the temples at every city where we moored. For, as I have said, although Amenmeses sat upon the throne, Seti still ruled in the hearts of the folk of Egypt. Moreover, as I sailed further up the Nile to districts where little was known of the Israelites, and the troubles they were bringing on the land, I found this to be so more and more. Why is it, the Great Ones would whisper in my ear, that his Highness the Prince Seti does not hold his father's place? Then I would tell them of the Hebrews, and they would laugh and say,

'Let the Prince unfurl his royal banner here, and we will show him what we think of the question of these Israelitish slaves. May not the Heir of Egypt form his own judgment on such a matter as to whether they should abide there in the north, or go away into that wilderness which they desire?'

To all of which, and much like it, I would only answer that their words should be reported. More I did not, and indeed did not dare to say, since everywhere I found that I was being followed and watched by the spies of Pharaoh.

At length I came to Thebes and took up my abode in a fine house that was the property of the Prince, which I found that a messenger had commanded should be made ready for me. It stood near by the entrance to the Avenue of Sphinxes, which leads to the greatest of all the Theban temples, where is that mighty columned hall built by the first Seti and his son, Rameses II, the Prince's grandfather.

Here, having entrance to the place, I would often wander at night, and in my spirit draw as near to heaven as ever it has been my lot to travel. Also, crossing the Nile to the western bank, I visited that desolate valley where the rulers of Egypt lie at rest. The tomb of Pharaoh Meneptah was still unsealed, and accompanied by a single priest with torches, I crept down its painted halls and looked upon the sarcophagus of him whom so lately I had seen seated in glory upon the throne, wondering, as I looked, how much or how little he knew of all that passed in Egypt to-day.

Moreover, I copied the papyri that I had come to seek, in which there was nothing worth preserving, and some of real value that I discovered in the ancient libraries of the temples, and purchased others. One of these indeed told a very strange tale that has given me much cause for thought, especially of late years now when all my friends are dead.

Thus I spent two months, and should have stayed longer

had not messengers reached me from the Prince saying that he desired my return. Of these, one followed within three days of the other, and his words were,

'Think you, Scribe Ana, that because I am no more Prince of Egypt I am no longer to be obeyed? If so, bear in mind that the gods may decree that one day I shall grow taller than ever I was before, and then be sure that I will remember your disobedience, and make you shorter by a head. Come swiftly, my friend, for I grow lonely, and need a man to talk with.'

To which I replied, that I returned as fast as the barge would carry me, it being so heavily laden with the manuscripts that I had copied and purchased.

So I started, being, to tell truth, glad to get away, for this reason. Two nights before, when I was walking alone from the great temple to the house, a woman dressed in many colours appeared and accosted me as such lost ones do. I tried to shake her off, but she clung to me, and I saw that she had drunk more than enough of wine. Presently she asked, in a voice that I thought familiar, if I knew who was the officer that had come to Thebes on the business of some Royal One and abode in the dwelling that was known as House of the Prince. I answered that his name was Ana.

'Once I knew an Ana very well,' she said, 'but I left him.'

'Why?' I asked, turning cold in my limbs, for although I could not see her face because of a hood she wore, now I began to be afraid.

'Because he was a poor fool,' she answered, 'no man at all, but one who was always thinking about writings and making them, and another came my way whom I liked better until he deserted me.'

'And what happened to this Ana?' I asked.

'I do not know. I suppose he went on dreaming, or perhaps he took another wife; if so, I am sorry for her. Only, if by any chance it is the same that has come to Thebes, he must be wealthy now, and I shall go and claim him and make him keep me well.'

'Had you any children?' I asked.

'Only one, thank the gods, and that died—thank the gods again, for otherwise it might have lived to be such as I am,' and she sobbed once in a hard fashion and then fell to her vile endearments.

As she did so, the hood slipped from her head and I saw that the face was that of my wife, still beauteous in a bold fashion, but grown dreadful with drink and sin. I trembled from head to foot, then said in the disguised voice that I had used to her,

'Woman, I know this Ana. He is dead and you were his ruin. Still, because I was his friend, take this and go reform your ways,' and I drew from my robe and gave to her a bag containing no mean weight of gold.

She snatched it as a hawk snatches, and seeing its contents by the starlight, thanked me, saying,

'Surely Ana dead is worth more than Ana alive. Also it is well that he is dead, for he is gone where the child went, which he loved more than life, neglecting me for its sake and thereby making me what I am. Had he lived, too, being as I have said a fool, he would have had more ill-luck with women, whom he never understood. Farewell, friend

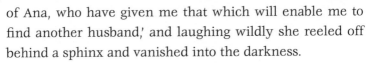

of Ana, who have given me that which will enable me to find another husband,' and laughing wildly she reeled off behind a sphinx and vanished into the darkness.

For this reason, then, I was glad to escape from Thebes. Moreover, that miserable one had hurt me sorely, making me sure of what I had only guessed, namely, that with women I was but a fool, so great a fool that then and there I swore by my guardian god that never would I look with love on one of them again, an oath which I have kept well whatever others I may have broken. Again she stabbed me through with the talk of our dead child, for it is true that when that sweet one took flight to Osiris my heart broke and in a fashion has never mended itself again. Lastly, I feared lest it might also be true that I had neglected the mother for the sake of this child which was the jewel of my worship, yes, and is, and thereby helped her on to shame. So much did this thought torment me that through an agent whom I trusted, who believed that I was but providing for one whom I had wronged, I caused enough to be paid to her to keep her in comfort.

She did marry again, a merchant about whom she had cast her toils, and in due course spent his wealth and brought him to ruin, after which he ran away from her. As for her, she died of her evil habits in the third year of the reign of Seti II. But, the gods be thanked she never knew that the private scribe of Pharaoh's chamber was that Ana who had been her husband. Here I will end her story.

Now as I was passing down the Nile with a heart more heavy than the great stone that served as anchor to the barge, we moored at dusk on the third night by the side of a vessel that was sailing up Nile with a strong northerly wind. On board this boat was an officer whom I had known at the Court of Pharaoh Meneptah, travelling to Thebes on duty. This man seemed so much afraid that I asked him if anything weighed upon his mind. Then he took me aside into a palm grove upon the bank, and seating himself on the pole whereby oxen turned a waterwheel, told me that strange things were passing at Tanis.

It seemed that the Hebrew prophets had once more appeared before Pharaoh, who since his accession had left the Israelites in peace, not attacking them with the sword as Meneptah had wished to do, it was thought through fear lest if he did so he should die as Meneptah died. As before, they had put up their prayer that the people of the Hebrews should be suffered to go to worship in the wilderness, and Pharaoh had refused them. Then when he went down to sail upon the river early in the morning of another day, they had met him and one of them struck the water with his rod, and it had turned to blood. Whereon Ki the Kherheb and his company also struck other water with their rods, and it turned to blood. That was six days ago, and now this officer swore to me that the blood was creeping up the Nile, a tale at which I laughed.

'Come then and see,' he said, and led me back to his boat, where all the crew seemed as fearful as he was himself.

He took me forward to a great water jar that stood upon the prow and, behold! it seemed to be full of blood, and in it was a fish dead, and—stinking.

'This water,' said he, 'I drew from the Nile with my own hands, not five hours sail to the north. But now we have

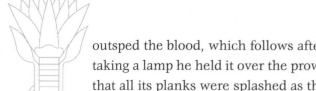

outsped the blood, which follows after us. Look again,' and taking a lamp he held it over the prow of the boat and I saw that all its planks were splashed as though with blood.

'Be advised by me, learned scribe,' he added, 'and fill every jar and skin that you can gather with sweet water, lest to-morrow you and your company should go thirsty,' and he laughed a very dreary laugh.

Then we parted without more words, for neither of us knew what to say, and about midnight he sailed on with the wind, taking his chance of grounding on the sandbanks in the darkness.

For my part I did as he bade me, though my rowers who had not spoken with his men, thought that I was mad to load up the barge with so much water.

At the first break of day I gave the order to start. Looking over the side of the barge it seemed to me as though the lights of dawn had fallen from the sky into the Nile whereof the water had become pink-hued. Moreover, this hue, which grew ever deeper, was travelling up stream, not down, against the course of nature, and could not therefore have been caused by red soil washed from the southern lands. The bargemen stared and muttered together. Then one of them, leaning over the side, scooped up water in the hollow of his hand and drew some into his mouth, only to spit it out again with a cry of fear.

' 'Tis blood,' he cried. 'Blood! Osiris has been slain afresh, and his holy blood fills the banks of Nile.'

So much were they afraid, indeed, that had I not forced them to hold to their course they would have turned and rowed up stream, or beached the boat and fled into the desert. But I cried to them to steer on northwards, for thus perhaps we should sooner be done with this horror, and they obeyed me. Ever as we went the hue of the water grew more red, almost to blackness, till at last it seemed as though we were travelling through a sea of gore in which dead fish floated by the thousand, or struggled dying on the surface. Also the stench was so dreadful that we must bind linen about our nostrils to strain the fœtid air.

We came abreast of a town, and from its streets one great wail of terror rose to heaven. Men stood staring as though they were drunken, looking at their red arms which they had dipped in the stream, and women ran to and fro upon the bank, tearing their hair and robes, and crying out such words as—

'Wizard's work! Bewitched! Accursed! The gods have slain each other, and men too must die!' and so forth.

Also we saw peasants digging holes at a distance from the shore to see perchance if they might come to water that was sweet and wholesome. All day long we travelled thus through this horrible flood, while the spray driven by the strong north wind spotted our flesh and garments, till we were like butchers reeking from the shambles. Nor could we eat any food because of the stench from this spray, which made it to taste salt as does fresh blood, only we drank of the water which I had provided, and the rowers who had held me to be mad now named me the wisest of men; one who knew what would befall in the future.

At length towards evening we noted that the water was growing much less red with every hour that passed, which was another marvel, seeing that above us, upstream, it was

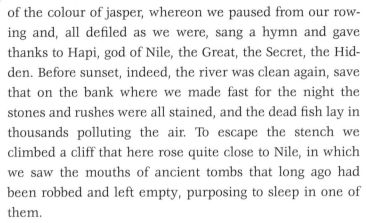

of the colour of jasper, whereon we paused from our row-
ing and, all defiled as we were, sang a hymn and gave
thanks to Hapi, god of Nile, the Great, the Secret, the Hidden. Before sunset, indeed, the river was clean again, save
that on the bank where we made fast for the night the
stones and rushes were all stained, and the dead fish lay in
thousands polluting the air. To escape the stench we
climbed a cliff that here rose quite close to Nile, in which
we saw the mouths of ancient tombs that long ago had
been robbed and left empty, purposing to sleep in one of
them.

A path worn by the feet of men ran to the largest of these
tombs, whence, as we drew near, we heard the sound of wailing. Looking in, I saw a woman and some children crouched
upon the floor of the tomb, their heads covered with dust
who, when they perceived us, cried more loudly than before,
though with harsh dry voices, thinking no doubt that we
were robbers or perhaps ghosts because of our bloodstained
garments. Also there was another child, a little one, that did
not cry, because it was dead. I asked the woman what
passed, but even when she understood that we were only
men who meant her no harm, she could not speak or do
more than gasp 'Water! Water!' We gave her and the children
to drink from the jars which we had brought with us, which
they did greedily, after which I drew her story from her.

She was the wife of a fisherman who made his home in
this cave, and said that seven days before the Nile had
turned to blood, so that they could not drink of it, and had
no water save a little in a pot. Nor could they dig to find it,
since here the ground was all rock. Nor could they escape,

since when he saw the marvel, her husband in his fear had leapt from his boat and waded to land and the boat had floated away.

I asked where was her husband, and she pointed behind her. I went to look, and there found a man hanging by his neck from a rope that was fixed to the capital of a pillar in the tomb, quite dead and cold. Returning sick at heart, I inquired of her how this had come about. She answered that when he saw that all the fish had perished, taking away his living, and that thirst had killed his youngest child, he went mad, and creeping to the back of the tomb, without her knowledge hung himself with a net rope. It was a dreadful story.

Having given the widow of our food, we went to sleep in another tomb, not liking the company of those dead ones. Next morning at the dawn we took the woman and her children on board the barge, and rowed them three hours' journey to a town where she had a sister, whom she found. The dead man and the child we left there in the tomb, since my men would not defile themselves by touching them.

So, seeing much terror and misery on our journey, at last we came safe to Memphis. Leaving the boatmen to draw up the barge, I went to the palace, speaking with none, and was led at once to the Prince. I found him in a shaded chamber seated side by side with the Lady Merapi, and holding her hand in such a fashion that they reminded me of the life-sized Ka statues of a man and his wife, such as I have seen in the ancient tombs, cut when the sculptors knew how to fashion the perfect likenesses of men and women. This they no longer do to-day, I think because the priests have taught them that it is not lawful. He was talk-

ing to her in a low voice, while she listened, smiling sweetly as she ever did, but with eyes, fixed straight before her
that were, as it seemed to me, filled with fear. I thought
that she looked very beautiful with her hair outspread over
her white robe, and held back from her temples by a little
fillet of gold. But as I looked, I rejoiced to find that my
heart no longer yearned for her as it had upon that night
when I had seen her seated beneath the trees without the
pleasure-house. Now she was its friend, no more, and so
she remained until all was finished, as both the Prince and
she knew well enough.

When he saw me Seti sprang from his seat and came to
greet me, as a man does the friend whom he loves. I kissed
his hand, and going to Merapi, kissed hers also noting that
on it now shone that ring which once she had rejected as
too large.

'Tell me, Ana, all that has befallen you,' he said in his
pleasant, eager voice.

'Many things, Prince; one of them very strange and terrible,' I answered.

'Strange and terrible things have happened here also,'
broke in Merapi, 'and, alas! this is but the beginning of woes.'

So saying, she rose, as though she could trust herself to
speak no more, bowed first to her lord and then to me, and
left the chamber.

I looked at the Prince and he answered the question in
my eyes.

'Jabez has been here,' he said, 'and filled her heart with
forebodings. If Pharaoh will not let the Israelites go, by
Amon I wish he would let Jabez go to some place whence

he never could return. But tell me, have you also met blood travelling against the stream of Nile? It would seem so,' and he glanced at the rusty stains that no washing would remove from my garments.

I nodded and we talked together long and earnestly, but in the end were no wiser for all our talking. For neither of us knew how it came about that men by striking water with a rod could turn it into what seemed to be blood, as the Hebrew prophet and Ki both had done, or how that blood could travel up the Nile against the stream and everywhere endure for a space of seven days; yes, and spread too to all the canals in Egypt, so that men must dig holes for water and dig them fresh each day because the blood crept in and poisoned them. But both of us thought that this was the work of the gods, and most of all of that god whom the Hebrews worship.

'You remember, Ana,' said the Prince, 'the message which you brought to me from Jabez, namely that no harm should come to me because of these Israelites and their curses. Well, no harm has come as yet, except the harm of Jabez, for he came. On the day before the news of this blood plague reached us, Jabez appeared disguised as a merchant of Syrian stuffs, all of which he sold to me at three times their value. He obtained admission to the chambers of Merapi, where she is accustomed to see whom she wills, and under pretence of showing her his stuffs, spoke with her and, as I fear, told her what you and I were so careful to hide, that she would bring trouble on me. At the least she has never been quite the same since, and I have thought it wise to make her swear by an oath,

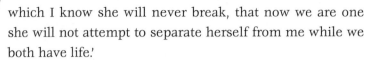

which I know she will never break, that now we are one she will not attempt to separate herself from me while we both have life.'

'Did he wish her to go away with him, Prince?'

'I do not know. She never told me so. Still I am sure that had he come with his evil talk before that day when you returned from Tanis, she would have gone. Now I hope there are reasons that will keep her where she is.'

'What then did he say, Prince?'

'Little beyond what he had already said to you, that great troubles were about to fall on Egypt. He added that he was sent to save me and mine from these troubles because I had been a friend to the Hebrews, in so far as that was possible. Then he walked through this house and all round its gardens, as he went reciting something that was written on a roll, of which I could not understand the meaning, and now and again prostrating himself to pray to his god. Thus, where the canal enters the garden and where it leaves the garden he stayed to pray, as he did at the well whence drinking water is drawn. Moreover, led by Merapi, he visited all my cornlands and those where my cattle are herded, reciting and praying until the servants thought that he was mad. After this he returned with her and, as it chanced, I overheard their parting. She said to him,

' "The house you have blessed and it is safe; the fields you have blessed and they are safe; will you not bless me also, O my Uncle, and any that are born of me?"

'He answered, shaking his head, "I have no command, my Niece, either to bless or to curse you, as did that fool whom the Prince slew. You have chosen your own path apart from your people. It may be well, or it may be ill, or perhaps both, and henceforth you must walk it alone to wherever it may lead. Farewell, for perhaps we shall meet no more."

'Thus speaking they passed out of earshot, but I could see that still she pleaded and still he shook his head. In the end, however, she gave him an offering, of all that she had I think, though whether this went to the temple of the Hebrews or into his own pouch I know not. At least it seemed to soften him, for he kissed her on the brow tenderly enough and departed with the air of a happy merchant who has sold his wares. But of all that passed between them Merapi would tell me nothing. Nor did I tell her of what I had overheard.'

'And then?'

'And then, Ana, came the story of the Hebrew prophet who made the water into blood, and of Ki and his disciples who did likewise. The latter I did not believe, because I said it would be more reasonable had Ki turned the blood back into water, instead of making more blood of which there was enough already.'

'I think that magicians have no reason.'

'Or can do mischief only, Ana. At any rate after the story came the blood itself and stayed with us seven whole days, leaving much sickness behind it because of the stench of the rotting fish. Now for the marvel—here about my house there was no blood, though above and below the canal was full of it. The water remained as it has always been and the fish swam in it as they have always done; also that of the well kept sweet and pure. When this came to be known thousands crowded to the place, clamouring for water; that is until they found that outside the gates it grew red in their vessels, after which, although some still came, they drank the water where they stood, which they must do quickly.'

'And what tale do they tell of this in Memphis, Prince?' I asked astonished.

'Certain of them say that not Ki but I am the greatest magician in Egypt—never, Ana, was fame more lightly earned. And certain say that Merapi, of whose doings in the temple at Tanis some tale has reached them, is the real magician, she being an Israelite of the tribe of the Hebrew prophets. Hush! She returns.'

14

KI COMES TO MEMPHIS

Now of all the terrors of which this turning of the water into blood was the beginning in Egypt, I, Ana, the scribe, will not write, for if I did so, never in my life-days should I, who am old, find time to finish the story of them. Over a period of many, many moons they came, one by one, till the land grew mad with want and woe. Always the tale was the same. The Hebrew prophets would visit Pharaoh at Tanis and demand that he should let their people go, threatening him with vengeance if he refused. Yet he did refuse, for some madness had hold of him, or perhaps the god of the Israelites laid an enchantment on him, why I know not.

Thus but a little while after the terror of blood came a plague of frogs that filled Egypt from north to south, and when these were taken away made the air to stink. This miracle Ki and his company worked also, sending the frogs into Goshen, where they plagued the Israelites. But however it came about, at Seti's palace at Memphis and on the land that he owned around it there were no frogs, or at least but few of them, although at night from the fields about the sound of their croaking went up like the sound of beaten drums.

Next came a plague of lice, and these Ki and his companions would have also called down upon the Hebrews, but they failed, and afterwards struggled no more against the magic of the Israelites. Then followed a plague of flies, so that the air was black with them and no food could be kept sweet. Only in Seti's palace there were no flies, and in the garden but a few. After this a terrible pest began among the cattle, whereof thousands died. But of Seti's great herd not one was even sick, nor, as we learned, was there a hoof the less in the land of Goshen.

This plague struck Egypt but a little while after Merapi had given birth to a son, a very beautiful child with his mother's eyes, that was named Seti after his father. Now the marvel of the escape of the Prince and his household and all that was his from these curses spread abroad and made much talk, so that many sent to inquire of it.

Among the first came old Bakenkhonsu with a message from Pharaoh, and a private one to myself from the Princess Userti, whose pride would not suffer her to ask aught of Seti. We could tell him nothing except what I have written, which at first he did not believe. Having satisfied himself, however, that the thing was true, he said that he had fallen sick and could not travel back to Tanis. Therefore he asked leave of the Prince to rest a while in his house, he who had been the friend of his father, his grandfather, and his great-grandfather. Seti laughed, as indeed did the cunning old man himself, and there with us Bakenkhonsu remained till the end, to our great joy, for he was the most pleasant of all companions and the most learned. As for his message, one of his servants took back the answer to Pharaoh and to Userti, with the news of his master's grievous sickness.

Some eight days or so later, as I stood one morning basking in the sun at that gate of the palace gardens which overlooks the temple of Ptah, idly watching the procession of priests passing through its courts and chanting as they went (for because of the many sicknesses at this time I left the palace but rarely), I saw a tall figure approaching me draped against the morning cold. The man drew near, and addressing me over the head of the guard, asked if he could see the lady Merapi. I answered No, as she was engaged in nursing her son.

'And in other things, I think,' he said with meaning, in a voice that seemed familiar to me. 'Well, can I see the Prince Seti?'

I answered No, he was also engaged.

'In nursing his own soul, studying the eyes of the lady Merapi, the smile of his infant, the wisdom of the scribe Ana, and the attributes of the hundred and one gods that are known to him, including that of Israel, I suppose,' said the familiar voice, adding, 'Then can I see this scribe Ana, who I understand, being lucky, holds himself learned.'

Now, angered at the scoffing of this stranger (though all the time I felt that he was none), I answered that the scribe Ana was striving to mend his lack of luck by the pursuit of the goddess of learning in his study.

'Let him pursue,' mocked the stranger, 'since she is the only woman that he is ever likely to catch. Yet it is true that once one caught him. If you are of his acquaintance ask him of his talk with her in the avenue of the Sphinxes outside the great temple at Thebes and of what it cost him in gold and tears.'

Hearing this I put my hand to my forehead and rubbed my eyes, thinking that I must have fallen into a dream there in the sunshine. When I lifted it again all was the same as before. There stood the sentry, indifferent to that which had no interest for him; the cock that had moulted its tail still scratched in the dirt; the crested hoopoe still sat spreading its wings on the head of one of the two great statues of Rameses which watched the gate; a water-seller in the distance still cried his wares, but the stranger was gone. Then I knew that I had been dreaming and turned to go also, to find myself face to face with him.

'Man,' I said, indignantly, 'how in the name of Ptah and all his priests did you pass a sentry and through that gate without my seeing you?'

'Do not trouble yourself with a new problem when already you have so many to perplex you, friend Ana. Say, have you yet solved that of how a rod like this turned itself into a snake in your hand?' and he threw back his hood, revealing the shaved head and the glowing eyes of the Kherheb Ki.

'No, I have not,' I answered, 'and I thank you,' for here he proffered me the staff, 'but I will not try the trick again. Next time the beast might bite. Well, Ki, as you can pass in here without my leave, why do you ask it? In short, what do you want with me, now that those Hebrew prophets have put you on your back?'

'Hush, Ana. Never grow angry, it wastes strength, of which we have so little to spare, for you know, being so wise, or perhaps you do not know, that at birth the gods give us a certain store of it, and when that is used we die and have to go elsewhere to fetch more. At this rate your life will be short, Ana, for you squander it in emotions.'

'What do you want?' I repeated, being too angry to dispute with him.

'I want to find an answer to the question you asked so roughly: Why the Hebrew prophets have, as you say, put me on my back?'

'Not being a magician, as you pretend you are, I can give you none, Ki.'

'Never for one moment did I suppose that you could,' he replied blandly, stretching out his hands, and leaving the staff which had fallen from them standing in front of him. (It was not till afterwards that I remembered that this accursed bit of wood stood there of itself without visible support, for it rested on the paving-stone of the gateway.) 'But, as it chances, you have in this house the master, or rather the mistress of all magicians, as every Egyptian knows to-day, the lady Merapi, and I would see her.'

'Why do you say she is a mistress of magicians?' I asked indignantly.

'Why does one bird know another of its own kind? Why does the water here remain pure, when all other water turns to blood? Why do not the frogs croak in Seti's halls, and why do the flies avoid his meat? Why, also, did the

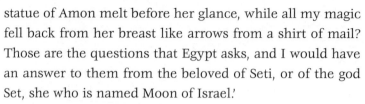

statue of Amon melt before her glance, while all my magic fell back from her breast like arrows from a shirt of mail? Those are the questions that Egypt asks, and I would have an answer to them from the beloved of Seti, or of the god Set, she who is named Moon of Israel.'

'Then why not go seek it for yourself, Ki? To you, doubtless, it would be a small matter to take the form of a snake or a rat, or a bird, and creep or run or fly into the presence of Merapi.'

'Mayhap it would not be difficult, Ana. Or, better still, I might visit her in her sleep, as I visited you on a certain night at Thebes, when you told me of a talk you had held with a woman in the avenue of Sphinxes, and of what it cost you in gold and tears. But, as it chances, I wish to appear as a man and a friend, and to stay a while. Bakenkhonsu tells me that he finds life here at Memphis very pleasant, free too from the sicknesses which just now seem to be so common in Egypt; so why should not I do the same, Ana?'

I looked at his round, ripe face, on which was fixed a smile unchanging as that worn by the masks on mummy coffins, from which I think he must have copied it, and at the cold, deep eyes above, and shivered a little. To tell truth I feared this man, whom I felt to be in touch with presences and things that are not of our world, and thought it wisest to withstand him no more.

'That is a question which you had best put to my master Seti who owns this house. Come, I will lead you to him,' I said.

So we went to the great portico of the palace, passing in and out through the painted pillars, towards my own apartments, whence I purposed to send a message to the Prince. As it chanced this was needless, since presently we saw him seated in a little bay out of reach of the sun. By his side was Merapi, and on a woven rug between them lay their sleeping infant, at whom both of them gazed adoringly.

'Strange that this mother's heart should hide more might than can be boasted by all the gods of Egypt. Strange that those mother's eyes can rive the ancient glory of Amon into dust!' Ki said to me in so low a voice that it almost seemed as though I heard his thought and not his words, which perhaps indeed I did.

Now we stood in front of these three, and the sun being behind us, for it was still early, the shadow of the cloaked Ki fell upon the babe and lay there. A hateful fancy came to me. It looked like the veiled form of an embalmer bending over one new dead. The babe felt it, opened its large eyes and wailed. Merapi saw it, and snatched up her child. Seti too rose from his seat, exclaiming, 'Who comes?'

Thereon, to my amazement, Ki prostrated himself and uttered the salutation which may only be given to the King of Egypt: 'Life! Blood! Strength! Pharaoh! Pharaoh! Pharaoh!'

'Who dares utter those words to me?' said Seti. 'Ana, what madman do you bring here?'

'May it please the Prince, *he* brought *me* here,' I replied faintly.

'Fellow, tell me who bade you say such words, than which none were ever less welcome.'

'Those whom I serve, Prince.'

'And whom do you serve?'

'The gods of Egypt.'

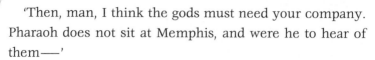

'Then, man, I think the gods must need your company. Pharaoh does not sit at Memphis, and were he to hear of them—'

'Pharaoh will never hear them, Prince, until he hears all things.'

They stared at each other. Then, as I had done by the gate Seti rubbed his eyes and said,

'Surely this is Ki. Why, then, did you look otherwise just now?'

'The gods can change the fashion of their messenger a thousand times in a flash, if so they will, O Prince.'

Now Seti's anger passed, and turned to laughter.

'Ki, Ki,' he said, 'you should keep these tricks for Court. But, since you are in the mood, what salutation have you for this lady by my side?'

Ki considered her, till she who ever feared and hated him shrank before his gaze.

'Crown of Hathor, I greet you. Beloved of Isis, shine on perfect in the sky, shedding light and wisdom ere you set.'

Now this saying puzzled me. Indeed, I did not fully understand it until Bakenkhonsu reminded me that Merapi's name was Moon of Israel, that Hathor, goddess of love, is crowned with the moon in all her statues, that Isis is the queen of mysteries and wisdom, and that Ki who thought Merapi perfect in love and beauty, also the greatest of all sorceresses, was likening her to these.

'Yes,' I answered, 'but what did he mean when he talked about her setting?'

'Does not the moon always set, and is it not sometimes eclipsed?' he asked shortly.

'So does the sun,' I answered.

'True; so does the sun! You are growing wise, very wise indeed, friend Ana. Oho—ho!'

To return: When Seti heard these words, he laughed again, and said,

'I must think that saying over, but it is clear that you have a pretty turn for praise. Is it not so, Merapi, Crown of Hathor, and Holder of the wisdom of Isis?'

But Merapi, who, I think, understood more than either of us, turned pale, and shrank further away, but outwards into the sunshine.

'Well, Ki,' went on Seti, 'finish your greetings. What for the babe?'

Ki considered it also.

'Now that it is no longer in the shadow, I see that this shoot from the royal root of Pharaoh grows so fast and tall that my eyes cannot reach its crest. He is too high and great for greetings, Prince.'

Then Merapi uttered a little cry, and bore the child away.

'She is afraid of magicians and their dark sayings,' said Seti, looking after her with a troubled smile.

'That she should not be, Prince, seeing that she is the mistress of all our tribe.'

'The lady Merapi a magician? Well, after a fashion, yes— where the hearts of men are concerned, do you not think so, Ana? But be more plain, Ki. It is still early, and I love riddles best at night.'

'What other could have shattered the strong and holy house where the majesty of Amon dwells on earth? Not even those prophets of the Hebrews as I think. What other

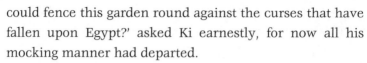

could fence this garden round against the curses that have fallen upon Egypt?' asked Ki earnestly, for now all his mocking manner had departed.

'I do not think she does these things, Ki. I think some Power does them through her, and I know that she dared to face Amon in his temple because she was bidden so to do by the priests of her people.'

'Prince,' he answered with a short laugh, 'a while ago I sent you a message by Ana, which perhaps other thoughts may have driven from his memory. It was as to the nature of that Power of which you speak. In that message I said that you were wise, but now I perceive that you lack wisdom like the rest of us, for if you had it, you would know that the tool which carves is not the guiding hand, and the lightning which smites is not the sending strength. So with this fair love of yours, and so with me and all that work marvels. We do not the things we seem to do, who are but the tool and the lightning. What I would know is who or what guides her hand and gives her the might to shield or to destroy.'

'The question is wide, Ki, or so it seems to me who, as you say, have little wisdom, and whoever can answer it holds the key of knowledge. Your magic is but a small thing which seems great because so few can handle it. What miracle is it that makes the flower to grow, the child to be born, the Nile to rise, and the sun and stars to shine in heaven? What causes man to be half a beast and half a god and to grow downward to the beast or upward to the god— or both? What is faith and what is unbelief? Who made these things, through them to declare the purposes of life, of death, and of eternity? You shake your head, you do not know; how then can I know who, as you point out, am but foolish? Go get your answer from the lady Merapi's self, only mayhap you will find your questions countered.'

'I'll take my chance. Thanks to Merapi's lord! A boon, O Prince, since you will not suffer that other name which comes easiest to the lips of one to whom the Present and the Future are sometimes much alike.'

Seti looked at him keenly, and for the first time with a tinge of fear in his eyes.

'Leave the Future to itself, Ki,' he exclaimed. 'Whatever may be the mind of Egypt, just now I hold the Present enough for me,' and he glanced first at the chair in which Merapi had been seated and then at the cloth upon which his son had lain.

'I take back my words. The Prince is wiser than I thought. Magicians know the future because at times it rushes down upon them and they must. It is that which makes them lonely, since what they know they cannot say. But only fools will seek it.'

'Yet now and again they lift a corner of the veil, Ki. Thus I remember certain sayings of your own as to one who would find a great treasure in the land of Goshen and thereafter suffer some temporal loss, and—I forget the rest. Man, cease smiling at me with your face and piercing me through with your sword-like eyes. You can command all things, what boon then do you seek from me?'

'To lodge here a little while, Prince, in the company of Ana and Bakenkhonsu. Hearken, I am no more Kherheb. I have quarrelled with Pharaoh, perhaps because a little breath from that great wind of the future blows through my

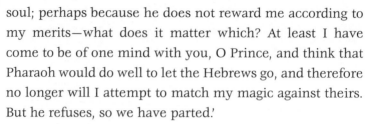

soul; perhaps because he does not reward me according to my merits—what does it matter which? At least I have come to be of one mind with you, O Prince, and think that Pharaoh would do well to let the Hebrews go, and therefore no longer will I attempt to match my magic against theirs. But he refuses, so we have parted.'

'Why does he refuse, Ki?'

'Perhaps because it is written that he must refuse. Or perhaps because, thinking himself the greatest of all kings instead of but a plaything of the gods, pride locks the doors of his heart that in a day to come the tempest of the Future, whereof I have spoken, may wreck the house which holds it. I do not know why he refuses, but her Highness Userti is much with him.'

'For one who does not know, you have many reasons and all of them different, O instructed Ki,' said Seti.

Then he paused, walking up and down the portico, and I who knew his mind guessed that he was wondering whether he would do well to suffer Ki, whom at times he feared because his objects were secret and never changed, to abide in his house, or whether he should send him away. Ki also shivered a little, as though he felt the shadow cold, and descended from the portico into the bright sunshine. Here he held out his hand and a great moth dropped from the roof and lit upon it, whereon he lifted it to his lips, which moved as though he were talking to the insect.

'What shall I do?' muttered Seti, as he passed me.

'I do not altogether like his company, nor, I think, does the lady Merapi, but he is an ill man to offend, Prince,' I answered. 'Look, he is talking with his familiar.'

Seti returned to his place, and shaking off the moth which seemed loth to leave him, for twice it settled on his head, Ki came back into the shadow.

'Where is the use of your putting questions to me, Ki, when, according to your own showing, already you know the answer that I shall give? What answer shall I give?' asked the Prince.

'That painted creature which sat upon my hand just now, seemed to whisper to me that you would say, O Prince, "Stay, Ki, and be my faithful servant, and use any little lore you have to shield my house from ill." '

Then Seti laughed in his careless fashion, and replied,

'Have your way, since it is a rule that none of the royal blood of Egypt may refuse hospitality to those who seek it, having been their friends, and I will not quote against your moth what a bat whispered in my ears last night. Nay, none of your salutations revealed to you by insects or by the future,' and he gave him his hand to kiss.

When Ki was gone, I said,

'I told you that night-haunting thing was his familiar.'

'Then you told me folly, Ana. The knowledge that Ki has he does not get from moths or beetles. Yet now that it is too late I wish that I had asked the lady Merapi what her will was in this matter. You should have thought of that, Ana, instead of suffering your mind to be led astray by an insect sitting on his hand, which is just what he meant that you should do. Well, in punishment, day by day it shall be your lot to look upon a man with a countenance like—like what?'

'Like that which I saw upon the coffin of the good god,

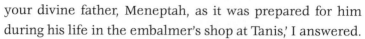

your divine father, Meneptah, as it was prepared for him during his life in the embalmer's shop at Tanis,' I answered.

'Yes,' said the Prince, 'a face smiling eternally at the Nothingness which is Life and Death, but in certain lights, with eyes of fire.'

On the following day, by her invitation, I walked with the lady Merapi in the garden, the head nurse following us, bearing the royal child in her arms.

'I wish to ask you about Ki, friend Ana,' she said. 'You know he is my enemy, for you must have heard the words he spoke to me in the temple of Amon at Tanis. It seems that my lord has made him the guest of this house—oh look!' and she pointed before her.

I looked, and there a few paces away, where the shadow of the overhanging palms was deepest, stood Ki. He was leaning on his staff, the same that had turned to a snake in my hand, and gazing upwards like one who is lost in thought, or listens to the singing of birds. Merapi turned as though to fly, but at that moment Ki saw us, although he still seemed to gaze upwards.

'Greeting, O Moon of Israel,' he said bowing. 'Greeting, O Conqueror of Ki!'

She bowed back, and stood still, as a little bird stands when it sees a snake. There was a long silence, which he broke by asking,

'Why seek that from Ana which Ki himself is eager to give? Ana is learned, but is his heart the heart of Ki? Above all, why tell him that Ki, the humblest of your servants, is your enemy?'

Now Merapi straightened herself, looked into his eyes, and answered,

'Have I told Ana aught that he did not know? Did not Ana hear the last words you said to me in the temple of Amon at Tanis?'

'Doubtless he heard them, Lady, and therefore I am glad that he is here to hear their meaning. Lady Merapi, at that moment, I, the Sacrificer to Amon, was filled—not with my own spirit, but with the angry spirit of the god whom you had humbled as never before had befallen him in Egypt. The god through me demanded of you the secret of your magic, and promised you his hate, if you refused. Lady, you have his hate, but mine you have not, since I also have his hate because I, and he through me, have been worsted by your prophets. Lady, we are fellow-travellers in the Valley of Trouble.'

She gazed at him steadily, and I could see that of all that passed his lips she believed not one word. Making no answer to him and his talk of Amon, she asked only,

'Why do you come here to do me ill who have done you none?'

'You are mistaken, Lady,' he replied. 'I come here to refuge from Amon, and from his servant Pharaoh, whom Amon drives on to ruin. I know well that, if you will it, you can whisper in the ear of the Prince and presently he will put me forth. Only then——' and he looked over her head to where the nurse stood rocking the sleeping child.

'Then what, Magician?'

Giving no answer, he turned to me.

'Learned Ana, do you remember meeting me at Tanis one night?'

I shook my head, though I guessed well enough what night he meant.

'Your memory weakens, learned Ana, or rather is confused, for we met often, did we not?'

Then he stared at the staff in his hand. I stared also, because I could not help it, and saw, or thought I saw, the dead wood begin to swell and curve. This was enough for me and I said hastily,

'If you mean the night of the Coronation, I do recall——'

'Ah! I thought you would. You, learned Ana, who like all scribes observe so closely, will have noted how little things—such as the scent of a flower, or the passing of a bird, or even the writhing of a snake in the dust—often bring back to the mind events or words it has forgotten long ago.'

'Well—what of our meeting?' I broke in hastily.

'Nothing at all—or only this. Just before it you were talking with the Hebrew Jabez, the lady Merapi's uncle, were you not?'

'Yes, I was talking with him in an open place, alone.'

'Not so, learned Scribe, for you know we are never alone— quite. Could you but see it, every grain of sand has an ear.'

'Be pleased to explain, O Ki.'

'Nay, Ana, it would be too long, and short jests are ever the best. As I have told you, you were not alone, for though there were some words that I did not catch, I heard much of what passed between you and Jabez.'

'What did you hear?' I asked wrathfully, and next instant

wished that I had bitten through my tongue before it shaped the words.

'Much, much. Let me think. You spoke about the lady Merapi, and whether she would do well to bide at Memphis in the shadow of the Prince, or to return to Goshen into the shadow of a certain—I forget the name. Jabez, a well-instructed man, said he thought that she might be happier at Memphis, though perhaps her presence there would bring a great sorrow upon herself and—another.'

Here again he looked at the child, which seemed to feel his glance, for it woke up and beat the air with its little hands.

The nurse felt it also, although her head was turned away, for she started and then took shelter behind the bole of one of the palm-trees. Now Merapi said in a low and shaken voice,

'I know what you mean, Magician, for since then I have seen my uncle Jabez.'

'As I have also, several times, Lady, which may explain to you what Ana here thinks so wonderful, namely that I should have learned what they said together when he thought that they were alone, which, as I have told him, no one can ever be, at least in Egypt, the land of listening gods——'

'And spying sorcerers,' I exclaimed.

'——And spying sorcerers,' he repeated after me, 'and scribes who take notes, and learn them by heart, and priests with ears as large as asses, and leaves that whisper—and many other things.'

'Cease your gibes, and say what you have to say,' said Merapi, in the same broken voice.

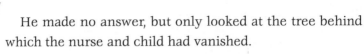

He made no answer, but only looked at the tree behind which the nurse and child had vanished.

'Oh! I know, I know,' she exclaimed in tones that were like a cry. 'My child is threatened! You threaten my child because you hate me.'

'Your pardon, Lady. It is true that evil threatens this royal babe, or so I understood from Jabez, who knows so much. But it is not I that threaten it, any more than I hate you, in whom I acknowledge a fellow of my craft, but one greater than myself that it is my duty to obey.'

'Have done! Why do you torment me?'

'Can the priests of the Moon-goddess torment Isis, Mother of Magic, with their prayers and offerings? And can I who would make a prayer and an offering—'

'What prayer, and what offering?'

'The prayer that you will suffer me to shelter in this house from the many dangers that threaten me at the hands of Pharaoh and the prophets of your people, and an offering of such help as I can give by my arts and knowledge against blacker dangers which threaten—another.'

Here once more he gazed at the trunk of the tree beyond which I heard the infant wail.

'If I consent, what then?' she asked, hoarsely.

'Then, Lady, I will strive to protect a certain little one against a curse which Jabez tells me threatens him and many others in whom runs the blood of Egypt. I will strive, if I am allowed to bide here—I do not say that I shall succeed, for as your lord has reminded me, and as you showed me in the temple of Amon, my strength is smaller than that of the prophets and prophetesses of Israel.'

'And if I refuse?'

'Then, Lady,' he answered in a voice that rang like iron, 'I am sure that one whom you love—as mothers love—will shortly be rocked in the arms of the god whom we name Osiris.'

'*Stay,*' she cried and, turning, fled away.

'Why, Ana, she is gone,' he said, 'and that before I could bargain for my reward. Well, this I must find in your company. How strange are women, Ana! Here you have one of the greatest of her sex, as you learned in the temple of Amon. And yet she opens beneath the sun of hope and shrivels beneath the shadow of fear, like the touched leaves of that tender plant which grows upon the banks of the river; she who, with her eyes set on the mystery that is beyond, whereof she hears the whispering winds, should tread both earthly hope and fear beneath her feet, or make of them stepping stones to glory. Were she a man she would do so, but her sex wrecks her, she who thinks more of the kiss of a babe than of all the splendours she might harbour in her breast. Yes, a babe, a single wretched little babe. You had one once, did you not, Ana?'

'Oh! to Set and his fires with you and your evil talk,' I said, and left him.

When I had gone a little way, I looked back and saw that he was laughing, throwing up his staff as he laughed, and catching it again.

'Set and his fires,' he called after me. 'I wonder what they are like, Ana. Perhaps one day we shall learn, you and I together, Scribe Ana.'

So Ki took up his abode with us, in the same lodgings as

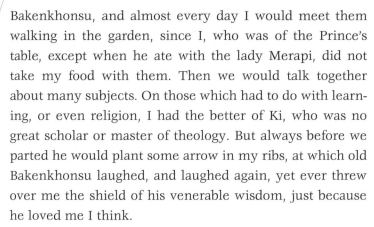

Bakenkhonsu, and almost every day I would meet them walking in the garden, since I, who was of the Prince's table, except when he ate with the lady Merapi, did not take my food with them. Then we would talk together about many subjects. On those which had to do with learning, or even religion, I had the better of Ki, who was no great scholar or master of theology. But always before we parted he would plant some arrow in my ribs, at which old Bakenkhonsu laughed, and laughed again, yet ever threw over me the shield of his venerable wisdom, just because he loved me I think.

It was after this that the plague struck the cattle of Egypt, so that tens of thousands of them died, though not all as was reported. But, as I have said, of the herds of Seti none died, nor, as we were told, did any of those of the Israelites in the land of Goshen. Now there was great distress in Egypt, but Ki smiled and said that he knew it would be so, and that there was much worse to come, for which I could have smitten him over the head with his own staff, had I not feared that, if I did so, it might once more turn to a serpent in my hand.

Old Bakenkhonsu looked upon the matter with another face. He said that since his last wife died, I think some fifty years before, he had found life very dull because he missed the exercises of her temper, and her habit of presenting things as these never had been nor could possibly ever be. Now, however, it grew interesting again, since the marvels which were happening in Egypt, being quite contrary to Nature, reminded him of his last wife and her arguments. All of which was his way of saying that in those years we lived in a new world, whereof for the Egyptians Set the Evil One seemed to be the king.

But still Pharaoh would not let the Hebrews go, perhaps because he had vowed as much to Meneptah who set him on the throne, or perhaps for those other reasons, or one of them, which Ki had given to the Prince.

Then came the curse of sores afflicting man, woman, and child throughout the land, save those who dwelt in the household of Seti. Thus the watchman and his family whose lodge was without the gates suffered, but the watchman and his family who lived within the gates, not twenty paces away, did not suffer, which caused bitterness between their women. In the same way Ki, who resided as a guest of the Prince at Memphis, suffered from no sores, whereas those of his College who remained at Tanis were more heavily smitten than any others, so that some of them died. When he heard this, Ki laughed and said that he had told them it would be so. Also Pharaoh himself and even her Highness Userti were smitten, the latter upon the cheek, which made her unsightly for a while. Indeed, Bakenkhonsu heard, I know not how, that so great was her rage that she even bethought her of returning to her lord Seti, in whose house she had learned people were safe, and the beauty of her successor, Moon of Israel, remained unscarred and was even greater than before, tidings that I think Bakenkhonsu himself conveyed to her. But in the end this her pride, or her jealousy, prevented her from doing.

Now the heart of Egypt began to turn towards Seti in good earnest. The Prince, they said, had opposed the policy of the oppression of the Hebrews, and because he could not prevail had abandoned his right to the throne, which Pharaoh Amenmeses had purchased at the price of accepting that policy whereof the fruits had been proved to be destruction. Therefore, they reasoned, if Amenmeses were deposed, and the Prince reigned, their miseries would cease. So they sent deputations to him secretly, praying him to rise against Amenmeses and promising him support. But he would listen to none of them, telling them that he was happy as he was and sought no other state. Still Pharaoh grew jealous, for all these things his spies reported to him, and set about plots to destroy Seti.

Of the first of these Userti warned me by a messenger, but the second and worse Ki discovered in some strange way, so that the murderer was trapped at the gates and killed by the watchman, whereon Seti said that after all he had been wise to give hospitality to Ki, that is, if to continue to live were wisdom. The lady Merapi also said as much to me, but I noted that always she shunned Ki, whom she held in mistrust and fear.

15

THE NIGHT
OF FEAR

Then came the hail, and some months after the hail the locusts, and Egypt went mad with woe and terror. It was known to us, for with Ki and Bakenkhonsu in the palace we knew everything, that the Hebrew prophets had promised this hail because Pharaoh would not listen to them. Therefore Seti caused it to be put about through all the land that the Egyptians should shelter their cattle, or such as were left to them, at the first sign of storm. But Pharaoh heard of it and issued a proclamation that this was not to be done, inasmuch as it would be an insult to the gods of Egypt. Still many did so and these saved their cattle. It was strange to see that wall of jagged ice stretching from earth to heaven and destroying all upon which it fell. The tall date-palms were stripped even of their bark; the soil was churned up; men and beasts if caught abroad were slain or shattered.

I stood at the gate and watched it. There, not a yard away, fell the white hail, turning the world to wreck, while

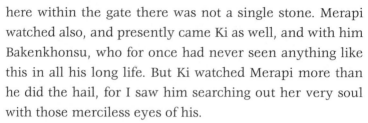

here within the gate there was not a single stone. Merapi watched also, and presently came Ki as well, and with him Bakenkhonsu, who for once had never seen anything like this in all his long life. But Ki watched Merapi more than he did the hail, for I saw him searching out her very soul with those merciless eyes of his.

'Lady,' he said at length, 'tell your servant, I beseech you, how you do this thing?' and he pointed first to the trees and flowers within the gate and then to the wreck without.

At first I thought that she had not heard him because of the roar of the hail, for she stepped forward and opened the side wicket to admit a poor jackal that was scratching at the bars. Still this was not so, for presently she turned and said,

'Does the Kherheb, the greatest magician in Egypt, ask an unlearned woman to teach him of marvels? Well, Ki, I cannot, because I neither do it nor know how it is done.'

Bakenkhonsu laughed, and Ki's painted smile grew as it were brighter than before.

'That is not what they say in the land of Goshen, Lady,' he answered, 'and not what the Hebrew women say here in Memphis. Nor is it what the priests of Amon say. These declare that you have more magic than all the sorcerers on the Nile. Here is the proof of it,' and he pointed to the ruin without and the peace within, adding, 'Lady, if you can protect your own home, why cannot you protect the innocent people of Egypt?'

'Because I cannot,' she answered angrily. 'If ever I had such power it is gone from me, who am now the mother of an Egyptian's child. But I have none. There in the temple of Amon some Strength worked through me, that is all, which never will visit me again because of my sin.'

'What sin, Lady?'

'The sin of taking the Prince Seti to lord. Now, if any god spoke through me it would be one of those of the Egyptians, since He of Israel has cast me out.'

Ki started as though some new thought had come to him, and at this moment she turned and went away.

'Would that she were high-priestess of Isis that she might work for us and not against us,' he said.

Bakenkhonsu shook his head.

'Let that be,' he answered. 'Be sure that never will an Israelitish woman offer sacrifice to what she would call the abomination of the Egyptians.'

'If she will not sacrifice to save the people, let her be careful lest the people sacrifice her to save themselves,' said Ki in a cold voice.

Then he too went away.

'I think that if ever that hour comes, then Ki will have his share in it,' laughed Bakenkhonsu. 'What is the good of a shepherd who shelters here in comfort, while outside the sheep are dying, eh, Ana?'

It was after the plague of locusts, which ate all there was left to eat in Egypt, so that the poor folk who had done no wrong and had naught to say to the dealings of Pharaoh with the Israelites starved by the thousand, and during that of the great darkness, that Laban came. Now this darkness lay upon the land like a thick cloud for three whole days and nights. Nevertheless, though the shadows were deep, there was no true darkness over the house of Seti at Mem-

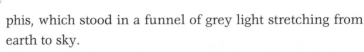

phis, which stood in a funnel of grey light stretching from earth to sky.

Now the terror was increased tenfold, and it seemed to me that all the hundreds of thousands of Memphis were gathered outside our walls, so that they might look upon the light, such as it was, if they could do no more. Seti would have admitted as many as the place would hold, but Ki bade him not, saying, that if he did so the darkness would flow in with them. Only Merapi did admit some of the Israelitish women who were married to Egyptians in the city, though for her pains they only cursed her as a witch. For now most of the inhabitants of Memphis were certain that it was Merapi who, keeping herself safe, had brought these woes upon them because she was a worshipper of an alien god.

'If she who is the love of Egypt's heir would but sacrifice to Egypt's gods, these horrors would pass from us,' said they, having, as I think, learned their lesson from the lips of Ki. Or perhaps the emissaries of Userti had taught them.

Once more we stood by the gate watching the people flitting to and fro in the gloom without, for this sight fascinated Merapi, as a snake fascinates a bird. Then it was that Laban appeared. I knew his hooked nose and hawk-like eyes at once, and she knew him also.

'Come away with me, Moon of Israel,' he cried, 'and all shall yet be forgiven you. But if you will not come, then fearful things shall overtake you.'

She stood staring at him, answering never a word, and just then the Prince Seti reached us and saw him.

'Take that man,' he commanded, flushing with anger,

and guards sprang into the darkness to do his bidding. But Laban was gone.

On the second day of the darkness the tumult was great, on the third it was terrible. A crowd thrust the guard aside, broke down the gates and burst into the palace, humbly demanding that the lady Merapi would come to pray for them, yet showing by their mien that if she would not come they meant to take her.

'What is to be done?' asked Seti of Ki and Bakenkhonsu.

'That is for the Prince to judge,' said Ki, 'though I do not see how it can harm the lady Merapi to pray for us in the open square of Memphis.'

'Let her go,' said Bakenkhonsu, 'lest presently we should all go further than we would.'

'I do not wish to go,' cried Merapi, 'not knowing for whom I am to pray or how.'

'Be it as you will, Lady,' said Seti in his grave and gentle voice. 'Only, hearken to the roar of the mob. If you refuse, I think that very soon every one of us will have reached a land where perhaps it is not needful to pray at all,' and he looked at the infant in her arms.

'I will go,' she said.

She went forth carrying the child and I walked behind her. So did the Prince, but in that darkness he was cut off by a rush of thousands of folk and I saw him no more till all was over. Bakenkhonsu was with me leaning on my arm, but Ki had gone on before us, for his own ends as I think. A huge mob moved through the dense darkness, in which here and there lights floated like lamps upon a quiet sea. I did not know where we were going until the light of one of

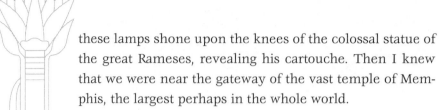

these lamps shone upon the knees of the colossal statue of the great Rameses, revealing his cartouche. Then I knew that we were near the gateway of the vast temple of Memphis, the largest perhaps in the whole world.

We went on through court after pillared court, priests leading us by the hand, till we came to a shrine commanding the biggest court of all, which was packed with men and women. It was that of Isis, who held at her breast the infant Horus.

'O friend Ana,' cried Merapi, 'give help. They are dressing me in strange garments.'

I tried to get near to her but was thrust back, a voice, which I thought was that of Ki, saying,

'On your life, fool!'

Presently a lamp was held up, and by the light of it I saw Merapi seated in a chair dressed like a goddess, in the sacerdotal robes of Isis and wearing the vulture cap headdress—beautiful exceedingly. In her arms was the child dressed as the infant Horus.

'Pray for us, Mother Isis,' cried thousands of voices, 'that the curse of blackness may be removed.'

Then she prayed, saying,

'O my God, take away this curse of blackness from these innocent people,' and all of those present, repeated her prayer.

At that moment the sky began to lighten and in less than the half of an hour the sun shone out. When Merapi saw how she and the child were arrayed she screamed aloud and tore off her jewelled trappings, crying,

'Woe! Woe! Woe! Great woe upon the people of Egypt!'

But in their joy at the new found light few hearkened to

her who they were sure had brought back the sun. Again Laban appeared for a moment.

'Witch! Traitress!' he cried. 'You have worn the robes of Isis and worshipped in the temple of the gods of the Egyptians. The curse of the God of Israel be on you and that which is born of you.'

I sprang at him but he was gone. Then we bore Merapi home swooning.

So this trouble passed by, but from that time forward Merapi would not suffer her son to be taken out of her sight.

'Why do you make so much of him, Lady?' I asked one day.

'Because I would love him well while he is here, Friend,' she answered, 'but of this say nothing to his father.'

A while went by and we heard that still Pharaoh would not let the Israelites go. Then the Prince Seti sent Bakenkhonsu and myself to Tanis to see Pharaoh and to say to him,

'I seek nothing for myself and I forget those evils which you would have worked on me through jealousy. But I say unto you that if you will not let these strangers go great and terrible things shall befall you and all Egypt. Therefore, hear my prayer and let them go.'

Now Bakenkhonsu and I came before Pharaoh and we saw that he was greatly aged, for his hair had gone grey about his temples and the flesh hung in bags beneath his eyes. Also not for one minute could he stay still.

'Is your lord, and are you also of the servants of this Hebrew prophet whom the Egyptians worship as a god because he has done them so much ill?' he asked. 'It may well be so, since I hear that my cousin Seti keeps an

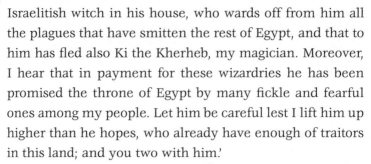

Israelitish witch in his house, who wards off from him all the plagues that have smitten the rest of Egypt, and that to him has fled also Ki the Kherheb, my magician. Moreover, I hear that in payment for these wizardries he has been promised the throne of Egypt by many fickle and fearful ones among my people. Let him be careful lest I lift him up higher than he hopes, who already have enough of traitors in this land; and you two with him.'

Now I said nothing who saw that the man was mad, but Bakenkhonsu laughed out loud and answered,

'O Pharaoh, I know little, but I know this although I be old, namely, that after men have ceased to speak your name I shall still hold converse with the wearer of the Double Crown in Egypt. Now will you let these Hebrews go, or will you bring death upon Egypt?'

Pharaoh glared at him and answered, 'I will not let them go.'

'Why not, Pharaoh? Tell me, for I am curious.'

'Because I cannot,' he answered with a groan. 'Because something stronger than myself forces me to deny their prayer. Begone!'

So we went, and this was the last time that I looked upon Amenmeses at Tanis.

As we left the chamber I saw the Hebrew prophet entering the presence. Afterwards a rumour reached us that he had threatened to kill all the people in Egypt, but that still Pharaoh would not let the Israelites depart. Indeed, it was said that he had told the prophet that if he appeared before him any more he should be put to death.

Now we journeyed back to Memphis with all these tidings and made report to Seti. When Merapi heard them she went half mad, weeping and wringing her hands. I asked her what she feared. She answered death, which was near to all of us. I said,

'If so, there are worse things, Lady.'

'For you mayhap who are faithful and good in your own fashion, but not for me. Do you not understand, friend Ana, that I am one who has broken the law of the god I was taught to worship?'

'And which of us is there who has not broken the law of the god we were taught to worship, Lady? If in truth you have done anything of the sort by flying from a murderous villain to one who loves you well, which I do not believe, surely there is forgiveness for such sins as this.'

'Aye, perhaps, but, alas! the thing is blacker far. Have you forgotten what I did? Dressed in the robes of Isis I worshipped in the temple of Isis with my boy playing the part of Horus on my bosom. It is a crime that can never be forgiven to a Hebrew woman, Ana, for my God is a jealous God. Yet it is true that Ki tricked me.'

'If he had not, Lady, I think there would have been none of us left to trick, seeing that the people were crazed with dread of the darkness and believed that it could be lifted by you alone, as indeed happened,' I added somewhat doubtfully.

'More of Ki's tricks! Oh! do you not understand that the lifting of the darkness at that moment was Ki's work, because he wished the people to believe that I am indeed a sorceress?'

'Why?' I asked.

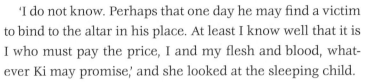

'I do not know. Perhaps that one day he may find a victim to bind to the altar in his place. At least I know well that it is I who must pay the price, I and my flesh and blood, whatever Ki may promise,' and she looked at the sleeping child.

'Do not be afraid, Lady,' I said. 'Ki has left the palace and you will see him no more.'

'Yes, because the Prince was angry with him about the trick in the temple of Isis. Therefore suddenly he went, or pretended to go, for how can one tell where such a man may really be? But he will come back again. Bethink you, Ki was the greatest magician in Egypt; even old Bakenkhonsu can remember none like to him. Then he matches himself against the prophets of my people and fails.'

'But did he fail, Lady? What they did he did, sending among the Israelites the plagues that your prophets had sent among us.'

'Yes, some of them, but he was outpaced, or feared to be outpaced at last. Is Ki a man to forget that? And if Ki chances really to believe that I am his adversary and his master at this black work, as because of what happened in the temple of Amon thousands believe to-day, will he not mete me my own measure soon or late? Oh! I fear Ki, Ana, and I fear the people of Egypt, and were it not for my lord beloved, I would flee away into the wilderness with my son, and get me out of this haunted land! Hush! he wakes.'

From this time forward until the sword fell there was great dread in Egypt. None seemed to know exactly what they dreaded, but all thought that it had to do with death. People went about mournfully looking over their shoulders as though someone were following them, and at night they gathered together in knots and talked in whispers. Only the Hebrews seemed to be glad and happy. Moreover, they were making preparations for something new and strange. Thus those Israelitish women who dwelt in Memphis began to sell what property they had and to borrow of the Egyptians. Especially did they ask for the loan of jewels, saying that they were about to celebrate a feast and wished to look fine in the eyes of their countrymen. None refused them what they asked because all were afraid of them. They even came to the palace and begged her ornaments from Merapi, although she was a countrywoman of their own who had showed them much kindness. Yes, and seeing that her son wore a little gold circlet on his hair, one of them begged that also, nor did she say her nay. But, as it chanced, the Prince entered, and seeing the woman with this royal badge in her hand, grew very angry and forced her to restore it.

'What is the use of crowns without heads to wear them?' she sneered, and fled away laughing, with all that she had gathered.

After she had heard that saying Merapi grew even sadder and more distraught than she was before, and from her the trouble crept to Seti. He too became sad and ill at ease, though when I asked him why he vowed he did not know, but supposed it was because some new plague drew near.

'Yet,' he added, 'as I have made shift to live through nine of them, I do not know why I should fear a tenth.'

Still he did fear it, so much that he consulted Bakenkhonsu as to whether there were any means by which the anger of the gods could be averted.

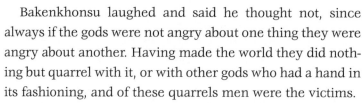

Bakenkhonsu laughed and said he thought not, since always if the gods were not angry about one thing they were angry about another. Having made the world they did nothing but quarrel with it, or with other gods who had a hand in its fashioning, and of these quarrels men were the victims.

'Bear your woes, Prince,' he added, 'if any come, for ere the Nile has risen another fifty times at most, whether they have or have not been, will be the same to you.'

'Then you think that when we go west we die indeed, and that Osiris is but another name for the sunset, Bakenkhonsu.'

The old Councillor shook his great head, and answered,

'No. If ever you should lose one whom you greatly love, take comfort, Prince, for I do not think that life ends with death. Death is the nurse that puts it to sleep, no more, and in the morning it will wake again to travel through another day with those who have companioned it from the beginning.'

'Where do all the days lead it to at last, Bakenkhonsu?'

'Ask that of Ki; I do not know.'

'To Set with Ki; I am angered with him,' said the Prince, and went away.

'Not without reason, I think,' mused Bakenkhonsu, but when I asked him what he meant, he would not or could not tell me.

So the gloom deepened and the palace, which had been merry in its way, became sad. None knew what was coming, but all knew that something was coming and stretched out their hands to strive to protect that which they loved best from the stroke of the warring gods. In the case of Seti and Merapi this was their son, now a beautiful little lad who could run and prattle, one too of a strange health and vigour for a child of the inbred race of the Ramessids. Never for a minute was this boy allowed to be out of the sight of one or other of his parents; indeed I saw little of Seti in those days and all our learned studies came to nothing, because he was ever concerned with Merapi in playing nurse to this son of his.

When Userti was told of it, she said in the hearing of a friend of mine,

'Without a doubt that is because he trains his bastard to fill the throne of Egypt.'

But, alas! all that the little Seti was doomed to fill was a coffin.

It was a still, hot evening, so hot that Merapi had bid the nurse bring the child's bed and set it between two pillars of the great portico. There on the bed he slept, lovely as Horus the divine. She sat by his side in a chair that had feet shaped like to those of an antelope. Seti walked up and down the terrace beyond the portico leaning on my shoulder, and talking by snatches of this or that. Occasionally as he passed he would stay for a while to make sure by the bright moonlight that all was well with Merapi and the child, as of late it had become a habit with him to do. Then without speaking, for fear lest he should awake the boy, he would smile at Merapi, who sat there brooding, her head resting on her hand, and pass on.

The night was very still. The palm leaves did not rustle, no jackals were stirring, and even the shrill-voiced insects had ceased their cries. Moreover, the great city below was

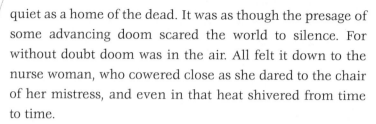

quiet as a home of the dead. It was as though the presage of some advancing doom scared the world to silence. For without doubt doom was in the air. All felt it down to the nurse woman, who cowered close as she dared to the chair of her mistress, and even in that heat shivered from time to time.

Presently little Seti awoke, and began to prattle about something he had dreamed.

'What did you dream, my son?' asked his father.

'I dreamed,' he answered in his baby talk, 'that a woman, dressed as Mother was in the temple, took me by the hand and led me into the air. I looked down, and saw you and Mother with white faces and crying. I began to cry too, but the woman with the feather cap told me not to as she was taking me to a beautiful big star where Mother would soon come to find me.'

The Prince and I looked at each other and Merapi feigned to busy herself with hushing the child to sleep again. It drew towards midnight and still no one seemed minded to go to rest. Old Bakenkhonsu appeared and began to say something about the night being very strange and unrestful, when, suddenly, a little bat that was flitting to and fro above us fell upon his head and thence to the ground. We looked at it, and saw that it was dead.

'Strange that the creature should have died thus,' said Bakenkhonsu, when, behold! another fell to the ground near by. The black kitten which belonged to little Seti saw it fall and darted from beside his bed where it was sleeping. Before ever it reached the bat, the creature wheeled round, stood upon its hind legs, scratching at the air about it, then uttered one pitiful cry and fell over dead.

We stared at it, when suddenly far away a dog howled in a very piercing fashion. Then a cow began to bale as these beasts do when they have lost their calves. Next, quite close at hand but without the gates, there arose the ear-curdling cry of a woman in agony, which on the instant seemed to be echoed from every quarter, till the air was full of wailing.

'Oh, Seti! Seti!' exclaimed Merapi, in a voice that was rather a hiss than a whisper, 'look at your son!'

We sprang to where the babe lay, and looked. He had awakened and was staring upward with wide-opened eyes and frozen face. The fear, if such it were, passed from his features, though still he stared. He rose to his little feet, always looking upwards. Then a smile came upon his face, a most beautiful smile; he stretched out his arms, as though to clasp one who bent down towards him, and fell backwards—quite dead.

Seti stood still as a statue; we all stood still, even Merapi. Then she bent down, and lifted the body of the boy.

'Now, my lord,' she said, 'there has fallen on you that sorrow which Jabez my uncle warned you would come, if ever you had aught to do with me. Now the curse of Israel has pierced my heart, and now our child, as Ki the evil prophesied, has grown too great for greetings, or even for farewells.'

Thus she spoke in a cold and quiet voice, as one might speak of something long expected or foreseen, then made

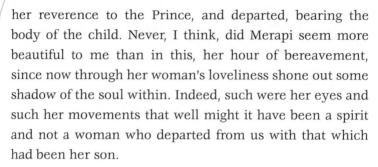

her reverence to the Prince, and departed, bearing the body of the child. Never, I think, did Merapi seem more beautiful to me than in this, her hour of bereavement, since now through her woman's loveliness shone out some shadow of the soul within. Indeed, such were her eyes and such her movements that well might it have been a spirit and not a woman who departed from us with that which had been her son.

Seti leaned on my shoulder looking at the empty bed, and at the scared nurse who still sat behind, and I felt a tear drop upon my hand. Old Bakenkhonsu lifted his massive face, and looked at him.

'Grieve not over much, Prince,' he said, 'since, ere as many years as I have lived out have come and gone, this child will be forgotten and his mother will be forgotten, and even you, O Prince, will live but as a name that once was great in Egypt. And then, O Prince, elsewhere the game will begin afresh, and what you have lost shall be found anew, and the sweeter for its sheltering from the vile breath of men. Ki's magic is not all a lie, or if his is, mine holds some shadow of the truth, and when he said to you yonder in Tanis that not for nothing were you named Lord of Rebirths, he spoke words that you should find comfortable to-night.'

'I thank you, Councillor,' said Seti, and turning, followed Merapi.

'Now I suppose we shall have more deaths,' I exclaimed, scarcely knowing what I said in my sorrow.

'I think not, Ana,' answered Bakenkhonsu, 'since the shield of Jabez, or of his god, is over us. Always he foretold that trouble would come to Merapi, and to Seti through Merapi, but that is all.'

I glanced at the kitten.

'It strayed here from the town three days ago, Ana. And the bats also may have flown from the town. Hark to the wailing. Was ever such a sound heard before in Egypt?'

16

JABEZ SELLS HORSES

Bakenkhonsu was right. Save the son of Seti alone, none died who dwelt in or about his house, though elsewhere all the first-born of Egypt lay dead, and the first-born of the beasts also. When this came to be known throughout the land a rage seized the Egyptians against Merapi who, they remembered, had called down woe on Egypt after she had been forced to pray in the temple and, as they believed, to lift the darkness from Memphis.

Bakenkhonsu and I and others who loved her pointed out that her own child had died with the rest. To this it was answered, and here I thought I saw the fingers of Userti and of Ki, that it was nothing, since witches did not love children. Moreover, they said she could have as many as she liked and when she liked, making them to look like children out of clay figures and to grow up into evil spirits to torment the land. Lastly, people swore that she had been heard to say that, although to do it she must kill her own lord's son, she would not on that account forego her vengeance on the Egyptians, who once had treated her as a slave and murdered her father. Further, the Israelites themselves, or some of them, mayhap Laban among them, were reported to have told the Egyptians that it was the sorceress who had bewitched Prince Seti who brought such great troubles on them.

So it happened that the Egyptians came to hate Merapi, who of all women was the sweetest and the most to be loved, and to her other supposed crimes, added this also, that by her witcheries she had stolen the heart of Seti away from his lawful wife and made him to turn that lady, the Royal Princess of Egypt, even from his gates, so that she was forced to dwell alone at Tanis. For in all these matters none blamed Seti, whom everyone in Egypt loved, because it was known that he would have dealt with the Israelites in a very different fashion, and thus averted all the woes that had desolated the ancient land of Khem. As for this matter of the Hebrew girl with the big eyes who chanced to have thrown a spell upon him, that was his ill-fortune, nothing more. Amongst the many women with whom they believed he filled his house, as was the way of princes, it was not strange that one favourite should be a witch. Indeed, I am certain that only because he was known to love her, was Merapi saved from death by poison or in some other secret fashion, at any rate for a while.

Now came the glad tidings that the pride of Pharaoh was broken at last (for his first-born child had died with the others), or that the cloud of madness had lifted from his brain, whichever it might be, and that he had decreed that the

Children of Israel might depart from Egypt when and whither they would. Then the people breathed again, seeing hope that their miseries might end.

It was at this time that Jabez appeared once more at Memphis, driving a number of chariot horses, which he said he wished to sell to the Prince, as he did not desire them to pass into any other hands. He was admitted and stated the price of his horses, according to which they must have been beasts of great value.

'Why do you wish to sell your horses?' asked Seti.

'Because I go with my people into lands where there is little water and there they might die, O Prince.'

'I will buy the horses. See to it, Ana,' said Seti, although I knew well that already he had more than he needed.

The Prince rose to show that the interview was ended, whereon Jabez, who was bowing his thanks, said hurriedly,

'I rejoice to learn, O Royal One, that things have befallen as I foretold, or rather was bidden to foretell, and that the troubles which have afflicted Egypt have passed by your dwelling.'

'Then you rejoice to learn a falsehood, Hebrew, since the worst of those troubles has made its home here. My son is dead,' and he turned away.

Jabez lifted his shifty eyes from the floor and glanced at him.

'Prince,' he said, 'I know and grieve because this loss has cut you to the heart. Yet it was no fault of mine or of my people. If you think, you will remember that both when I built a wall of protection about this place because of your good deeds to Israel, O Prince, and before, I warned, and caused you to be warned, that if you and my niece, Moon of Israel, came together a great trouble might fall on you through her who, having become the woman of an Egyptian in defiance of command, must bear the fate of Egyptian women.'

'It may be so,' said the Prince. 'The matter is not one of which I care to talk. If this death was wrought by the magic of your wizards I have only this to say—that it is an ill payment to me in return for all that I have striven to do on behalf of the Hebrews. Yet, what else could I expect from such a people in such a world? Farewell.'

'One prayer, O Prince. I would ask your leave to speak with my niece, Merapi.'

'She is veiled. Since the murder of her child by wizardry, she sees no man.'

'Still I think she will see her uncle, O Prince.'

'What then do you wish to say to her?'

'O Prince, through the clemency of Pharaoh we poor slaves are about to leave the land of Egypt never to return. Therefore, if my niece remains behind, it is natural that I should wish to bid her farewell, and to confide to her certain matters connected with our race and family, which she might desire to pass on to her children.'

Now, when he heard this word 'children' Seti softened.

'I do not trust you,' he said. 'You may be charged with more of your Hebrew curses against Merapi, or you may say words to her that will make her even unhappier than she is. Yet if you would wish to see her in my presence——'

'My lord Prince, I will not trouble you so far. Farewell. Be pleased to convey——'

'Or if that does not suit you,' interrupted Seti, 'in the presence of Ana here you can do so, unless she refuses to receive you.'

Jabez reflected for a moment, and answered,

'Then in the presence of Ana let it be, since he is a man who knows when to be silent.'

Jabez made obeisance and departed, and at a sign from the Prince I followed him. Presently we were ushered into the chamber of the lady Merapi, where she sat looking most sad and lonely, with a veil of black upon her head.

'Greeting, my uncle,' she said, after glancing at me, whose presence I think she understood. 'Are you the bearer of more prophecies? I pray not, since your last were overtrue,' and she touched the black veil with her finger.

'I am the bearer of tidings, and of a prayer, Niece. The tidings are that the people of Israel are about to leave Egypt. The prayer, which is also a command, is—that you make ready to accompany them——'

'To Laban?' she asked, looking up.

'No, my niece. Laban would not wish as a wife one who has been the mistress of an Egyptian, but to play your part, however humble, in the fortunes of our people.'

'I am glad that Laban does not wish what he never could obtain, my uncle. Tell me, I pray you, why should I hearken to this prayer, or this command?'

'For a good reason, Niece—that your life hangs on it. Heretofore you have been suffered to take your heart's desire. But if you bide in Egypt where you have no longer a mission to fulfil, having done all that was sought of you in

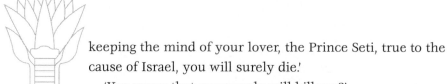

keeping the mind of your lover, the Prince Seti, true to the cause of Israel, you will surely die.'

'You mean that our people will kill me?'

'No, not our people. Still you will die.'

She took a step towards him, and looked him in the eyes.

'You are certain that I shall die, my uncle?'

'I am, or at least others are certain.'

Now she laughed; it was the first time I had seen her laugh for several moons.

'Then I will stay here,' she said.

Jabez stared at her.

'I thought that you loved this Egyptian, who indeed is worthy of any woman's love,' he muttered into his beard.

'Perhaps it is because I love him that I wish to die. I have given him all I have to give; there is nothing left of my poor treasure except what will bring trouble and misfortune on his head. Therefore the greater the love—and it is more great than all those pyramids massed to one—the greater the need that it should be buried for a while. Do you understand?'

He shook his head.

'I understand only that you are a very strange woman, different from any other that I have known.'

'My child, who was slain with the rest, was all the world to me, and I would be where he is. Do you understand now?'

'You would leave your life, in which, being young, you may have more children, to lie in a tomb with your dead son?' he asked slowly, like one astonished.

'I only care for life while it can serve him whom I love, and if a day comes when he sits upon the throne how will a daughter of the hated Israelites serve him then? Also I do not wish for more children. Living or dead, he that is gone owns all my heart; there is no room in it for others. That love at least is pure and perfect, and having been embalmed by death, can never change. Moreover, it is not in a tomb that I shall lie with him, or so I believe. The faith of these Egyptians which we despise tells of a life eternal in the heavens, and thither I would go to seek that which is lost, and to wait that which is left behind awhile.'

'Ah!' said Jabez. 'For my part I do not trouble myself with these problems, who find in a life temporal on the earth enough to fill my thoughts and hands. Yet, Merapi, you are a rebel, and whether in heaven or on earth, how are rebels received by the king against whom they have rebelled?'

'You say I am a rebel,' she said, turning on him with flashing eyes. 'Why? Because I would not dishonour myself by marrying a man I hate, one also who is a murderer, and because while I live I will not desert a man whom I love to return to those who have done me naught but evil. Did God then make women to be sold like cattle of the field for the pleasure and the profit of him who can pay the highest?'

'It seems so,' said Jabez, spreading out his hands.

'It seems that you think so, who fashion God as you would wish him to be, but for my part I do not believe it, and if I did, I should seek another king. My uncle, I appeal from the priest and the elder to That which made both them and me, and by Its judgment I will stand or fall.'

'Always a very dangerous thing to do,' reflected Jabez aloud, 'since the priest is apt to take the law into his own hands before the cause can be pleaded elsewhere. Still, who am I that I should set up my reasonings against one

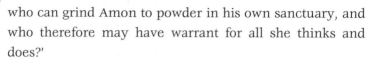

who can grind Amon to powder in his own sanctuary, and who therefore may have warrant for all she thinks and does?'

Merapi stamped her foot.

'You know well it was you who brought me the command to dare the god Amon in his temple. It was not I——' she began.

'I do know,' replied Jabez waving his hand. 'I know also that is what every wizard says, whatever his nation or his gods, and what no one ever believes. Thus because, having faith, you obeyed the command and through you Amon was smitten, among both the Israelites and the Egyptians you are held to be the greatest sorceress that has looked upon the Nile, and that is a dangerous repute, my niece.'

'One to which I lay no claim, and never sought.'

'Just so, but which all the same has come to you. Well, knowing as without doubt you do all that will soon befall in Egypt, and having been warned, if you needed warning, of the danger with which you yourself are threatened, you still refuse to obey this second command which it is my duty to deliver to you?'

'I refuse.'

'Then on your own head be it, and farewell. Oh! I would add that there is certain property in cattle, and the fruit of lands which descends to you from your father. In the event of your death——'

'Take it all, my uncle, and may it prosper you. Farewell.'

'A great woman, friend Ana, and a beautiful,' said the old Hebrew, after he had watched her go. 'I grieve that I shall never see her again, and, indeed, that no one will see her for very long; for, remember, she is my niece of whom I am fond. Now I too must be going, having completed my errand. All good fortune to you, Ana. You are no longer a soldier, are you? No? Believe me, it is as well, as you will learn. My homage to the Prince. Think of me at times, when you grow old, and not unkindly, seeing that I have served you as best I could, and your master also, who I hope will soon find again that which he lost awhile ago.'

'Her Highness, Princess Userti,' I suggested.

'The Princess Userti amongst other things, Ana. Tell the Prince, if he should deem them costly, that those horses which I sold him are really of the finest Syrian blood, and of a strain that my family has owned for generations. If you should chance to have any friend whose welfare you desire, let him not go into the desert soldiering during the next few moons, especially if Pharaoh be in command. Nay, I know nothing, but it is a season of great storm. Farewell, friend Ana, and again farewell.'

'Now what did he mean by that?' thought I to myself, as I departed to make my report to Seti. But no answer to the question rose in my mind.

Very soon I began to understand. It appeared that at length the Israelites were leaving Egypt, a vast horde of them, and with them tens of thousands of Arabs of various tribes who worshipped their god and were, some of them, descended from the people of the Hyksos, the shepherds who once ruled in Egypt. That this was true was proved to us by the tidings which reached us that all the Hebrew women who dwelt in Memphis, even those of them who were married to Egyptians, had departed

from the city, leaving behind them their men and sometimes their children. Indeed, before these went, certain
of them who had been friends visited Merapi and asked
her if she were not coming also. She shook her head as
she replied,

'Why do you go? Are you so fond of journeyings in the
desert that for the sake of them you are ready never again
to look upon the men you love and the children of your
bodies?'

'No, Lady,' they answered, weeping. 'We are happy here
in white-walled Memphis and here, listening to the murmur of Nile, we would grow old and die, rather than strive
to keep house in some desert tent with a stranger or alone.
Yet fear drives us hence.'

'Fear of what?'

'Of the Egyptians who, when they come to understand
all that they have suffered at our hands in return for the
wealth and shelter which they have given us for many generations, whereby we have grown from a handful into a
great people, will certainly kill any Israelite whom they
find left among them. Also we fear the curses of our priests
who bid us to depart.'

'Then *I* should fear these things also,' said Merapi.

'Not so, Lady, seeing that being the only beloved of the
Prince of Egypt who, rumour tells us, will soon be Pharaoh
of Egypt, by him you will be protected from the anger of
the Egyptians. And being, as all know well, the greatest
sorceress in the world, the over-thrower of Amon-Ra the
mighty, and one who by sacrificing her child was able to
ward away every plague from the household where she

dwelt, you have naught to fear from priests and their magic.'

Then Merapi sprang up, bidding them to leave her to her fate and to be gone to their own, which they did hastily enough, fearing lest she should cast some spell upon them. So it came about that presently the fair Moon of Israel and certain children of mixed blood were all of the Hebrew race that were left in Egypt. Then, notwithstanding the miseries and misfortunes that during the past few years by terror, death, and famine had reduced them to perhaps one half of their number, the people of Egypt rejoiced with a great joy.

In every temple of every god processions were held and offerings made by those who had anything left to offer, while the statues of the gods were dressed in fine new garments and hung about with garlandings of flowers. Moreover, on the Nile and on the sacred lakes boats floated to and fro, adorned with lanterns as at the feast of the Rising of Osiris. As titular high-priest of Amon, an office of which he could not be deprived while he lived, Prince Seti attended these demonstrations, which indeed he must do, in the great temple of Memphis, whither I accompanied him. When the ceremonies were over he led the procession through the masses of the worshippers, clad in his splendid sacerdotal robes, whereon every throat of the thousands present there greeted him in a shout of thunder as 'Pharaoh!' or at least as Pharaoh's heir.

When at length the shouting died, he turned upon them and said,

'Friends, if you would send me to be of the company that sits at the table of Osiris and not at Pharaoh's feasts,

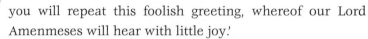

you will repeat this foolish greeting, whereof our Lord Amenmeses will hear with little joy.'

In the silence that followed a voice called out,

'Have no fear, O Prince, while the Hebrew witch sleeps night by night upon your bosom. She who could smite Egypt with so many plagues can certainly shelter you from harm;' whereon the roars of acclamation went up again.

It was on the following day that Bakenkhonsu the aged returned with more tidings from Tanis, where he had been upon a visit. It seemed that a great council had been held there in the largest hall of one of the largest temples. At this council, which was open to all the people, Amenmeses had given report on the matter of the Israelites who, he stated, were departing in their thousands. Also offerings were made to appease the angry gods of Egypt. When the ceremony was finished, but before the company broke up in a heavy mood, her Highness the Princess Userti rose in her place, and addressed Pharaoh.

'By the spirits of our fathers,' she cried, 'and more especially by that of the good god Meneptah, my begetter, I ask of you, Pharaoh, and I ask of you, O people, whether the affront that has been put upon us by these Hebrew slaves and their magicians is one that the proud land of Egypt should be called upon to bear? Our gods have been smitten and defied; woes great and terrible, such as history tells not of, have fallen upon us through magic; tens of thousands, from the first-born child of Pharaoh down, have perished in a single night. And now these Hebrews, who have murdered them by sorcery, for they are sorcerers all, men and women together, especially one of them who sits at

Memphis, of whom I will not speak because she has wrought me private harm, by the decree of Pharaoh are to be suffered to leave the land. More, they are to take with them all their cattle, all their threshed corn, all the treasure they have hoarded for generations, and all the ornaments of price and wealth that they have wrung by terror from our people, borrowing that which they never purpose to return. Therefore I, the Royal Princess of Egypt, would ask of Pharaoh, is this the decree of Pharaoh?'

'Now,' said Bakenkhonsu, 'Pharaoh sat with hanging head upon his throne and made no answer.'

'Pharaoh does not speak,' went on Userti. 'Then I ask, is this the decree of the Council of Pharaoh and of the people of Egypt? There is still a great army in Egypt, hundreds of chariots and thousands of foot-men. Is this army to sit still while these slaves depart into the desert there to rouse our enemies of Syria against us and return with them to butcher us?'

'At these words,' continued Bakenkhonsu, 'from all that multitude there went up a shout of "No." '

'The people say No. What saith Pharaoh?' cried Userti.

There followed a silence, till suddenly Amenmeses rose and spoke,

'Have it as you will, Princess, and on your head and the heads of all these whom you have stirred up let the evil fall if evil comes, though I think it is your husband, the Prince Seti, who should stand where you stand and put up this prayer in your place.'

'My husband, the Prince Seti, is tied to Memphis by a rope of witch's hair, or so they tell me,' she sneered, while the people murmured in assent.

'I know not,' went on Amenmeses, 'but this I know that always the Prince would have let these Hebrews go from among us, and at times, as sorrow followed sorrow, I have thought that he was right. Truly more than once I also would have let them go, but ever some Strength, I know not what, descended on my heart, turning it to stone, and wrung from me words that I did not desire to utter. Even now I would let them go, but all of you are against me, and, perchance, if I withstand you, I shall pay for it with my life and throne. Captains, command that my armies be made ready, and let them assemble here at Tanis that I myself may lead them after the people of Israel and share their dangers.'

Then with a mighty shouting the company broke up, so that at the last all were gone and only Pharaoh remained seated upon his throne, staring at the ground with the air, said Bakenkhonsu, rather of one who is dead than of a living king about to wage war upon his foes.

To all these words the Prince listened in silence, but when they were finished he looked up and asked,

'What think you, Bakenkhonsu?'

'I think, O Prince,' answered the wise old man, 'that her Highness did ill to stir up this matter, though doubtless she spoke with the voices of the priests and of the army, against which Pharaoh was not strong enough to stand.'

'What you think, I think,' said Seti.

At this moment the lady Merapi entered.

'I hear, my lord,' she said, 'that Pharaoh purposes to pursue the people of Israel with his host. I come to pray my lord that he will not join himself to the host of Pharaoh.'

'It is but natural, Lady, that you should not wish me to

make war upon your kin, and to speak truth I have no mind that way,' replied Seti, and, turning, left the chamber with her.

'She is not thinking of her kin but of her lover's life,' said Bakenkhonsu. 'She is not a witch as they declare, but it is true that she knows what we do not.'

'Yes,' I answered, 'it is true.'

17
THE DREAM
OF MERAPI

A while went by; it may have been fourteen days, during which we heard that the Israelites had started on their journey. They were a mighty multitude who bore with them the coffin and the mummy of their prophet, a man of their blood, Vizier, it is reported, to that Pharaoh who welcomed them to Egypt hundreds of years before. Some said they went this way and some that, but Bakenkhonsu, who knew everything, declared that they were heading for the Lake of Crocodiles, which others name Sea of Reeds, whereby they would cross into the desert beyond, and thence to Syria. I asked him how, seeing that at its narrowest part, this lake was six thousand paces in width, and that the depth of its mud was unfathomable. He replied that he did not know, but that I might do well to inquire of the lady Merapi.

'So you have changed your mind, and also think her a witch,' I said, to which he answered:

'One must breathe the wind that blows, and Egypt is so

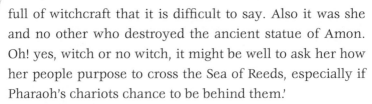

full of witchcraft that it is difficult to say. Also it was she and no other who destroyed the ancient statue of Amon. Oh! yes, witch or no witch, it might be well to ask her how her people purpose to cross the Sea of Reeds, especially if Pharaoh's chariots chance to be behind them.'

So I did ask her, but she answered that she knew nothing of the matter, and wished to know nothing, seeing that she had separated from her people, and remained in Egypt.

Then Ki came, I know not whence, and having made his peace with Seti as to the dressing of Merapi in the robes of Isis which, he vowed, was done by the priests against his wish, told us that Pharaoh and a great host had started to pursue the Israelites. The Prince asked him why he had not gone with the host, to which he replied that he was no soldier, also that Pharaoh hid his face from him. In return he asked the Prince why *he* had not gone.

Seti answered, because he had been deprived of his command with his other officers and had no wish to take share in this business as a private citizen.

'You are wise, as always, Prince,' said Ki.

It was on the following night, very late, while the Prince, Ki, Bakenkhonsu and I, Ana, sat talking, that suddenly the lady Merapi broke in upon us as she had risen from her bed, wild-eyed, and with her hair flowing down her robes.

'I have dreamed a dream!' she cried. 'I dreamed that I saw all the thousands of my people following after a flame that burned from earth to heaven. They came to the edge of a great water and behind them rushed Pharaoh and all the hosts of the Egyptians. Then my people ran on to the face of the water, and it bore them as though it were sound land. Now the soldiers of Pharaoh were following, but the gods of Egypt appeared, Amon, Osiris, Horus, Isis, Hathor, and the rest, and would have turned them back. Still they refused to listen, and dragging the gods with them, rushed out upon the water. Then darkness fell, and in the darkness sounds of wailing and of a mighty laughter. It passed, the moon rose, shining upon emptiness. I awoke, trembling in my limbs. Interpret me this dream if you can, O Ki, Master of Magic.'

'Where is the need, Lady,' he answered, awaking as though from sleep, 'when the dreamer is also the seer? Shall the pupil venture to instruct the teacher, or the novice to make plain the mysteries to the high-priestess of the temple? Nay, Lady, I and all the magicians of Egypt are beneath your feet.'

'Why will you ever mock me?' she said, and as she spoke, she shivered.

Then Bakenkhonsu opened his lips, saying,

'The wisdom of Ki has been buried in a cloud of late, and gives no light to us, his disciples. Yet the meaning of this dream is plain, though whether it be also true I do not know. It is that all the host of Egypt, and with it the gods of Egypt, are threatened with destruction because of the Israelites, unless one to whom they will hearken can be found to turn them from some purpose that I do not understand. But to whom will the mad hearken, oh! to whom will they hearken?' and lifting his great head, he looked straight at the Prince.

'Not to me, I fear, who now am no one in Egypt,' said Seti.

'Why not to you, O Prince, who to-morrow may be

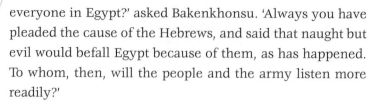

everyone in Egypt?' asked Bakenkhonsu. 'Always you have pleaded the cause of the Hebrews, and said that naught but evil would befall Egypt because of them, as has happened. To whom, then, will the people and the army listen more readily?'

'Moreover, O Prince,' broke in Ki, 'a lady of your household has dreamed a very evil dream, of which, if naught be said, it might be held that it was no dream, but a spell of power aimed against the majesty of Egypt; such a spell as that which cast great Amon from his throne, such a spell as that which has set a magic fence around this house and field.'

'Again I tell you that I weave no spells, O Ki, who with my own child have paid the price of them.'

'Yet spells were woven, Lady, and as has been known from of old, strength is perfected in sacrifice alone,' Ki answered darkly.

'Have done with your talk of spells, Magician,' exclaimed the Prince, 'or if you must speak of them, speak of your own, which are many. It was Jabez who protected us here against the plagues, and the statue of Amon was shattered by some god.'

'I ask your pardon, Prince,' said Ki bowing, 'it was *not* this lady but her uncle who fenced your house against the plagues which ravaged Egypt, and it was *not* this lady but some god working in her which overthrew Amon of Tanis. The Prince has said it. Yet this lady has dreamed a certain dream which Bakenkhonsu has interpreted although I cannot, and I think that Pharaoh and his captains should be told of the dream, that on it they may form their own judgment.'

'Then why do you not tell them, Ki?'

'It has pleased Pharaoh, O Prince, to dismiss me from his service as one who failed and to give my office of Kherheb to another. If I appear before the face of Pharaoh I shall be killed.'

Now I, Ana, listening, wished that Ki would appear before the face of Pharaoh, although I did not believe that he could be killed by him or by anybody else, since against death he had charms. For I was afraid of Ki, and felt in myself that again he was plotting evil to Merapi whom I knew to be innocent.

The Prince walked up and down the chamber as was his fashion when lost in thought. Presently he stopped opposite to me and said,

'Friend Ana, be pleased to command that my chariots be made ready with a general's escort of a hundred men and spare horses to each chariot. We ride at dawn, you and I, to seek out the army of Pharaoh and pray audience of Pharaoh.'

'My lord,' said Merapi in a kind of cry, 'I pray you go not, leaving me alone.'

'Why should I leave you, Lady? Come with me if you will.' She shook her head, saying,

'I dare not. Prince, there has been some charm upon me of late that draws me back to my own people. Twice in the night I have awakened and found myself in the gardens with my face set towards the north, and heard a voice in my ears, even that of my father who is dead, saying,

' "Moon of Israel, thy people wander in the wilderness and need thy light."

'It is certain therefore that if I came near to them I

should be dragged down as wood is dragged of an eddy, nor would Egypt see me any more.'

'Then I pray you bide where you are, Merapi,' said the Prince, laughing a little, 'since it is certain that where you go I must follow, who have no desire to wander in the wilderness with your Hebrew folk. Well, it seems that as you do not wish to leave Memphis and will not come with me, I must stay with you.'

Ki fixed his piercing eyes upon the pair of them.

'Let the Prince forgive me,' he said, 'but I swear it by the gods that never did I think to live to hear the Prince Seti Meneptah set a woman's whims before his honour.'

'Your words are rough,' said Seti, drawing himself up, 'and had they been spoken in other days, mayhap, Ki——'

'Oh! my lord,' said Ki prostrating himself till his forehead touched the ground, 'bethink you then how great must be the need which makes me dare to speak them. When first I came hither from the court of Tanis, the spirit that is within me speaking through my lips gave certain titles to your Highness, for which your Highness was pleased to reprove me. Yet the spirit in me cannot lie and I know well, and bid all here make record of my words, that to-night I stand in the presence of him who ere two moons have passed will be crowned Pharaoh.'

'Truly you were ever a bearer of ill-tidings, Ki, but if so, what of it?'

'This your Highness: Were it not that the spirits of Truth and Right compel me for their own reasons, should I, who have blood that can be shed or bones that can be broken, dare to hurl hard words at him who will be Pharaoh?

Should I dare to cross the will of the sweet dove who nestles on his heart, the wise, white dove that murmurs the mysteries of heaven, whence she came, and is stronger than the vulture of Isis and swifter than the hawk of Ra; the dove that, were she angry, could rend me into more fragments than did Set Osiris?'

Now I saw Bakenkhonsu begin to swell with inward laughter like a frog about to croak, but Seti answered in a weary voice,

'By all the birds of Egypt with the sacred crocodiles thrown in, I do not know, since that mind of yours, Ki, is not an open writing which can be read by the passer-by. Still, if you would tell me what is the reason with which the goddesses of Truth and Justice have inspired you——'

'The reason is, O Prince, that the fate of all Egypt's army may be hidden in your hand. The time is short and I will be plain. Deny it as she will this lady here, who seems to be but a thing of love and beauty, is the greatest sorceress in Egypt, as I whom she has mastered know well. She matched herself against the high god of Egypt and smote him to the dust, and has paid back upon him, his prophets, and his worshippers the ills that he would have worked to her, as in a like case any of our fellowship would do. Now she has dreamed a dream, or her spirit has told her that the army of Egypt is in danger of destruction, and I know that this dream is true. Hasten then, O Prince, to save the hosts of Egypt, which you will surely need when you come to sit upon its throne.'

'I am no sorceress,' cried Merapi, 'and yet—alas! that I must say it—this smiling-featured, cold-eyed wizard's

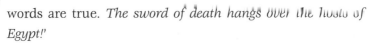

words are true. *The sword of death hangs over the hosts of Egypt!"*

'Command that the chariots be made ready,' said Seti again.

Eight days had gone by. It was sunset and we drew rein over against the Sea of Reeds. Day and night we had followed the army of Pharaoh across the wilderness on a road beaten down by his chariot wheels and soldiers, and by the tens of thousands of the Israelites who had passed that way before them. Now from the ridge where we had halted we saw it encamped beneath us, a very great army. Moreover, stragglers told us that beyond, also encamped, was the countless horde of the Israelites, and beyond these the vast Sea of Reeds which barred their path. But we could not see the Israelites or the water on the further side of them for a very strange reason. Between these and the army of Pharaoh rose a black wall of cloud, built as it were from earth to heaven. One of those stragglers of whom I have spoken, told us that this cloud travelled before the Israelites by day, but at night was turned into a pillar of fire. Only on this day, when the army of Pharaoh approached, it had moved round and come between the people of Israel and the army.

Now when the Prince, Bakenkhonsu, and I heard these things we looked at each other and were silent. Only presently the Prince laughed a little, and said,

'We should have brought Ki with us, even if we had to carry him bound, that he might interpret this marvel, for it is sure that no one else can.'

'It would be hard to keep Ki bound, Prince, if he wished

to go free,' answered Bakenkhonsu. 'Moreover, before ever we entered the chariots at Memphis he had departed south for Thebes. I saw him go.'

'And I gave orders that he should not be allowed to return, for I hold him an ill guest, or so thinks the lady Merapi,' replied Seti with a sigh.

'Now that we are here what would the Prince do?' I asked.

'Descend to the camp of Pharaoh and say what we have to say, Ana.'

'And if he will not listen, Prince?'

'Then cry our message aloud and return.'

'And if he will not suffer us to return, Prince?'

'Then stand still and live or die as the gods may decree.'

'Truly our lord has a great heart!' exclaimed Bakenkhonsu, 'and though I feel over young to die, I am minded to see the end of this matter with him,' and he laughed aloud.

But I who was afraid thought that *O-ho-ho* of his, which the sky seemed to echo back upon our heads, a strange and indeed a fearful sound.

Then we put on robes of ceremony that we had brought with us, but neither swords nor armour, and having eaten some food, drove on with the half of our guard towards the place where we saw the banners of Pharaoh flying about his pavilion. The rest of our guard we left encamped, bidding them, if aught happened to us, to return and make report at Memphis and in the other great cities. As we drew near to the camp the outposts saw us and challenged. But when they perceived by the light of the setting sun who it was that they challenged, a murmur went through them, of

'The Prince of Egypt! The Prince of Egypt!' for so they had never ceased to name Seti, and they saluted with their spears and let us pass.

So at length we came to the pavilion of Pharaoh, round about which a whole regiment stood on guard. The sides of it were looped up high because of the heat of the night which was great, and within sat Pharaoh, his captains, his councillors, his priests, his magicians, and many others at meat or serving food and drink. They sat at a table that was bent like a bow, with their faces towards the entrance, and Pharaoh was in the centre of the table with his fan-bearers and butlers behind him.

We advanced into the pavilion, the Prince in the centre, Bakenkhonsu leaning on his staff on the right hand, and I, wearing the gold chain that Pharaoh Meneptah had given me, on the left, but those with us remained among the guard at the entrance.

'Who are these?' asked Amenmeses, looking up, 'who come here unbidden?'

'Three citizens of Egypt who have a message for Pharaoh,' answered Seti in his quiet voice, 'which we have travelled fast and far to speak in time.'

'How are you named, citizens of Egypt, and who sends your message?'

'We are named, Seti Meneptah aforetime Prince of Egypt, and heir to its crown; Bakenkhonsu the aged Councillor, and Ana the scribe and King's Companion, and our message is from the gods.'

'We have heard those names, who has not?' said Pharaoh, and as he spoke all, or very nearly all, the company rose, or half rose, and bowed towards the Prince. 'Will you and your companions be seated and eat, Prince Seti Meneptah?'

'We thank the divine Pharaoh, but we have already eaten. Have we Pharaoh's leave to deliver our message?'

'Speak on, Prince.'

'O Pharaoh, many moons have gone by, since last we looked upon each other face to face, on that day when my father, the good god Meneptah, disinherited me, and afterwards fled hence to Osiris. Pharaoh will remember why I was thus cut off from the royal root of Egypt. It was because of the matter of these Israelites, who in my judgment had been evilly dealt by, and should be suffered to leave our land. The good god Meneptah, being so advised by you and others, O Pharaoh, would have smitten the Israelites with the sword, making an end of them, and to this he demanded my assent as the Heir of Egypt. I refused that assent and was cast out, and since then, you, O Pharaoh, have worn the double crown, while I have dwelt as a citizen of Memphis, living upon such lands and revenues as are my own. Between that hour and this, O Pharaoh, many griefs have smitten Egypt, and the last of them cost you your first-born, and me mine. Yet through them all, O Pharaoh, you have refused to let these Hebrews go, as I counselled should be done at the beginning. At length after the death of the first-born, your decree was issued that they might go. Yet now you follow them with a great army and purpose to do to them what my father, the good god Meneptah, would have done, had I consented, namely—to destroy them with the sword. Hear me, Pharaoh!'

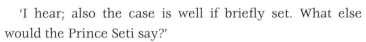

'I hear; also the case is well if briefly set. What else would the Prince Seti say?'

'This, O Pharaoh. That I pray you to return with all your host from the following of these Hebrews, not to-morrow or the next day, but at once—this night.'

'Why, O Prince?'

'Because of a certain dream that a lady of my household who is Hebrew has dreamed, which dream foretells destruction to you and the army of Egypt, unless you hearken to these words of mine.'

'I think that we know of this snake whom you have taken to dwell in your bosom, whence it may spit poison upon Egypt. It is named Merapi, Moon of Israel, is it not?'

'That is the name of the lady who dreamed the dream,' replied Seti in a cold voice, though I felt him tremble with anger at my side, 'the dream that if Pharaoh wills my companions here shall set out word for word to his magicians.'

'Pharaoh does not will it,' shouted Amenmeses smiting the board with his fist, 'because Pharaoh knows that it is but another trick to save these wizards and thieves from the doom that they have earned.'

'Am I then a worker of tricks, O Pharaoh? If I had been such, why have I journeyed hither to give warning, when by sitting yonder at Memphis to-morrow, I might once more have become heir to the double crown? For if you will not hearken to me, I tell you that very soon you shall be dead, and with you these'—and he pointed to all those who sat at table—'and with them the great army that lies without. Ere you speak, tell me, what is that black cloud which stands before the camp of the Hebrews? Is there no answer? Then I will give the answer. It is the pall that shall wrap the bones of every one of you.'

Now the company shivered with fear, yes, even the priests and the magicians shivered. But Pharaoh went mad with rage. Springing from his seat, he snatched at the double crown upon his head, and hurled it to the ground, and I noted that the golden uræus band about it, rolled away, and rested upon Seti's sandalled foot. He tore his robes and shouted,

'At least our fate shall be your fate, Renegade, who have sold Egypt to the Hebrew witch in payment of her kisses. Seize this man and his companions, and when we go down to battle against these Israelites to-morrow after the darkness lifts, let them be set with the captains of the van. So shall the truth be known at last.'

Thus Pharaoh commanded, and Seti, answering nothing, folded his arms upon his breast and waited.

Men rose from their seats as though to obey Pharaoh and sank back to them again. Guards started forward and yet remained standing where they were. Then Bakenkhonsu burst into one of his great laughs.

'O-ho-ho,' he laughed, 'Pharaohs have I seen come and go, one and two and three, and four and five, but never yet have I seen a Pharaoh whom none of his councillors or guards could obey however much they willed it. When you are Pharaoh, Prince Seti, may your luck be better. Your arm, Ana my friend, and lead on, Royal Heir of Egypt. The truth is shown to blind eyes that will not see. The word is spoken to deaf ears that will not hearken, and the duty

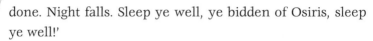

done. Night falls. Sleep ye well, ye bidden of Osiris, sleep ye well!'

Then we turned and walked from that pavilion. At its entrance I looked back, and in the low light that precedes the darkness, it seemed to me as though all seated there were already dead. Blue were their faces and hollow shone their eyes, and from their lips there came no word. Only they stared at us as we went, and stared and stared again.

Without the door of the pavilion, by command of the Prince, I called aloud the substance of the lady Merapi's dream, and warned all within earshot to cease from pursuing the people of Israel, if they would continue to live to look upon the sun. Yet even now, although to speak thus was treason against Pharaoh, none lifted a hand against the Prince, or against me his servant. Often since then I have wondered why this was so, and found no answer to my questionings. Mayhap it was because of the majesty of my master, whom all knew to be the true Pharaoh, and loved at heart. Mayhap it was because they were sure that he would not have travelled so far and placed himself in the power of Amenmeses save to work the armies of Egypt good, and not ill, and to bring them a message that had been spoken by the gods themselves.

Or mayhap it was because he was still hedged about by that protection which the Hebrews had vowed to him through their prophets with the voice of Jabez. At least so it happened. Pharaoh might command, but his servants would not obey. Moreover, the story spread, and that night many deserted from the host of Pharaoh and encamped about us, or fled back towards the cities whence they came. Also with them were not a few councillors and priests who had talked secretly with Bakenkhonsu. So it chanced that even if Pharaoh desired to make an end of us, as perhaps he purposed to do in the midnight watches, he thought it wisest to let the matter lie until he had finished with the people of Israel.

It was a very strange night, silent, with a heavy, stirless air. There were no stars, but the curtain of black cloud which seemed to hang beyond the camp of the Egyptians was alive with lightnings which appeared to shape themselves to letters that I could not read.

'Behold the Book of Fate written in fire by the hand of God!' said Bakenkhonsu, as he watched.

About midnight a mighty east wind began to blow, so strongly that we must lie upon our faces under the lea of the chariots. Then the wind died away and we heard tumult and shoutings, both from the camp of Egypt, and from the camp of Israel beyond the cloud. Next there came a shock as of earthquake, which threw those of us who were standing to the ground, and by a blood-red moon that now appeared we perceived that all the army of Pharaoh was beginning to move towards the sea.

'Whither go they?' I asked of the Prince who clung to my arm.

'To doom, I think,' he answered, 'but to what doom I do not know.'

After this we said no more, because we were too much afraid.

* * *

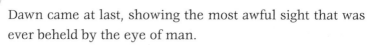

Dawn came at last, showing the most awful sight that was ever beheld by the eye of man.

The wall of cloud had disappeared, and in the clear light of the morning, we perceived that the deep waters of the Sea of Reeds had divided themselves, leaving a raised roadway that seemed to have been cleared by the wind, or perchance to have been thrown up by the earthquake. Who can say? Not I who never set foot upon that path of death. Along this wide road streamed the tens of thousands of the Israelites, passing between the water on the right hand, and the water on the left, and after them followed all the army of Pharaoh, save those who had deserted, and stood or lay around us, watching. We could even see the golden chariots that marked the presence of Pharaoh himself, and of his bodyguard, deep in the heart of the broken host that struggled forward without discipline or order.

'What now? Oh! what now?' murmured Seti, and as he spoke there was a second shock of earthquake. Then to the west on the sea there arose a mighty wave, whereof the crest seemed to be high as a pyramid. It rolled forward with a curved and foaming head, and in the hollow of it for a moment, no more, we saw the army of Egypt. Yet in that moment I seemed to see mighty shapes fleeing landwards along the crest of the wave, which shapes I took to be the gods of Egypt, pursued by a form of light and glory that drove them as with a scourge. They came, they went, accompanied by a sound of wailing, and the wave fell.

But beyond it, the hordes of Israel still marched—upon the further shore.

Dense gloom followed, and through the gloom I saw, or

thought I saw, Merapi, Moon of Israel, standing before us
with a troubled face and heard or thought I heard her cry,
    'Oh! help me, my lord Seti! Help me, my lord Seti!'
    Then she too was gone.

'Harness the chariots!' cried Seti, in a hollow voice.

18
THE CROWNING
OF MERAPI

Fast as sped our horses, rumour, or rather the truth, carried by those who had gone before us, flew faster. Oh! that journey was as a dream begotten by the evil gods. On we galloped through the day and through the night and lo! at every town and village women rushed upon us crying,

'Is it true, O travellers, is it true that Pharaoh and his host are perished in the sea?'

Then old Bakenkhonsu would call in answer,

'It is true that he who *was* Pharaoh and his host are perished in the sea. But lo! here is he who *is* Pharaoh,' and he pointed to the Prince, who took no heed and said nothing, save,

'On! On!'

Then forward we would plunge again till once more the sound of wailing died into silence.

It was sunset, and at length we drew near to the gates of Memphis. The Prince turned to me and spoke.

'Heretofore I have not dared to ask,' he said, 'but tell me, Ana. In the gloom after the great cliff of water fell and the shapes of terror swept by, did you seem to see a woman stand before us and did you seem to hear her speak?'

'I did, O Prince.'

'Who was that woman and what did she say?'

'She was one who bore a child to you, O Prince, which child is not, and she said, "Oh! help me, my lord Seti. Help me, my lord Seti!" '

His face grew ashen even beneath its veil of dust, and he groaned.

'Two who loved her have seen and two who loved her have heard,' he said. 'There is no room for doubt. Ana, she is dead!'

'I pray the gods——'

'Pray not, for the gods of Egypt are also dead, slain by the god of Israel. Ana, who has murdered her?'

With my finger I who am a draughtsman drew in the thick dust that lay on the board of the chariot the brows of a man and beneath them two deep eyes. The gilt on the board where the sun caught it looked like light in the eyes.

The Prince nodded and said,

'Now we shall learn whether great magicians such as Ki can die like other men. Yes, if need be, to learn that I will put on Pharaoh's crown.'

We halted at the gates of Memphis. They were shut and barred, but from within the vast city rose a sound of tumult.

'Open!' cried the Prince to the guard.

'Who bids me open?' answered the captain of the gate peering at us, for the low sun lay behind.

'Pharaoh bids you open.'

'Pharaoh!' said the man. 'We have sure tidings that Pharaoh and his armies are slain by wizardry in the sea.'

'Fool!' thundered the Prince, 'Pharaoh never dies. Pharaoh Amenmeses is with Osiris but the good god Seti Meneptah who *is* Pharaoh bids you open.'

Then the bronze gates rolled back, and those who guarded them prostrated themselves in the dust.

'Man,' I called to the captain, 'what means yonder shouting?'

'Sir,' he answered, 'I do not know, but I am told that the witch who has brought woe on Egypt and by magic caused the death of Pharaoh Amenmeses and his armies, dies by fire in the place before the temple.'

'By whose command?' I cried again as the charioteer flogged the horses, but no answer reached our ears.

We rushed on up the wide street to the great place that was packed with tens of thousands of the people. We drove the horses at them.

'Way for Pharaoh! Way for the Mighty One, the good god, Seti Meneptah, King of the Upper and the Lower Land!' shouted the escort.

The people turned and saw the tall shape of the Prince still clad in the robes of state which he had worn when he stood before Amenmeses in the pavilion by the sea.

'Pharaoh! Pharaoh! Hail to Pharaoh!' they cried, prostrating themselves, and the cry passed on through Memphis like a wind.

Now we were come to the centre of the place, and there in front of the great gates of the temple burned a vast pyre of wood. Before the pyre moved figures, in one of whom I knew Ki dressed in his magician's robe. Outside of these was a double circle of soldiers who kept the people back, which these needed, for they raved like madmen and shook their fists. A group of priests near the fire separated, and I saw that among them stood a man and a woman, the latter with dishevelled hair and torn robes as though she had been roughly handled. At this moment her strength seemed to fail her and she sank to the ground, lifting her face as she did so. It was the face of Merapi, Moon of Israel.

So she was not dead. The man at her side stooped as though to lift her up, but a stone thrown out of the shadow struck him in the back and caused him to straighten himself, which he did with a curse at the thrower. I knew the voice at once, although the speaker was disguised.

It was that of Laban the Israelite, he who had been betrothed to Merapi, and had striven to murder us in the land of Goshen. What did he here? I wondered dimly.

Ki was speaking. 'Hark how the Hebrew cat spits,' he said. 'Well, the cause has been tried and the verdict given, and I think that the familiar should feed the flames before the witch. Watch him now, and perhaps he will change into something else.'

All this he said, smiling in his usual pleasant fashion, even when he made a sign to certain black temple slaves who stood near. They leapt forward, and I saw the firelight shine upon their copper armlets as they gripped Laban. He fought furiously, shouting,

'Where are your armies, Egyptians, and where is your

dog of a Pharaoh? Go dig them from the Sea of Reeds. Farewell, Moon of Israel. Look how your royal lover crowns you at the last, O faithless——'

He said no more, for at this moment the slaves hurled him headlong into the heart of the great fire, which blackened for a little and burned bright again.

Then it was that Merapi struggled to her feet and cried in a ringing voice those very words which the Prince and I had seemed to hear her speak far away by the Sea of Reeds—'Oh! help me my lord Seti! Help me, my lord Seti!' Yes, the same words which had echoed in our ears days before they passed her lips, or so we believed.

Now all this while our chariots had been forcing their way foot by foot through the wall of the watching crowd, perhaps while a man might count a hundred, no more. As the echoes of her cry died away at length we were through and leaping to the ground.

'The witch calls on one who sups to-night at the board of Osiris with Pharaoh and his host,' sneered Ki. 'Well, let her go to seek him there if the guardian gods will suffer it,' and again he made a sign to the black slaves.

But Merapi had seen or felt Seti advancing from the shadows and seeing flung herself upon his breast. He kissed her on the brow before them all, then bade me hold her up and turned to face the people.

'Bow down. Bow down. Bow down!' cried the deep voice of Bakenkhonsu. 'Life! Blood! Strength! Pharaoh! Pharaoh! Pharaoh!' and what he said the escort echoed.

Then of a sudden the multitude understood. To their knees they fell and from every side rose the ancient salu-

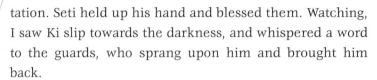

tation. Seti held up his hand and blessed them. Watching, I saw Ki slip towards the darkness, and whispered a word to the guards, who sprang upon him and brought him back.

Then the Prince spoke:

'Ye name me Pharaoh, people of Memphis, and Pharaoh I fear I am by descent of blood to-day, though whether I will consent to bear the burdens of government, should Egypt wish it of me, as yet I know not. Still he who wore the double crown is, I believe, dead in the midst of the sea; at the least I saw the waters overwhelm him and his army. Therefore, if only for an hour, I will be Pharaoh, that as Pharaoh I may judge of certain matters. Lady Merapi, tell me, I pray you, how came you to this pass?'

'My lord,' she answered, in a low voice, 'after you had gone to warn the army of Pharaoh because of that dream I dreamed, Ki, who departed on the same day, returned again. Through one of the women of the household, over whom he had power, or so I think, he obtained access to me when I was alone in my chamber. There he made me this offer:

' "Give me," he said, "the secret of your magic that I may be avenged upon the wizards of the Hebrews who have brought about my downfall, and upon the Hebrews themselves, and also upon all my other enemies, and thus once more become the greatest man in Egypt. In turn I will fulfil all your desires, and make you, and no other, Queen of Egypt, and be your faithful servant, and that of your lord Seti who shall be Pharaoh, until the end of your lives.

Refuse, and I will stir up the people against you, and before ever the Prince returns, if he returns at all, they who believe you to be an evil sorceress shall mete out to you the fate of a sorceress." '

'My lord, I answered to Ki what I have often told him before, that I had no magic to reveal to him, I who knew nothing of the black arts of sorcery, seeing that it was not I who destroyed the statue of Amon in the temple at Tanis, but that same Power which since then has brought all the plagues on Egypt. I said, too, that I cared nothing for the gifts he offered to me, as I had no wish to be Queen of Egypt. My lord, he laughed in my face, saying I should find that he was one ill to mock, as others had found before me. Then he pointed at me with his wand and muttered some spell over me, which seemed to numb my limbs and voice, holding me helpless till he had been gone a long while, and could not be found by your servants, whom I commanded in your name to seize, and keep him till your return.

'From that hour the people began to threaten me. They crowded about the palace gates in thousands, crying day and night that they were going to kill me, the witch. I prayed for help, but from me, a sinner, heaven has grown so far away that my prayers seem to fall back unheard upon my head. Even the servants in the palace turned against me, and would not look upon my face. I grew mad with fear and loneliness, since all fled before me. At last one night towards the dawn I went on to the terrace, and since no god would hear me, I turned towards the north whither I knew that you had gone, and cried to you to help me in those same words which I cried again just now before you appeared.' (Here the Prince looked at me and I Ana looked at him.) 'Then it was that from among the bushes of the garden appeared a man, hidden in a long, sheepskin cloak, so that I could not see his face, who said to me,

' "Moon of Israel, I have been sent by his Highness, the Prince Seti, to tell you that you are in danger of your life, as he is in danger of his, wherefore he cannot come to you. His command is that you come to him, that together you may flee away out of Egypt to a land where you will both be safe until all these troubles are finished."

' "How know I that you of the veiled face are a true messenger?" I asked. "Give me a sign."

'Then he held out to me that scarabæus of lapis-lazuli which your Highness gave to me far away in the land of Goshen, the same that you asked back from me as a love token when we plighted troth, and you gave me your royal ring, which scarabæus I had seen in your robe when you drove away with Ana.'

'I lost it on our journey to the Sea of Reeds, but said nothing of it to you, Ana, because I thought the omen evil, having dreamed in the night that Ki appeared and stole it from me,' whispered the Prince to me.

' "It is not enough," I answered. "This jewel may have been thieved away, or snatched from the dead body of the Prince, or taken from him by magic."

'The cloaked man thought a while and said, "This night, not an hour ago, Pharaoh and his chariots were overwhelmed in the Sea of Reeds. Let that serve as a sign."

' "How can this be?" I answered, "since the Sea of Reeds is far away, and such tidings cannot travel thence in an hour. Get you gone, false tempter."

' "Yet it is so," he answered.

' "When you prove it to me, I will believe, and come."

' "Good," ' he said, and was gone.

'Next day a rumour began to run that this awful thing had happened. It grew stronger and stronger, until all swore that it had happened. Now the fury of the people rose against me, and they ravened round the palace like lions of the desert, roaring for my blood. Yet it was as though they could not enter here, since whenever they rushed at the gates or walls, they fell back again, for some spirit seemed to protect the place. The days went by; the night came again and at the dawn, this dawn that is past, once more I stood upon the terrace, and once more the cloaked man appeared from among the trees.

' "Now you have heard, Moon of Israel," he said, "and now you must believe and come, although you think your-self safe because at the beginning of the plagues this, the home of Seti, was enchanted against evil, so that none within it can be harmed."

' "I have heard, and I think that I believe, though how the tidings reached Memphis in an hour I do not under-stand. Yet, stranger, I say to you that it is not enough."

'Then the man drew a papyrus roll from his bosom and threw it at my feet. I opened it and read. The writing was the writing of Ana as I knew well, and the signature was the signature of you, my lord, and it was sealed with your seal, and with the seal of Bakenkhonsu as a witness. Here

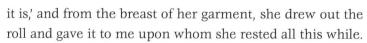

it is,' and from the breast of her garment, she drew out the roll and gave it to me upon whom she rested all this while.

I opened it, and by the light of torches the Prince, Bakenkhonsu, and I read. It was as she had told us in what seemed to be my writing, and signed and sealed as she had said. The words ran:

'To Merapi, Moon of Israel, in my house at Memphis.

'Come, Lady, Flower of Love, to me your lord, to whom the bearer of this will guide you safely. Come at once, for I am in great danger, as you are, and together only can we be safe.'

'Ana, what means this?' asked the Prince in a terrible voice. 'If you have betrayed me and her——'

'By the gods,' I began angrily, 'am I a man that I should live to hear even your Highness speak thus to me, or am I but a dog of the desert?'

I ceased, for at that moment Bakenkhonsu began to laugh.

'Look at the letter!' he laughed. 'Look at the letter.'

We looked, and as we looked, behold the writing on it turned first to the colour of blood and then faded away, till presently there was nothing in my hand but a blank sheet of papyrus.

'Oho-ho!' laughed Bakenkhonsu. 'Truly, friend Ki, you are the first of magicians, save those prophets of the Israelites who have brought you—Whither have they brought you, friend Ki?'

Then for the first time the painted smile left the face of Ki, and it became like a block of stone in which were set two angry jewels that were his eyes.

'Continue, Lady,' said the Prince.

'I obeyed the letter. I fled away with the man who said he had a chariot waiting. We passed out by the little gate.

' "Where is the chariot?" I asked.

' "We go by boat," he answered, and led the way towards the river. As we threaded the big palm grove men appeared from between the trees.

' "You have betrayed me," I cried.

' "Nay," he answered, "I am myself betrayed."

'Then for the first time I knew his voice for that of Laban.

'The men seized us; at the head of them was Ki.

' "This is the witch," he said, "who, her wickedness finished, flies with her Hebrew lover, who is also the familiar of her sorceries."

'They tore the cloak and the false beard from him and there before me stood Laban. I cursed him to his face. But all he answered was,

' "Merapi, what I have done I did for love of you. It was my purpose to take you away to our people, for here I knew that they would kill you. This magician promised you to me if I could tempt you from the safety of the palace, in return for certain tidings that I have given him."

'These were the only words that passed between us till the end. They dragged us to the secret prison of the great temple where we were separated. Here all day long Ki and the priests tormented me with questions, to which I gave no answer. Towards the evening they brought me out and led me here with Laban at my side. When the people saw me a great cry went up of "Sorceress! Hebrew witch!" They broke through the guard; they seized me, threw me to the

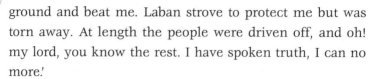

ground and beat me. Laban strove to protect me but was torn away. At length the people were driven off, and oh! my lord, you know the rest. I have spoken truth, I can no more.'

So saying her knees loosened beneath her and she swooned. We bore her to the chariot.

'You have heard, Ki,' said the Prince. 'Now, what answer?'

'None, O Pharaoh,' he replied coldly, 'for Pharaoh you are, as I promised that you should be. My spirit has deserted me, those Hebrews have stolen it away. That writing should have faded from the scroll as soon as it was read by yonder lady, and then I would have told you another story; a story of secret love, of betrayal and attempted flight with her lover. But some evil god kept it there until you also had read, you who knew that you had not written what appeared before your eyes. Pharaoh, I am conquered. Do your will with me, and farewell. Beloved you shall always be as you have always been, but happy never in this world.'

'O People,' cried Seti, 'I will not be judge in my own cause. You have heard, do you judge. For this wizard, what reward?'

Then there went up a great cry of 'Death! Death by fire. The death he had made ready for the innocent!'

That was the end, but they told me afterwards that, when the great pyre had burned out, in it was found the head of Ki looking like a red-hot stone. When the sunlight fell on it, however, it crumbled and faded away, as the writing had faded from the roll. If this be true I do not know, who was not present at the time.

*　*　*

We bore Merapi to the palace. She lived but three days, she whose body and spirit were broken. The last time I saw her was when she sent for me not an hour before death came. She was lying in Seti's arms babbling to him of their child and looking very sweet and happy. She thanked me for my friendship, smiling the while in a way which showed me that she knew it was more than friendship, and bade me tend my master well until we all met again elsewhere. Then she gave me her hand to kiss and I went away weeping.

After she was dead a strange fancy took Seti. In the great hall of the palace he caused a golden throne to be put up, and on this throne he set her in regal garments, with pectoral and necklaces of gems, crowned like a queen of Egypt, and thus he showed her to the lords of Memphis. Then he caused her to be embalmed and buried in a secret sepulchre, the place of which I have sworn never to reveal, but without any rites because she was not of the faith of Egypt.

There then she sleeps in her eternal house until the Day of Resurrection, and with her sleeps her little son.

It was within a moon of this funeral that the great ones of Egypt came to Memphis to name the Prince as Pharaoh, and with them came her Highness, the Queen Userti. I was present at the ceremony, which to me was very strange. There was the Vizier Nehesi; there was the high-priest Roi and with him many other priests; and there was even the old chamberlain Pambasa, pompous yet grovelling as before, although he had deserted the household of the Prince after his disinheritance for that of the Pharaoh

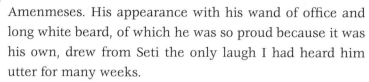

Amenmeses. His appearance with his wand of office and long white beard, of which he was so proud because it was his own, drew from Seti the only laugh I had heard him utter for many weeks.

'So you are back again, Chamberlain Pambasa,' he said.

'O most Holy, O most Royal,' answered the old knave, 'has Pambasa, the grain of dust beneath your feet, ever deserted the House of Pharaoh, or that of him who will be Pharaoh?'

'No,' replied Seti, 'it is only when you think that he will not be Pharaoh that you desert. Well, get you to your duties, rogue, who perhaps at bottom are as honest as the rest.'

Then followed the great and ancient ceremony of the Offering of the Crown, in which spoke priests disguised as gods and other priests disguised as mighty Pharaohs of the past; also the nobles of the Nomes and the chief men of cities. When all had finished Seti answered:

'I take this, my heritage,' and he touched the double crown, 'not because I desire it but because it is my heritage, and I know that while I live I must do my duty, as I swore that I would to one who has departed. Blow upon blow have smitten Egypt which, I think, had my voice been listened to, would never have fallen. Egypt lies bleeding and well-nigh dead. Let it be your work and mine to try to nurse her back to life. For no long while am I with you, who also have been smitten, how it matters not, yet while I am here, I who seem to reign will be your servant and that of Egypt. It is my decree that no feasts or ceremonial shall mark this my accession, and that the wealth which would have been scattered upon them shall be distributed among the widows and the children of those who perished in the Sea of Reeds. Depart!'

They went, humble yet happy, since here was a Pharaoh who knew the needs of Egypt, one too who loved her and who alone had shown himself wise of heart while others were filled with madness. Then her Highness entered, splendidly apparelled, crowned and followed by her household, and made obeisance.

'Greeting to Pharaoh,' she cried.

'Greeting to the Royal Princess of Egypt,' he answered.

'Nay, Pharaoh, the Queen of Egypt.'

By Seti's side there was another throne, that in which he had set dead Merapi with a crown upon her head. He turned and looked at it a while. Then, he said,

'I see that this seat is empty. Let the Queen of Egypt take her place here if so she wills.'

She stared at him as if she thought that he was mad, though doubtless she had heard something of that story, then swept up the steps and sat herself down in the royal chair.

'Your Majesty has been long absent,' said Seti.

'Yes,' she answered, 'but as my Majesty promised she would do, she has returned to her lawful place at the side of Pharaoh—never to leave it more.'

'Pharaoh thanks her Majesty,' said Seti, bowing low.

Some six years had gone by, when one night I was seated with the Pharaoh Seti Meneptah in his palace at Memphis, for there he always chose to dwell when matters of State allowed.

It was on the anniversary of the Death of the First-born,

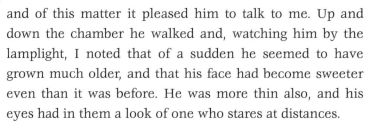

and of this matter it pleased him to talk to me. Up and down the chamber he walked and, watching him by the lamplight, I noted that of a sudden he seemed to have grown much older, and that his face had become sweeter even than it was before. He was more thin also, and his eyes had in them a look of one who stares at distances.

'You remember that night, Friend, do you not,' he said; 'perhaps the most terrible night the world has ever seen, at least in the little piece of it called Egypt.' He ceased, lifted a curtain, and pointed to a spot on the pillared portico without. 'There she sat,' he went on; 'there you stood; there lay the boy and there crouched his nurse—by the way, I grieve to hear that she is ill. You are caring for her, are you not, Ana? Say to her that Pharaoh will come to visit her—when he may, when he may.'

'I remember it all, Pharaoh.'

'Yes, of course you would remember, because you loved her, did you not, and the boy too, and even me, the father. And so you will love us always when we reach a land where sex with its walls and fires are forgotten, and love alone survives—as we shall love you.'

'Yes,' I answered, 'since love is the key of life, and those alone are accursed who have never learned to love.'

'Why accursed, Ana, seeing that, if life continues, they still may learn?' He paused a while, then went on: 'I am glad that he died, Ana, although had he lived, as the Queen will have no children, he might have become Pharaoh after me. But what is it to be Pharaoh? For six years now I have reigned, and I think that I am beloved; reigned over a broken land which I have striven to bind together, reigned over a sick land which I have striven to heal, reigned over a desolated land which I have striven to make forget. Oh! the curse of those Hebrews worked well. And I think that it was my fault, Ana, for had I been more of a man, instead of casting aside my burden, I should have stood up against my father Meneptah and his policy and, if need were, have raised the people. Then the Israelites would have gone, and no plagues would have smitten Egypt. Well, what I did, I did because I must, perhaps, and what has happened, has happened. And now my time comes to an end, and I go hence to balance my account as best I may, praying that I may find judges who understand, and are gentle.'

'Why does Pharaoh speak thus?' I asked.

'I do not know, Ana, yet that Hebrew wife of mine has been much in my mind of late. She was wise in her way, as wise as loving, was she not, and if we could see her once again, perhaps she would answer the question. But although she seems so near to me, I never can see her, quite. Can you, Ana?'

'No, Pharaoh, though one night old Bakenkhonsu vowed that he perceived her passing before us, and looking at me earnestly as she passed.'

'Ah! Bakenkhonsu. Well, he is wise too, and loved her in his fashion. Also the flesh fades from him, though mayhap he will live to make offerings at both our tombs. Well, Bakenkhonsu is at Tanis, or is it at Thebes, with her Majesty, whom he ever loves to observe, as I do. So he can tell us nothing of what he thought he saw. This chamber is hot, Ana, let us stand without.'

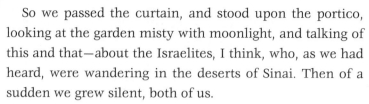

So we passed the curtain, and stood upon the portico, looking at the garden misty with moonlight, and talking of this and that—about the Israelites, I think, who, as we had heard, were wandering in the deserts of Sinai. Then of a sudden we grew silent, both of us.

A cloud floated over the face of the moon, leaving the world in darkness. It passed, and I became aware that we were no longer alone. There in front of us was a mat, and on the mat lay a dead child, the royal child named Seti; there by the mat stood a woman with agony in her eyes, looking at the dead child, the Hebrew woman named Moon of Israel.

Seti touched me, and pointed to her, and I pointed to the child. We stood breathless. Then of a sudden, stooping down, Merapi lifted up the child and held it towards its father. But, lo! now no longer was it dead; nay, it laughed and laughed, and seeing him, seemed to throw its arms about his neck, and to kiss him on the lips. Moreover, the agony in the woman's eyes turned to joy unspeakable, and she became more beautiful than a star. Then, laughing like the child, Merapi turned to Seti, beckoned, and was gone.

'We have seen the dead,' he said to me presently, 'and, oh! Ana, *the dead still live!*'

That night, ere dawn, a cry rang through the palace, waking me from my sleep. This was the cry:

'The good god Pharaoh is no more! The hawk Seti has flown to heaven!'

* * *

At the burial of Pharaoh, I laid the halves of the broken cup upon his breast, that he might drink therefrom in the Day of Resurrection.

Here ends the writing of the Scribe Ana, the Counsellor and Companion of the King, by him beloved.

THE END

THIS EXCLUSIVE EDITION
has been typeset for The Reincarnation Library
in Augustea Open, Meridien, and Veljovic
and printed by offset lithography on
archival quality paper
at Cushing-Malloy, Inc.

The text and endpapers are acid-free and meet
or surpass all guidelines established by
the Council of Library Resources
and the American National
Standards Institute™.

Book design by Charlotte Staub